The Hole in the Bottom of the Sea

The Winthorpe Mysteries, Part Two

By
Mike Bradford

Bookman
Publishing & Marketing
Providing Quality, Professional
Author Services
www.bookmanmarketing.com

This is a work of fiction. Names, dates and places are used fictionally and any similarity to actual persons or places is purely coincidental.

© Copyright 2005, Mike Bradford

All Rights Reserved.

No part of this book may be reproduced, stored in a retrieval system, or transmitted by any means, electronic, mechanical, photocopying, recording, or otherwise, without written permission from the author.

ISBN: 1-59453-591-4

Acknowledgements

The author would like to express thanks to the following persons who were instrumental and supportive in the writing of this story; Emma Brown, friend and persistent editor; Jim and Becky Brawner, Innkeepers wealthy in knowledge about the island of Kaua'i; Dr. Wayne Emery, advisor, critic and long time friend. Wonderful help was received from managers and wait-staff at many restaurants along the way. Several of their establishments and much of their advice appear in this effort. *Aloha* and *Mahalo* to the people of Kaua'i. Their aloha spirit and helpful words made this a magical effort. Finally, thanks and love to my wife, Julie, companion, advisor and patient mate.

For Brenda Oliver Brown
Co-worker and dear friend
The original Red Head

and

My friends Jim and Becky Brawner
They are my innkeepers in paradise

Prologue

The Fat Man deftly worked the controls of the Quicksilver MX ultralight aircraft as he banked slowly to make his approach and fly under Louisville's Kennedy Bridge. He held the craft steady and continued on through the shadows of the Second Street Bridge. The December day was perfect—still and crystal clear. A smile creased his weathered face as he diverted his eyes to the skyline of downtown Louisville. He turned his focus back to the glassy surface of the Ohio River and eased the controls forward—toward the water. His smile broadened as his wheels touched gently on the rippling river surface. The Rotex engine whined as he pulled up to touch down again—twice, three times. This was more fun than he had expected.

Mitzy Ellis strode across the deck of the riverfront bar to serve a double Gentleman Jack to a stranger at the rail. It was his second. She served all comers without prejudice, but secretly held a little disrespect for those who came to Louisville, Kentucky and ordered Tennessee whiskey. She studied his figure. She didn't care for his choice of poison, but she did like the cut of his butt. "Cute," she said. More than that, he looked like money. "There ya go!" she said, as she sat the whiskey down.

The man made a grunt that resembled a thank you.

Mitzy wondered about this stranger. She wondered why he chose to go out on the deck this crisp December day. She wondered why he seemed to have nothing more on his mind that watching the river do its thing. Why was he alone? He might be a real looser. On the other hand, he might be a man worth getting to know. She lingered beside him for a moment. She smoothed the curls of her red hair while staring at his classic profile. Turning to lean upon the rail, she gazed into the cold water as it flowed slowly by.

"Who's the guy in the airplane?" the man asked. His voice was firm with a hint of a sensual growl.

Mitzy followed his gaze to the ultralight coming under the bridge. "That damn fool is at it again! I don't know his name. I think he's some hot shot trying to make up for having a too small pecker! He flies down here and pulls this stunt. By the time the police show up he disappears." Mitzy froze. Her jaw went slack. "Oh, my God! Did you see that?" She heard the stranger say something, but her mind was blank as she stared at the empty surface of the Ohio. She turned to speak. The highball glass rested on a twenty-dollar bill. The stranger was gone.

The Fat Man panicked the instant the motor popped once and quit. Only the sound of cold water rushing over his feet filled his ears. The flood engulfed him, washing his scream away. The fragile airframe buckled, and the nylon-covered wings slapped together as they slipped beneath the swirling current. In an instant the Ohio River resumed its form and wandered on as it had through ages past. In the dark below, the Fat Man was first enshrouded by the crumpled wings then plummeted into the deep as the wings swept away. He clawed at his harness as he spun disoriented, aimlessly, hopelessly, eternally into the flow. Into the dark he fell. Metal crunched and broke away as his body slammed into the steel side of an ancient, sunken barge. The engine of the mangled craft scraped along the hulk, sweeping into a passage beneath the rust and decay. Fat Man followed, broken and lost. The twisted wings came too, into the hole—following, folding, wedging, packing, hiding. The muck of the Ohio collapsed behind the intruding mess. The water cleared as a cloud of debris swirled away.

He's there. He's still down there—the Fat Man—never to be seen again.

The Hole in the Bottom of the Sea

Chapter One

Life persists in the constant process of things slipping away. We are replenished from time to time, but never in equal kind. Even that which enriches us exacts a cost, leaving no such thing as pure gain. This belief is the essence of the story I am about to tell, for in this chapter of my life I experienced wonderful events that few can claim, but, in the end of the matter, I paid the price. I never asked for these events to happen; yet they came to me fair and square. My name is Davis Winthorpe. I do tasks.

The person that I have become was born amidst the salt spray and morning mist in a place by the sea. The realization of life as something full and rich for the savoring came to me during a September week I once spent in a house named *Fancy Dancer*.

My wife of two days, my love, my Kitty had chosen the seaside as the place for our honeymoon. We drove through the foothills of the Cumberland Mountains in Kentucky and up across the Blue Ridge of the Appalachians in North Carolina to the eastern shore and a place called *Maramassee Island*.

There our life together began. With joy, with hope and with confidence we sprang fresh upon the earth.

"It's more than I hoped for," she said softly to me. We stood upon the widow's walk above Fancy Dancer, watching the panorama spread before us. We had climbed the many steps to the top of the house before dawn to watch the mighty sun come sizzling up from the sea. Light of day began to drive away the stars. Sea birds soared above us, announcing the day with their raucous calls. We scarcely chanced to breathe as we waited for our first sunrise together as man and wife. The side of my face began to grow warm.

"The sun's in the wrong place!" I shouted.

"What!" Kitty exclaimed.

We turned to face the morning sun. To our left, up and over the housetops, the sun had made its way into the day.

"The sun is supposed to rise over the ocean! Our first sunrise together, and we missed it!"

Kitty's words rippled with laughter, "Winthorpe, you are a treasure! Didn't you know this island faces south?"

"Don't blame me. It was your idea to come here!"

We laughed. We clung to each other, watching another couple stroll down the beach.

Oh, the sun could have come up over the ocean, and we would have seen just another sunrise. Our beginning, though not as dreamed, gave us a wonderful story to tell.

The bonding of two people became complete in that special place. Our meeting and our early days had come to us under the most unusual of circumstances.

Not only was our knowledge of each other the product of a whirlwind affair, but the entire situation of our beginning was strangely shaped by the murder of one woman and a promise made to another. With closure in our minds over both of these situations we were free to be. That's it—*We were free to be.*

The days—the week unfolded like a time of rebirth for two well worn middle-aged lovers. What we had missed in living we found in each other. When the time for leaving the island came we felt as if we were saying goodbye to a dear friend. It seemed impossible that we were feasting upon the view from the bridge for the last time. I slowed the car just to linger a little longer.

"We *will* come back," she murmured.

"Yes," was all I could say. Words come hard for me in situations like that.

Back over the mountains we traveled, making our way to contact with reality. We made our way back up into the Bluegrass, across Kentucky to the Ohio River Valley and our home on Peachtree Avenue in Louisville. Realizing that we had not come back to my little house after the wedding, I gathered Kitty up into my arms to carry her across the threshold. I'd been successful with this maneuver a few days ago at Fancy Dancer. This time things went differently.

"Whoop!" Kitty shouted.

My wife, by nature, is not a tiny little thing. She still had a vanity case in her hand. Kitty rolled to her right to set down the case. She kept on rolling right out of my arms. The two of us crashed in a heap at the kitchen door.

"What the heck?"

"I'm so sorry!" she said. "With the case in my hand, I thought I would be too heavy."

"Are you Ok?" I asked.

Kitty placed her arms around my neck, kissing me full and hard. "I am now," she whispered into my ear.

"Welcome home, Mrs. Winthorpe."

What began at the kitchen door continued in various stages of passionate embrace all the way to the bedroom, actually all the way into both bedrooms. The ardor of honeymooning couples can at best be described as peculiar. I had always wanted to create one of those scenes in which articles of clothing were strewn in a trail from the door to the bed. That day I enjoyed the opportunity!

During the events of the preceding weeks, my neglect of my clients had allowed my work to completely go away. I do tasks for people. That sounds a little simple, but it works. I take on the odd little deeds that people need done to make life more convenient. I was running an errand for a certain gentleman when I met Kitty in New York City. To make the story short, when Kitty learned that my trip to New York was part of a cover up for a murder, she packed her bags and came to Louisville. That's what she said, and it was the truth—truth wrapped around a lie. Actually she had cut up her credit cards, cut off her telephone and disappeared. My wife, would you believe, became a woman in hiding, and I was still in

The Hole in the Bottom of the Sea

the dark. From what? From whom? I was still trying to learn the answers. Yeah, that's odd, but it didn't' keep us from falling in love. What fools we lovers make. She will trust me enough some day to tell the whole story. Then I will let you know.

We were not broke. I had run through the little cash I had, but Kitty had taken a large chunk of change out of her savings. We agreed that we could not spend that recklessly. Between us, we had gone through several thousand bucks. As much as I hated it, the time had come to get back to the grind. I had to turn away from love on the beach and go back to making a living.

I found no messages on my answering machine and had no prospects of a task to do. Relief came through a phone call to my friend and partner in this business, Winston Pence. While we were away, Win had come to my house to check messages. He told me he had done a couple of odd jobs while Kitty and I were honeymooning, and there was one outstanding request for our peculiar services.

"That guy down at the retirement home called. They done bought a new bus to use with the old folks. It's ready for delivery and he say none of them can go get it. They all goin' to a conference of some kind and don't have time."

"Where's the bus?"

"It's in Denton, Texas. That's somewhere outside of Dallas."

"What's the deal?"

"The people that did the custom work on the bus say they'll pay for an airline ticket, if the home will send someone to pick up the rig. I done told the man at the home we would do it. I called the other guy in Texas and told him we got to have two tickets, because I don't want to drive the rig back by myself"

"And?"

"The man said to buy the tickets and bring him the receipt. He'll pay us back."

"Oh good grief, Win, I just walked in the door. When is this supposed to happen?"

"The tickets are for a flight tomorrow," Win said. "I had to decide something, what with you being off running buck naked on a beach somewhere!"

"Well hell, Win, you did the right thing. Kitty will kill me, but business is business."

The trip to Dallas was a matter of getting back to the grind. The man from the custom shop met us at the airport with the brand new bus. Win and I threw our bags aboard and hit the road. By spelling each other through the night we were back in Louisville the next day. We parked the bus at the retirement center, collected the fee and headed home. I've told you about this venture to give you a glimpse of my life. And I could not resist telling about my homecoming.

After leaving Winston at his home on Adelia Avenue, I made my way back to my neighborhood. I made my left turn off Taylor Boulevard. I was heading for Peachtree and eager to get back to life with Kitty.

Men are highly visual characters, and married or not I was determined to get an eyeful of the woman I saw jogging down the sidewalk on Bicknell Avenue. Actually she was running, not jogging. The beauty was taking long graceful strides. Her motion seemed effortless, covering the ground at a rapid pace. She was clad in a skintight silver spandex body suit. A shocking pink T-shirt was cut off just below her bust. She had tied a shear scarf around her waist, folded with the point to one side. The scarf covered too much of what appeared to be a lovely rump.

"I have got to check this out," I said out loud.

The woman was running away from me and appeared to be a stranger to my neighborhood. This was a dish I had not cast eyes on before. She took a sharp right into a short alley before I could check out the rest of her figure. Thank God for such little blessings, I thought, as I turned the corner at Peachtree.

It was just a short way to our house. As I negotiated the left into the driveway I watched the rear view, wondering what route the object of my attention had taken. By the time I exited Plain Jane, the runner had slowed to a trot, and had cut across my front yard. It was Kitty.

"I just saw the most gorgeous woman running down Bicknell!"

"Oh—I'm—still running—off that—seafood." Kitty was sweat soaked. A matching hot pink headband was about her forehead. Radiance was upon her glistening face. With her cheeks fully flushed, her black and silver hair plastered to her face completed a picture of healthfulness. Kitty's smile, though broken by huffs and puffs, was more beautiful than ever.

"I don't think I've ever seen any one run quite like that," I said. It was more a question than a comment.

"I never jog," she puffed. "I always run with long strides to stretch my muscles." Kitty paused. "It's a trick I learned back during my days as a dancer. It would build my endurance for long routines. I run hard as I can until exhausted. Usually, I'm done in after a mile or so." She puffed some more. "Today I'm finished after only a couple of times around the block. I've gotten lazy since I met you, Davis."

"We could have run together at the beach."

"I did run. The mornings I left you sleeping I ran to the pier and back." A few more short puffs. "Besides," she said, flashing a full blush and a smile. "I've seen you run. I can't move that slow."

Dear Lord, I thought. Then I laughed. I knew running was not the thing this man did best. I said, "Mrs. Winthorpe, I believe you have a new outfit."

"I got a taxi today—went shopping. Davis, you must teach me to drive. Getting around Louisville isn't as easy as getting around The City."

"No problem. Tell me about the outfit."

"Just something to run in. These are too big. I had to cover up with something." She lifted her cut off T-shirt for an instant, revealing the outline of her breasts. Her nipples were rigid and full against the silver spandex.

The Hole in the Bottom of the Sea

Her casual comment and action sent an erotic rush through me. For me, like most men, arousal occurs in milliseconds. I was immediately fishing for a come on.

Kitty said, "You didn't know I was a dancer, did you?"

"Never dawned on me."

"Watch this!"

Kitty took about three effortless strides across our back yard. Leaping, she took to the air. She sailed completely over my picnic table, landing with spinning move as she curtsied and took a bow.

I stared—big eyed and slack jawed.

"Your turn, Mr. Winthorpe."

I did a shuffling jog across the yard, stepped onto the bench, walked across the table and carefully jumped from the opposite side before offering my version of a bow.

Kitty had begun to fan her face with her little top. I took both of her hands. Pulling her to me, I gently kissed her fingertips.

"How'd I do?"

Her expression answered my question. "Kitty, how did you do that? Jump the table—I mean?"

"No big deal," she replied. "After I dropped out of college, I came back to New York and tried to make it big time as a dancer. I made it into a couple of shows. Sang in the chorus. But, it wasn't my thing."

"Why not?"

Kitty blushed. "I'm too heavy. Compared to the other girls, I was a cow!"

"No!" I said.

"I lost over twenty pounds so I could compete. I just didn't like being that skinny. I work hard to keep in shape, but I also like the way I'm made. Mom used to tell me that I have a healthy attitude toward my body."

I was not in a position to argue, and I knew that I had a *very* healthy attitude toward her body.

"Let's go in. How was the trip?" she said.

"The trip was long and tiring. It was nearly a hundred degrees in Dallas. Are you going to jump the table again?"

"No, but I may jump you."

She was up the steps and across the deck before I could blink. By the time I was into the kitchen Kitty was into the hallway. She pulled her little top off over her head and tossed it at me.

"Going to join me?" she said, reaching for her zipper.

I dropped my clothes in the hall and joined her in the shower.

"You forgot to kiss me hello, dear husband," she whispered into my ear.

Kitty gathered me into her arms, holding me tight.

"You've had two long hard days, and I've missed you so. You just relax and let me wash all your weariness away." Her breath, hot upon my ear, gave me shivers as she whispered these words.

The warm water was like a blessing flowing over me. Kitty bathed me top to bottom. She filled the lavatory with hot water and warmed a bottle of something I assumed to be baby oil. My sweet lover gently spread the warm oil over the both of us, using her body much more than she used her hands.

"Now you're ready," she said.

This is true, I thought.

Kitty led me to our room where an old quilt was already spread across the bed. Laying me down on my stomach, she began to massage my fingers first, working her way down to my toes. Her touch seemed to push every last bit of tension out of me.

"Where did you learn to do that?" I mumbled.

"I learned this in Spain, from an expert. That's all you need to know about that!"

She rolled me onto my back and, gently, she came to me. Our lovemaking was slow and sweet.

"This is how you make love to an exhausted man," she whispered.

The last drop of energy seeped from me. Within moments I was asleep.

When I awoke, Kitty was still with me. She had pulled the quilt over me. She lay at my side, watching me sleep. Two heavy terry towels were on the foot of the bed.

"It's important to keep your body warm after a good massage," she said. "I'm glad you slept."

"Wow," I uttered softly.

"You came home before I was ready. I meant to have candlelight and a nice meal ready." Her tone was loving and oh so soft. I was experiencing the sensual side of her that I sensed the first moment I met her back in New York.

"Oh this is better, much, much better," I replied.

"Oh!" she said. "I meant to do this too!"

Kitty pulled me from the bed, handing me one of the large towels. We each removed the remaining oil from the other."

"Just pat it away," she said. "Don't rub it off. It's better for your skin if you leave as much as you can."

Kitty spoke as I patted her back, "Do you like me the way I am? Well, what I mean is, that comment I made about liking to be a little overweight, does that bother you?"

The question made me very self-conscious. Standing there in my natural state, I knew that I was awkwardly adorned with established love handles and the early stages of a definite potbelly. I was sallow skinned and way out of shape. I couldn't answer her without judging myself.

"Kitty, you're so beautiful. I have to wonder what it is you see in me." I dropped my towel, spreading my arms in full surrender.

She continued to pat herself dry, looking at me with a raised eyebrow. "I know why I like you. I can't find the words to say why I love you. I don't think you can bottle up love and put it into an explanation. I love you because you are you. I can't keep from loving you. I don't see the shape of you when I love you. All I see is love. I like you because of the kindness in your eyes, because of the freeness of your spirit. I like you because you're not on some ego trip, always competing with me and every other person you meet. Davis, I have fallen in love with two guys before you, and I didn't like either of them. Liking you makes loving you so much more wonderful."

She raised her arms as she finished her speech. She used both hands to smooth her oil soaked hair back along her head. My heart raced at the very appearance of her.

"I don't know how to say words like that," I confessed with a rough whisper. I felt like a grounded bird. Tears had formed in my eyes.

"I know," she said. There was roughness in her voice too. "And that's why I love you."

I didn't understand the meaning of what she said last. I didn't have to understand. She accepted me the way I was, and that was why I loved her too.

"Will you wash my hair for me?" she asked.

"Now and forever," I said. I only managed those three words.

She eased into my arms. I could feel her tears against my cheek.

With this woman, I said to myself. *Life and love are one and the same.*

The Hole in the Bottom of the Sea

Chapter Two

The weeks rolled off rapidly after my return from Dallas. In my journal I referred to that event as *my homecoming*. It was an experience that I didn't want to quickly forget. We were enjoying life together, but there was a restless spirit growing in both of us.

Kitty put it bluntly. "Davis, I'm bored."

"How's your search for a job going?"

"I haven't pursued that very aggressively. I want to be free to travel with you."

I appreciated her sweet sentiment. I was also taken by surprise. It was clear that two couldn't live as cheaply as one. Besides, I had a private little dream to move us into a better place. I turned the potential for argument aside. In spite of our married state, and the torrid nature of our journey through intimacy, we were still in the process of getting acquainted. I figured difficult days would come soon enough. I didn't see the sense of making our finances an issue. There's no sense in looking for trouble, for trouble will find us on it's own. I let the matter drop.

Several tasks came our way, but they didn't take away the nagging boredom. Life was too plain. Kitty and I made one quick trip to Pittsburgh for a client. Another situation took us to Ann Arbor, Michigan and back. Both were sans excitement.

I knew what was happening to us. It was daring, danger and intrigue that brought us together. Now the every day routine was testing our relationship. We were back to the ordinary. Life was dull. It was work. I'd never sought such a thing before, but I had discovered a new me and I wanted adventure! I didn't know it, but adventure would soon come looking for me.

Winter came, along with the Christmas spirit. December is unpredictable in the Ohio River Valley. Snow could be flying with a nasty chill, or one might be comfortable in shirtsleeves. I've even experienced both on the same day. This year brought one of those special gifts from Mother Nature. Sunny skies and balmy weather made for great December days.

Kitty was grousing around. "This doesn't seem like the Christmas season to me! I want snow! I want a big parade! I want stuffed shells!"

"Wait 'til tomorrow," I said. "The weather will change, and there will be a beautiful parade." I was wrong. The warm weather persisted and we had a wet parade. I also had no idea what stuffed shells were.

Kitty went out on a search for decorations. She stated that my well-worn collection of baubles was, "Lacking in theme and without *panache*."

"Whatever," I mumbled. Somehow the spirit was not yet upon me.

The prelude to mystery began with the coming of the mail one day. It was December thirteenth, nineteen ninety-three. I remember that well. I looked for a long time at the return address on one of the Christmas cards. It had been postmarked in Kansas City.

I still don't understand why that one card always catches me by surprise. I should have been expecting it, but, as usual, it took my breath away. I opened the card slowly. It was an elegant greeting, reflecting rich taste. The design was oriental. A scene depicting the birth of Christ adorned the card with writing along one side that I assumed to be Japanese. Each character in the scene appeared to be oriental. The clothing was unlike anything I had ever seen in a church play. As I opened the card, two crisp, new hundred-dollar bills came sliding out. Inside, these words appeared, "As always, I thank you. Merry Christmas." The bold signature was that of William Luzadder.

"An odd bit of greeting," I said aloud. "Merry Christmas and a pay-off!"

I had a task.

I heard Kitty shouting her good bye to the taxi driver. She insisted on the independence of going for things herself. She also enjoyed the open friendliness of the people of Louisville. My Kitty had become one who shouted hello and goodbye to all she met. I also grumbled to myself a bit. I had ignored her request for driving lessons. This woman did things with much zeal. I think I was still afraid of the thought of being in a car with Kitty behind the wheel.

"Bargains, Davis, bargains—look at all I found!" There was a childlike glow in her face.

The Hole in the Bottom of the Sea

I stuffed the two bills into my pocket. I wanted to have some fun with Kitty. At the time I assumed my task presented only a small adventure, so I wanted to make as much of it as I could.

"Put your treasures on the couch, Kitty. We have a job to do."

"I'm sorry, but what?"

I lowered the timbre of my voice. "An adventure, Kitty. I have a task, and your assistance is needed." It was only a tease. I anticipated a short trip downtown and a pleasant dinner. I didn't foresee the strange events that would begin to unfold.

Her eyes widened. "Davis, what are you up to?"

"This is a sad, dark story, Kitty, my sweet. We must prepare!" I gave her the most sinister look I could muster and said the last few words in an ominous and frightening style.

"Oh, good grief," she responded.

"I'll make the call. You wait here."

I dialed the number of my good friend, Maggie Branum, at a floral shop in Old Louisville. I waited for Maggie to come on the line.

"Branum! This is Winthorpe!" I announced tersely. "It's Christmas. We need to do the deed. You know the drill!"

Maggie said, "How's the new bride, and what's gotten into you?"

I wanted to keep up my front. I could explain to Maggie later. "You know what I need! This is no time for questions!"

"I gotcha," Maggie said. "Davis, you'd better have a good story to tell!"

"I said no questions!" I hung up the phone.

Kitty stood with arms akimbo, tapping one foot. She had that look on her face.

I didn't crack a smile. "We must prepare. There's no time to waste. Go outside and look across the back fence. There you will find a stack of bricks. Remove one. Wash it well." I gave the orders in rapid-fire succession.

"Aren't those our neighbor's bricks?"

"No questions," I commanded.

"Davis, What are you going to do?"

"I," I said, striking a dignified pose, "Am going to get a coat hanger."

I strode into the bedroom. Kitty was still sputtering in the living room. Hmmm, I thought, this could turn into foreplay.

"I'll be back!" I heard Kitty say, with a deep masculine tone. She was catching onto the game.

I found a coat hanger and went back to the kitchen.

Kitty returned with her prize. She presented the brick to me with aloof disdain, holding it between two fingers as if to present a dead rat. "Selected, washed, delivered! Is this acceptable?"

I inspected the object carefully, sighting through the holes and along the edges. "It is adequate. We must go to the car."

Maggie was used to my peculiar nature. I knew she would have my order ready upon our arrival. I pointed

The Hole in the Bottom of the Sea

my Toyota north on Taylor Boulevard toward Old Louisville.

"You wait in car, five, maybe eight minutes. Be useful. Put money in the meter," I said, as I parked.

She said, "I have heard and will obey."

On the way I'd met her constant inquiries with stern silence. She was having fun now. The sense of anticipation, which often gets the best of her, was fully in control.

Only moments passed and I was back with what I had come for. Maggie had prepared a wreath for me. It was smallish and done in a Christmas motif. Pinecones, small, silk poinsettia blooms and other typical stuff adorned the offering. I carefully placed the wreath in the middle of the back seat.

"Davis, tell me what you're up to. Tell me now!" Kitty demanded.

"Be still. We are going to the river."

Kitty isn't really one to use rough language, but she found some clearly understandable and well-seasoned phrases to cast my way.

I pulled Plain Jane into the parking area near Tow Boat Annie's. Tow Boat Annie's was a bit of an odd combination of a barge and a towboat hooked together. All that aside, it was a floating restaurant on the banks of the Ohio. During my life before Kitty I used it as a good place for conversation and pretty decent food. I used to go there on a summer's day and while away an hour or so while nursing a little Coke and Southern Comfort. I would listen to outrageous stories, and tell a few of my own. If I state the facts, I have to say that I don't go to this old hangout as much. I find too many memories there for my feeble heart. As you read more of this story from way back when, you will understand why I say that.

We drove under the Interstate at the riverfront, parked near the restaurant and headed down the gangway.

My friend, the Red Head, saw us coming. "Davis Winthorpe, where have you been?" The Red Head was a part-time waitress at the place. She was a petite gal with fire in her step. She had a pair of dancing hazel eyes that filled me with fun every time I looked into them. My friend was not a gal with a fancy figure, but then she didn't have to be. The woman was all personality. And in my typical fashion, I used her. She filled the role of an honest confidant. Without batting an eye, she could tell me everything I never wanted to hear about myself. Nine times out of ten the Red Head was right on target. That's why I enjoyed her. Besides, a good friend is a lot cheaper than a shrink.

"You here for your Christmas thing?" she chimed.

"Introductions first, I want you to meet Kitty."

Kitty had worn a royal blue, shirtwaist dress that day. The outfit was made of a silken material, cut to the mid-calf and full. With her long lines, full figure, graceful step and sparkling eyes, she sort of took charge of the room. Red looked her up and down. I could sense that sparks might be about to fly.

The Hole in the Bottom of the Sea

"Davis, every time you find a new girl you break my heart!"

Snickers came from some of my buddies at the bar.

"Not a girl friend, Red. She's my wife!"

"Dear God!" she said. Her tone was soft. She seemed to be wondering what to say next. "When did this happen?"

"We met in September, fell in love in September, got married in September. Bang, bang, bang. Just like that."

Red reached out to Kitty with open arms. The two didn't match at all. At five-foot ten Kitty dwarfed the smaller woman. Kitty looked into those hazel eyes. I think she too saw the friend inside.

"Davis, this is a good woman. How'd you get so lucky?"

"Thank you," Kitty said. "I don't believe Davis said your name."

"Hell's bells, call me Red. My mom named me Mitzy. Believe me I ain't no Mitzy. Kitty, I'm glad to meet you. I've had to keep Davis straight for way too long. You can work on him now."

"No," Kitty replied. "Davis has such a long way to go. I'm sure he'll still need your attention from time to time."

"Kitty, if he doesn't treat you right, come and see me. I know some boys across the river who will straighten him out! And Kitty, if you don't treat him right. Well, you'll have to talk to me." Red flashed her biggest smile at Kitty. Then she pursed her lips and twisted them to one side. "What'll you have?" she said.

"Fix us two whitefish on rye, Mitzy. Throw in some onion rings and sweet tea. I need to go up on the deck," I said.

The conversation was getting just a little inside my comfort zone. There were a few things I needed to tell Kitty about this woman. From the quizzical look on Kitty's face, I knew that I would get my opportunity in short order.

"Don't call me Mitzy!" the Red Head shouted after us.

As we had gotten out of the car, I had gathered up the brick, the hanger and the wreath. I had not wanted Kitty to feel awkward by carrying this odd assortment of items while meeting my friends at Tow Boat Annie's.

She was full of wonder as I spread the items on one of the tables. "Davis, I suppose at some point this will begin to make a little sense."

"Perhaps," I replied, cautiously. "It depends on what you mean by making a little sense." I twisted the coat hanger apart to use as a wire.

"So, what's the story on Mitzy?"

She sure didn't waste time on getting back to that one. I figured a direct approach would serve me best. I began to loop the coat hanger wire through the holes in the brick.

"Mitzy is dear to me, but our relationship is an odd one. I don't even know where she lives. I've never talked to her outside this place. Sometimes I feel we're as intimate as lovers, but I've never even touched her.

The Hole in the Bottom of the Sea

We've never even shaken hands. She's only part-time here, and I feel fortunate when I come in and catch her working."

"And?" Kitty prodded me on.

"And—she's a straight shooter. Whatever I say, she doesn't hesitate to tell me what I need to hear. It's like she sees straight to my insides."

"Oh good grief, Davis, she's the Woman at the Bar!"

"I'm sorry—say again." The tone in Kitty's voice was almost insulting to me.

"The Woman at the Bar, the person you can talk to; she's your alter ego. She's an anchor. We all need one. That's not odd. That's life."

"It seems odd that she's a woman. You know, like, we talk about stuff I'd never tell Winston or one of the guys." I said this softly; almost hoping it would not be heard. "Does it bother you that she's a woman?"

"Not as long as you know where the line is," Kitty said. "Mitzy knows her own heart. I don't want to burst your bubble, but she talks to twenty guys like you every day."

I worked silently, using the wire to tie the wreath to the brick. What Kitty said did hurt a bit. I guess I had a little fantasy in my mind that I was very special to the Red Head. "What do you mean when you say that she knows her own heart?"

"Mitzy likes you." Kitty paused. "I think she's in love with you."

I straightened up abruptly, pursed my lips without thinking and turned my head quickly to give her a direct glare. I caught myself thinking of my dad. I didn't mean to copy him, but he would do the same thing when my words had crossed his comfort zone. I didn't like what I had heard Kitty say. I wasn't a spring chicken any more. I had been through a divorce, and lost both my mom and my dad. I had needed this friend to talk to. I suddenly realized my fantasy with Red was that of her being a surrogate parent onto whom I could heartlessly dump my troubles. Suddenly I didn't like myself as well as I did a few minutes ago. My chin was quivering as I turned my gaze out across the river. I didn't understand the sudden melancholy that had come over me.

"Kitty, she's never done one thing to even hint at such a thing!" I spat the words out.

"She knows you don't love her, and she also knows that you two would never get along. You've never looked close enough to see, and she's OK with knowing that you have no idea how she feels."

All of a sudden I was very sure that I was not happy with Kitty knowing so much, or seeing through me so easily. The game was over.

"Excuse me!" I said abruptly as I walked to the edge of the deck.

Kitty got out of the way.

"This is from your brother," I said, as I dropped the wreath into the Ohio River.

Kitty squawked with genuine surprise. "You sunk my brick!"

I continued to watch the water.

"Davis, that was our neighbor's brick!"

I kept my silence.

"How much did that wreath cost?"

I had nothing to say. I wanted the other conversation to go away.

"What the hell are you doing?"

Bingo, subject changed. I began to tell Kitty the story.

"Tow Boat Annie's used to be on the Indiana side." I pointed to the old mooring across the river. "See where parking area comes down to the water?"

"I don't see where you mean," she said.

"Don't worry. It's over there. A few years ago, about this time of the year, this guy named Raymond Luzadder died over there in front of Tow Boat Annie's."

"Like, what? Fell overboard, heart attack—what?"

I could see the ginger rising in my girl.

"No, stranger than that. Luzadder was one of those rich hot shots. He was from Louisville, but he moved away and made it big in electronics, computers or something. He got into all sorts of action sports; skydiving, white water rafting, climbing, stuff like that. I think he was sort of a jet-set playboy."

"So, how'd he die?"

"Luzadder took up flying. He was into ultralights. You know. They're made like hang gliders, but with a seat underneath and a motor."

"I know what you mean. I've seen them. What happened?"

Mike Bradford

"He would come down here along the river to fly. He would swoop under the bridges and do what they call touch-and-go landings on the water. He would cruise along close to the water and touch his wheels to the surface. I've seen him do it! I thought he was crazy. I think it was illegal too.

"Davis! What happened to him?"

"Well, one day, a little before Christmas, he comes under the bridge. Red—Mitzy, was watching. He touches the water three or four times and then he's gone! The motor quits and Luzadder goes straight into the drink."

"Dear Lord," Kitty gasped. "Just like that?"

"Just like that."

"So why the wreath?"

"They never found him. Never even found the ultralight. The currents in the river are weird here. The water picks up speed as it heads for the falls. There's construction, wreckage, sunken barges and who knows what else out there."

"OK, but that doesn't explain the wreath."

"Yeah, right. Luzadder has this brother. He's another rich dude. The brother, William, lives in Kansas City. One day, right after Thanksgiving, the brother calls me. He had seen my ad in the *Courier-Journal*. He told me that he'd been coming here each year before Christmas to drop a wreath into the drink near the place where his brother went down. He said that his health had gotten sort of unpredictable and the trip was getting to be hard on him. He asked me to do the deed in his place—drop a wreath. So, the last three years, about this time, a Christmas card comes with a couple of hundred in it. I buy a wreath, tie on a brick, come to Tow Boat Annie's, drop the wreath overboard and pocket what's left of the dough."

"You said the man died on the other side."

"Right, over there," I said, pointing to the Indiana side of the river.

"Why do you drop the wreath over here?"

"I've thought about that, but, what the heck, I like coming to Tow Boat Annie's. I figure neither of the Luzadder brothers will ever know the difference."

Kitty stood quietly, gazing into the water. She shielded her eyes from the late afternoon sun and looked across the Ohio River toward the fateful site.

She said, "He went into the hole in the bottom of the sea."

"I'm sorry," I responded. "What?"

"You know, the children's song; 'There's a hole, there's a hole, there's a hole in the bottom of the sea,' like that."

"Yeah, right," I said. "I guess you could say that."

"He's gone there and we'll never see him again." Kitty spoke with sadness in her voice. It was strange how this little story had affected her.

I put my arm around her. "Our food is probably ready."

She continued to watch the river, she pondered the circumstances several seconds longer before she leaned into me accepting the warmth of my body. I felt her shiver. She spoke softly, "Davis, Mitzy certainly deserves more than a handshake."

The food was good. Spirits in the restaurant were high, but we ate in silence. Kitty was now my dear lover. She'd also become my understanding friend in deed—the one I needed. I think I knew all along that this change had taken place in my life. I had a new confidant. I watched the Red Head as she worked tables and teased with the regulars. I was embarrassed inside. For the first time I was seeing her as a person. I wondered where she lived. I wondered what pain and what joy was in her life. *She's not just a listening post. She's somebody.* Another discomfort was there. I was seeing her as a woman, and I liked what I saw. *I wonder what I've missed.* I looked across the table at my Kitty. My wonder went away.

"More than a handshake?" I said.

"More than a handshake," she replied.

I put the other hundred on the table, under the edge of my plate. I smiled at Kitty and walked to the Red Head. Without warning, I gathered Mitzy into my arms and hugged her close.

Her feet came off the floor as I squeezed her. She sputtered protests, squirming to be released.

"I'll see you again soon, Red," I whispered into her ear.

I knew that I would not.

The Hole in the Bottom of the Sea

Chapter Three

Nothing more needed to be said about the man who drowned in the Ohio River. According to Kitty, he had gone to the hole in the bottom of the sea and I was content to leave him there, but things were soon to change. In early April of 1994 I received a phone call that put us on a new course.

"Mr. Winthorpe," the voice said. The person on the other end of the phone line sounded tired—there was a hint of trouble in the way he formed his words. It was a very peculiar thing how I received a sudden chill from the way he said my name.

"This is Davis Winthorpe."

"Mr. Winthorpe, this is William Luzadder."

He caught me by surprise. I stammered a bit. "Yes, well, uh, good afternoon, Mr. Luzadder. Uh, What can I do for you?"

My first thought was that I was about to lose a client. My self-centered nature always seems to jump up first. The two-hundred Luzadder sent me each year wasn't much, but it was easy money. It had tended to come in handy, showing up just before Christmas each year.

"Mr. Winthorpe, I have a most unusual request. I hesitate to tell you what I want in fear that you will not, uh, respond," he said. Then he paused.

Ouch, the word *respond* and the way he said it sent my red flags flying.

"Perhaps if you told me what you want," I replied. I was nudging him a bit. I wanted to hear more, but I was not about to commit to this conversation on such a foggy beginning.

"Will you come to Kansas City to see me? If you will just do that, I'm sure I can present my unusual request to you and you will be able to ease my mind. At least I'm hoping you can help me to get some foolish notions out of my head."

Luzadder was a stranger to me. I had never met the man. What he already had me doing for him was a little screwy. I do tasks, but I don't take care of foolish notions. My inclination was to make up an excuse and say no, but, what the heck—it was a job. I could listen to the man ramble a bit, nod my head, give advice, go eat a Kansas City steak and come home. Three hundred a day plus expenses was on my mind. Kitty was still out of work and the way my jobs went had us on a feast or famine sort of a lifestyle.

"Will the middle of next week be soon enough? I promised my wife I would take her to visit her brother this weekend." I said.

"Oh, yes, surely—why, yes, it is. I was almost certain you would say no!"

An odd feeling crept over me. I listened to the man's voice brighten. He sounded younger and stronger just because I had agreed to travel hundreds of miles and listen to *foolish notions*. I had to know more.

The Hole in the Bottom of the Sea

"You're a good client, Mr. Luzadder. I appreciate you too much to ever say no. Can you give me any clue to what this is about?"

The phone was silent. Then he spoke, "I'm, well, I —Mr. Winthorpe, I just can't say what I have to say into the phone. It, well, it sounds so silly. In my mind, I just have this picture of me saying this out loud and you laughing it off. If you hear my need, I just fear you won't come. Is there any way you can understand?"

"Understand? I don't have to understand. You've got my curiosity up. You'd have a hard time stopping me from coming to Kansas City. We'll take this trip over the weekend and will leave as soon as we can get out of town on Wednesday. I can't wait to hear your foolish notions!"

"I await your arrival with great anticipation, Mr. Winthorpe. I sense that you have a wonderful open mind. In the meantime I will prepare my comments and work up my courage! And, don't be concerned about your expenses. I am comfortably well off. I'll pay you generously. Bring your wife or a friend. Travel goes quicker when someone is with you. I will cover their needs as well."

"One condition, Mr. Luzadder," I responded.

"One condition?"

"Please stop calling me Mr. Winthorpe. I've never gotten used to that. Please call me Davis."

"That's a deal! Will you call me William?"

"I'll see you next week, William and I'll bring my wife. Her name is Kitty. How's that?"

"Agreed, Davis! Agreed!"

"Agreed!" I replied.

Luzadder gave me specific directions on how to find his home and wished us well before hanging up the phone.

Well, call me William, I mused. *It's William, but not Bill.*

The words *foolish notions* were buzzing in my mind. As a dyed-in-the-wool Louisville boy, this sounded to me like a great name for a racehorse.

"*Foolish Notions*," I said out loud. I thought it over. When I get rich I'll buy me a racehorse and call it *Foolish Notions*. No, wait, that's a great name for a boat. No, wait, when I get really rich I'll buy one of those beach cottages over in North Carolina. I'll buy me a beach house and name it *Foolish Notions*. What a plan!"

"Kitty!" I shouted. "I have a foolish notion."

"Now?" she responded. She came in from the deck, folding a paperback book under her arm. We finally were having days warm enough to sit outside and read. She'd missed all of my conversation with Luzadder. Kitty and I were still having tons of fun—each discovering the sensual side of the other. She really wasn't ready for lovemaking at the drop of a hat, but that was one of her favorite ways to tease. When I would make some peculiar statement, she would say *now* as if she thought I was asking about sex. At least I *think* she was teasing.

"Let's go to Kansas City," I said.

The Hole in the Bottom of the Sea

"Yeah, but—uh, what?" she sputtered. She pointed up, back and to either side with a questioning look on her face.

"West," I said. "Due west."

Kitty held out her left hand and made chopping motions across it with her right hand. The question was still on her face. We had been together since September and already she had me communicating with sign language.

"Louisville, Indiana, Illinois, St. Louis, Missouri, Kansas City," I answered.

"Let's drive. I've never seen Illinois." She said Illinois with the "S" on the end. That's very irritating to a Midwesterner. "When do we leave?"

Kitty laid her paperback on the kitchen table and came to my arms. A tight wonderful hug was mine to enjoy. I took her face in my hands and gave her one of those honeymoon kisses. She relaxed against me, laying her head against my shoulder.

"After we get back from Tennessee," I replied, softly.

"Why are we going?"

As I supplied her with the details of the conversation, Kitty remembered the story of William and Raymond Luzadder, but was not impressed with the strange request.

"Let me see if I have this straight," she said. "A man who pays you two hundred dollars to go down to the Ohio to tie a brick to a wreath and sink it in the river calls you to tell you that he has something weird on his mind, but he's afraid that, if he tells you what it is over the phone, you will laugh and not come. So, he asks you to drive all the way to Kansas City so he can tell you face to face, and you say yes?"

"No, he said he would cover our expenses. You added the part about driving."

"Whatever—this is something weird leading to something weirder."

I said, "Well, Sweets, it's a task."

"Davis, It's a mystery!"

The game was on.

The Hole in the Bottom of the Sea

Chapter Four

I had Kansas City on my mind as I drove toward Tennessee. I was anxious to meet her mysterious brother, but the Luzadder thing kept bubbling to the top of my thoughts. I had married Kitty without any knowledge of those who are dear and kin to her. I did know that her brother was named Sal. He, like Kitty, had flown the coop and started a new life. He had moved south, bought a restaurant, changed his name and started over. That was about all I knew. This was an area of Kitty's life that I had learned to avoid. She would talk about it in vague generalities with passive aggressive behavior. She said that it was time to visit Sal and I obeyed. We planned a route that took us into the foothills of the Appalachians to Tennessee and a place called Johnson City to find the brother and his new life.

"It will be years before we can live close to each other," Kitty said.

I knew she was referring to the family of her brother. She stared silently through a misting rain as we dropped out of the hills into Middlesboro, Kentucky. Most of the trip was like that. She was melancholy over this bitter sweet trip and I was preoccupied with William Luzadder's strange remarks.

"Maybe so." I said.

She looked at me and smiled a sweet little smile.

I didn't reply. I forgot about Luzadder. I wondered if I would ever really know Kitty and understand what was going on.

She had kept a promise once made to her mother to separate herself from those whom Kitty referred to as her father's people. It was Sal and Kitty, running because of a promise. What was this all about? I was befuddled. The details as to whom and what her father was also continued to escape me, but it was the keeping of that fateful promise that brought the two of us together. Yes! It was the promise that brought me into the life of this exuberant woman. Such a mixture of the difficult and the wondrous, I thought. But then, that's life.

It was dark as we searched Johnson City for a restaurant named Fraschetta. We found the place on the main drag, in a small strip mall—near a Mexican restaurant. Once inside we found that Fraschetta was warm and inviting. Little candles in wine bottles glowed on each table. Tiny white lights adorned silk trees on the far wall. A good crowd had gathered. A soft voiced tenor was crooning, "You fill my heart with gladness, you take away all my sadness. You ease my trouble. That's what you do…"

Winthorpe, I said to myself. This is going to be good!

The Hole in the Bottom of the Sea

"Holy Mother! Peter James and John!" The sound came booming from the area of the open kitchen. "Rosie, Rosie, it's Kit! Get the boys! You two, get in here!"

Salvatore Servideo, now Fraschetta, scooped my Kitty up into powerful arms. Rosie joined us. She came, wiping her hands on her long white apron. Two boys, dark and full of life with eyes that sparkled in the candlelight, joined the fray. For the first time in my life I enjoyed the beauty of kissing faces that were bathed with tears.

"Is this the bum you told me about?"

"Oh, Sal! Can't you be nicer?" Rosie scolded.

"No!" Kitty said. "This is some other bum!"

"So, you take good care of my sister, or what!" Sal's demand was delivered with a good-natured grin.

This was a new experience for me. Five people were shouting at each other. All talked at the same time, and all seemed to understand. The entire clientele watched the scene unfold. If I'd found the opportunity to speak, I would not have known what to say.

"What, cat got your tongue? Kitty, does he talk—what?" Sal's booming voice filled the room.

"He talks enough to say *I do*," Kitty responded.

"Hey! You married my sister?"

Suddenly I was the one caught up in his arms. The man nearly squeezed the breath out of me. Sal held me by the shoulders and said, "You don't know how much this means to me." He dropped his voice to a lower tone and continued, whispering in my ear. "My heart tells me you are a good man. You *will* be good to my sister. You don't and I'll know. Then we talk. Understand?" He continued to hold me firmly by the shoulders, kissing me on my cheek.

I stammered, looking for words. "Hi, Sal, I'm Davis."

"Hey, everybody!" Sal boomed to his patrons. "This is Davis. He married my sister, Kitty! When you get married?"

"Sal, I'm sorry. It was in September—six months, maybe."

Sal gave her a look. "Six months they're married! So what! Sing to 'em" Sal, who could be described as tone deaf, began to sing. "Here comes the bride, Big fat and wide! Com'on, join in. Here comes the bride, Big fat and wide!"

Soon the whole crowd joined in the off-key ditty. As the energy of the crowd ran out, the crooner came to our rescue.

"This one's for Davis and Kitty. Congratulations and best wishes!" The sweet voiced man played on a keyboard and began to sing *The Tennessee Waltz*.

Sal led us to a corner and urged us to dance. All eyes were upon us. Air was under my feet. The world was mine.

Sal Fraschetta was a total surprise to me. He presented none of the fine features I saw in Kitty. There's nothing delicate about my Kitty. By fine features, I mean to say that there's a distinctive elegance about her looks and carriage. Sal was a different lot. He barged or bolted everywhere he went.

The Hole in the Bottom of the Sea

In many ways he had a greater presence than his sister, but he didn't outshine her. Rather, he dwarfed her with his exuberance. Sal was not that tall but rounded and powerful. He looked almost fat, but was solid to the touch. His hair was blondish and cut close into a flat-top. An oversized nose dominated the rough features of his face. With teeth that were large and prominent, he could flash a smile that oozed with schoolboy like charm. Strangely enough his penetrating eyes were blue, almost gray—so unlike his dark sister. With well-weathered and sun-bronzed skin, he made the complete picture of a man's man. Sal's features were not handsome at all. Yet, he was very pleasant to look at.

Rosie was quite the contrast. She seemed to flow into the wake of Sal, always calming, always reminding him of a better way to behave. He ignored her advice completely, though she never tired of offering it. Rosie was the tallest of the four of us, slim to the point of appearing gaunt, and small breasted with a raw-boned frame. She was so different from Kitty. Just as dark and with olive skin, she bore a perfectly even complexion. She, Like Sal, possessed a large nose, but her mouth was wide and narrow. She was exotic in appearance with dark eyes that seemed to pierce to the inside of me. What Sal expressed with bravado, Rosie expressed with a look. Every word she spoke fell as a note from a song. Music was in her voice. Especially when she spoke in Italian phrases. Rosie was warmth to my soul. She took my breath away.

The boys, whom I guessed to be about six and four years of age, bore no resemblance to those who parented them. They did have Rosie's blue black hair, perfect skin and piercing eyes, but, by contrast, they were beautiful. Nicholas, the older, was soft voiced with untamed curls. Leonard, the younger, was courser, with hair that lay in gentle waves. He had the voice of his father. It was obvious that the younger assumed he was the one in charge. Sal addressed them as Nicky and Lenny. He always said their names together, as if it was one word. Rosie also called them by their nicknames, but always separately. "Nicky, you do this. Lenny, you go help," she would say. And it was Rosie who would stop the train. "Nicholas, I am talking to you!"

For the younger, her insistence was more pronounced, "Leonardo Demitri Servideo..." The rest of her plea to Lennie was always in Italian. I couldn't understand. Kitty said it had something to do with walking on his mother's heart. Rosie would scold the boy while, in the same motion, gathering him up to kiss his gentle curls.

Rosie would approach Nicky more softly. She would touch his face as she spoke her native tongue. Kitty told me that Rosie's pet phrase for little Nick roughly came out as *angel child.*

We all stayed together late into the night, sampling dish after dish of exquisite offerings.

"Don't eat too much of that. You got to try this!" Sal would say. He told me the *Chicken Marsala* I enjoyed on the coast wasn't the real stuff.

"You eat this!" he commanded.

His masterpiece, though, was a savory dish that he translated to me as being chicken with bowties, *pollo fa foli*. We drank rich wine, and, oh, the bread!

This family continued to express the pent up concerns caused by months of separation. They continued to address one another loudly. To my southern ears it was the sound of anger. I came to realize it was this family's way of expressing love.

I watched as the night passed. I watched Sal and Kitty together, kissing and hugging. They touched nose to nose and held each other's face. Kitty's joy seemed so complete. Never before did I feel such a sense of family.

"Famiglia bella!" Sal exclaimed, lifting a glass in toast.

Lenny was asleep in my arms. I had never known the joy of a brother of my own. Mom and I were to only ones in our Louisville home. Oh, how I missed my mother's eyes.

My head nodded. It was late. I was worn down after a long day, but I was so warm inside. This family was a little screwy, but I knew that I would never be alone again.

The Hole in the Bottom of the Sea

Chapter Five

We drove back from Tennessee on Monday, ran some errands on Tuesday and prepared to hit the road again.

We threw a few things into one suitcase. Kitty loaded up her little bag of secret things and stuffed her oversized purse to the brim. We dumped everything into the back seat, piled into Plane Jane and headed for highways west.

"You got Junior?" she asked.

"On my person," I replied. Junior is a five shot Smith and Wesson revolver—a hammerless belly gun. I hated the thing, and, up to that time, I'd never fired it. I wasn't sure if I even could shoot at someone—on the other hand it gave me some sort of confidence. No, I take that back. Junior gave me a stupid sort of confidence. In the sum total of things, I guess that there's no fool like and armed fool. "You got that cannon you carry?"

"Yeah, it's tucked away." When traveling, Kitty puts this huge, chrome plated, six-shot forty-four in that big purse of hers. I think the thing must weigh seven pounds "Davis, are you making fun of me?"

"It is sort of big."

"Big guns make big holes. It beats that pop-gun you got tucked in your belt!"

The Hole in the Bottom of the Sea

This argument was mine to lose. This was not my subject and I knew it. I had never seen what any kind of a bullet would do to a man—not even to an animal. I figured Kitty didn't know either. At least she knew how to use the thing. Her brother, Sal, had taught her to carry a gun for protection. He had taken her to a range and had made her learn the art of making big holes with big bullets. I pressed hard on the accelerator, maneuvering Plain Jane onto I-64 west. I turned to Kitty, "Here's hoping we never have to find out."

The redbuds were in full glory as we drove across the pleasant rolling hills of southern Indiana. Kitty was greatly intrigued by the signs directing travelers to a town named Santa Claus. I promised to take her there on another day. The hills fell away to flatlands in Illinois. The interchanges rose up above the landscape to provide the traveler with a view of well-kept farms, tree lines and even an occasional oil well. Kitty's actions were predictable. In spite of her desire to see the state, Kitty slept all the way across Illinois. I awakened her as we began to descend into the Mississippi River Valley at St. Louis. I wanted her to see the Arch and the bumper-to-bumper traffic.

"This is the Gateway to the West," I informed her.

"I thought you said Louisville was the Gateway to the West."

"It was," I said. "First there was New York Harbor. Then there was the confluence at Pittsburgh. Then came the Falls of the Ohio at Louisville. Then came

Mike Bradford

Cairo where the Ohio joins the Mississippi. Then we find ourselves at the wagon trails and railheads at St. Louis. Each, in its turn, was the Gateway to the West."

"Davis, this isn't going to be one of your lectures is it?" she teased.

"I'm done, but you have to admit. We Americans had to get all the way to California somehow. Do you know that as one travels from Kansas City to Denver there is a town every so many miles apart, and that the distance between the towns is the distance it took for the steam engines to run out of water. Every so many miles they had to take on water and a town grew up where these water tanks were located?"

"Davis!" she exclaimed. "Now, California I understand. That's really west."

"Well, Hawaii, while not our western most state, is farther west than California." I knew I had her irritated. I couldn't resist another nudge.

"Davis, why do you always have to know everything? Do you suppose we can get a trip to Hawaii out of this?"

"Not a chance," I responded.

William Luzadder greeted us warmly at the door of his sprawling, ranch style home. It was one of those upscale houses with a huge yard in a fine old neighborhood. I guessed the house had been built in the mid-sixties before they developed the choped up lines that we see in more modern abodes. I liked the house and I liked William Luzadder. He was a what-you-see-is-what-you-get sort of a guy. He was older

The Hole in the Bottom of the Sea

but not elderly with that well-worn look that can come from years of labor and stress. I figured he could tell us of some difficult years. He was a tall man, carrying too much weight. His once-black, curly hair was now steel gray. A thin scar that began just below the corner of his left eye and circled to the corner of his mouth accented his piercing blue eyes. His hands were large, stubby fingered and rough. His two-fisted handshake conveyed a strong and warm character. His wife bore the sweet name of Alice.

Alice had prepared for our coming. She busied herself and made mighty efforts at plying us with sweets and refreshments. I got nice feel from the Luzadder house. The place did not have the look of a home where entertainment was an important focus. It was efficient, cozy, and practical. This was by no means a showplace. Somehow it reminded me of the house on Peachtree Avenue. It was peculiar, but that reminder left me cold. I didn't want to wind up a few years down the road living with Kitty in a cozy house with no sense of life and no joy through involvement. I decided right then to go back to Louisville and plan a party. *All work and no play make Jack a dull boy* were the words that had popped into my mind.

Luzadder did not come right to the point. We waded through about twenty minutes of small talk. He was a football fan and loved to root for the Chiefs. I was pretty sure I was talking to a Republican and a protestant. It was his opinion that Kansas City is too big and not as genteel as Louisville. The place is too cold in the winter and too hot in the summer. The wind blows too much.

"May we take you to dinner?" Luzadder asked. "Alice wanted to cook a big meal, but this is Kansas City. You can't visit our town without eating real Kansas City steak!"

I slipped my foot over onto Kitty's little tootsies and pressed down. I knew she was just a breath away from asking if there were Italian restaurants nearby. She gave me a glare—I spoke first. "Gladly, can we take Plain Jane?"

"What, I'm sorry?"

"Can we take our car? We call her Plain Jane."

"Lord, why?"

"No reason. Kitty can't remember makes of cars. She just names them."

William cast a sidelong look at Kitty as if he was weighing an impossible situation.

"Shall we pile in?" I said.

"No, no, no, you're our guests," William replied, with a big smile.

He disappeared into the back of the house. Within moments I heard the unmistakable high-C sound of the horns on a Cadillac. Alice led us out to the drive where I was delighted at the sight of a metallic turquoise 1967 Cadillac four-door hardtop. The ride had a black vinyl top and matching leather interior. The car was original, perfect and immaculate.

"Heavens to Betsy!" I exclaimed. "Did you restore this?"

The Hole in the Bottom of the Sea

"Humpf," he grunted, as if insulted. "Restore, hell, I bought this baby new and maintained it myself. Every inch is original. They don't build cars like this anymore. There's not a Japanese part on it, and you can bet it wasn't built in Canada!"

I felt a little uncomfortable as we backed out past my rusting Toyota. Plain Jane was hardly a ride to brag about. I had bought it used and had neglected it all by myself.

The Luzadders took us to a restaurant called the *Hereford House*. It was a nice enough place on the south side of the downtown area. William informed us that the restaurant had a national reputation. "Top of the line, Davis, top of the line!"

"You just have to try their Kansas City strip. It's the steak that made our city famous!" Alice chirped.

"Well all right!" I agreed. Kitty nodded approval.

The Luzadders ordered a petit filet, soup and salad. They suggested we split the thirty-two ounce steak for two. I got the feeling we'd just been set up.

After a fashionably long period of time, the servers returned pushing a cart. We were presented with our own private salad bar. Soon to follow was two full pounds of prime beef. Braised vegetables were piled high. Large fresh looking tomato halves, smothered with Parmesan were presented, still sizzling from the broiler.

"Holy Mother," Kitty said.

The Luzadders just smiled.

I remember my dad once telling of a time that he ate to a standstill. I finally understood what he meant by that.

The trim little dark-haired waitress chimed, "Do you care for dessert?"

The Luzadders ordered a nice peach cobbler. The Winthorpes sat and stared.

"I guess I can't put this off any longer," William said.

I kept quiet. From the way Kitty was shifting in her seat, I just knew she was about to burst with curiosity.

"Mr. Winthorpe, someone is putting flowers on my mother's grave. I want to know who it is."

Luzadder had blurted these words out with an intensity that made it seem like some big deal. Kitty made a sound like the air had just gone out of her. I was at a loss for a comeback. I shrugged and said, "Tell me more."

"My brother and I grew up in Louisville, over in the highlands. After our mother died, Raymond sort of took over the home place as headquarters for his escapades. I don't know how the hell he made so much money, but he always seemed to be rolling in dough. He was in and out of Louisville five or six times a year. He brought friends—mostly women. Ray always had some sort of long drawn out bash during Derby Week. Christmas was party time for him. It goes on and on. I just stayed out of the way. I didn't care about the house. I had enough to take care of here."

"How does this tie in to flowers on your mother's grave?" I asked.

"After Ray died, I took over the house and rented it out. I have an agent who sees to the place, but once a year or so I try to get over and check it out. I don't travel well anymore. I try to go in May or June, when the weather is nice."

"And?" I nudged.

"When I'm in Louisville I go to visit my mother's grave. It's in the old St. Louis Cemetery. Two years ago I found dead, dried out flowers on her grave. Last summer flowers were there again. This time they were fresh looking. I don't know what gives."

"Why is this a problem?"

"There's no other family besides me. That grave was untouched for years. All of a sudden someone is decorating my mother's resting place. I thought it might have been a neighbor, or someone from where she attended church, but she died almost twenty years ago. It doesn't add up."

My inquisitive nature began to take control. In all honesty, I had been indifferent to this man and his situation, but there was something compelling about the whole notion of some mysterious donor of flowers. I was starting to care.

"What about your father?" Kitty asked.

I think I flinched. I knew that if she got interested there would be no stopping until the mystery was solved.

"Hell, he's both the ruination of me and the key to my success!" Luzadder exclaimed. He spat the words

Mike Bradford

out with a tinge of contempt. He continued, "I was seventeen when my father shot himself. I was in my senior year of high school with plans for college. I had this big notion about being a veterinarian, but our old man blew that all to hell. The S.O.B. left us with a mortgage, unpaid bills and zip in the bank. I went to work in the stockyards to support the three of us. I've been killing myself at hard labor ever since."

"Sounds like you were dealt a rough hand," I said. I wanted to tell him to get over it. My dad died when I was young. Mom worked. I worked. We made a life for ourselves. Life isn't always what you want it to be, and I never called my dad a S.O.B. I was ready to stop liking William Luzadder, but I wanted to know more.

"How did Raymond handle it?" I asked.

"Ray was eight years old and spoiled rotten. After the suicide our mother poured all of her attention on Ray. I couldn't work hard enough or bring home enough money to get any praise from her. Ray was her baby." His tone got colder with every word.

Kitty said, "So you kept them up?"

"For a while," he said. "Then *they* hit it big time."

"How's that?" I asked.

"Her older sister, Grace, died—left mom a whole pile of money. Mom paid off the mortgage. She bought a new Thunderbird, and began to give Ray what she called the *advantages of life*."

"I see," I said—Interrupting. I had started to understand the pattern.

"She took Raymond to the country club for golf lessons. She bought him one of those moped's so he could *visit his friends.* Three times, mind you, not once, but three times she took him to Hawaii. Damn, she put Ray through college.

"And you?" Kitty asked.

"Me—hell, she told me that I was older and should understand. She said that I needed to take my responsibilities seriously. My twenty-first birthday came and went. She didn't even mention it. I hit the road—never looked back. Well, that's an overstatement. I did check back on them. It's just that, well, we were never a family."

I took a guess. "I assume it's safe to say you and Raymond were not close."

The man's chin started to quiver. "I loved him so, and I hated him. I couldn't resolve the two emotions. I wanted so much to have this little brother to goof off with. I wanted to stick up for him, teach him to chase girls. As it happened, I was never home. When I was home, I was exhausted. Ray took up with a different crowd. Before too long, he didn't want his friends meeting his brother, Will. He told me I smelled like the stockyard."

Tears had come to the older man's eyes. I was at a loss as to what to say.

Kitty spoke. "Mr. Luzadder." Her voice was soft. When touched by something she would speak in a gentle purr. "I sense so much grief in you—and anger. If we can, we'll help you deal with your concerns. What more needs to be said about the flowers on your mother's grave?"

"Could we get out of here?" Luzadder said. He pushed his chair back abruptly. Alice was immediately busy gathering up her things.

I kept my silence as we drove back to the Luzadder home. We were traveling boys in the front, girls in the back. Kitty and Alice were chattering. William and I were both content to let the time pass.

The garage door was opening. "You walk the women in. I'll be in shortly," he instructed.

I got out of the Caddy.

Alice went straight to making coffee for us. In just moments William appeared from the garage encumbered with something rolled up in newspaper.

"Oh, Will," Alice chided.

"I kept the damn things," Luzadder said, unrolling the bundle on the kitchen table. "Here's what puzzles me. Both times the flowers were just like these."

"What is this?" I asked, fingering one of the well-dried flowers. It was peculiar in shape. I knew I had seen a flower like that before, but, still, I couldn't place it.

"Bird-of-paradise," Kitty supplied. "It's tropical. All of those flowers are tropical."

William said, "I could understand chrysanthemums, or glads, or—petunias, for that matter, but these are weird looking things. I get one strange feeling when I look at this stuff. I want to know who's putting them on my mother's grave!"

"Did your mother ever have a lover?" Kitty asked, abruptly.

The Hole in the Bottom of the Sea

Luzadder threw his head back and looked off to one side. He put one hand over his mouth and then both hands on his hips. "The thought never occurred to me. You almost made me blow my stack, but, well—that would be one explanation."

"Except for all the time that passed," I said.

"Right, where was her honey all those years?"

"Mr. Luzadder," I said.

"Mr. Winthorpe?"

"I'm not an investigator. In simplest of terms, I'm an errand boy. Why am I in Kansas City?" I held my arms out wide. "I am honestly enthralled by this story. It's compelling. It's fascinating, but why do you need me, us, here?"

Luzadder poured himself a cup of coffee. He walked to the kitchen door and stared into the darkness. "Coffee?" he said.

We had no chance to answer.

Alice busied herself with cups and saucers.

He continued, "You do that thing for me every Christmas with the wreath. You know what happened to my brother." Luzadder stopped. He was waiting for a response.

"Yes, and?" That's all I knew to say.

"I thought you might hear what I have to say and at least have a sympathetic ear. I'm a guilt driven man, Davis. I let anger rule my actions toward my mother and my brother. I never understood what dad did. I couldn't talk to mom. If I questioned her at all, I faced rebuke and anger. I was a frustrated young man and I made one ugly choice after another. I walked out on the only family I had. There's me, and there's Alice, and there's that Cadillac. So, once a year I go to my mother's grave. I stand and talk to her. She still doesn't tell me anything. Once a year I have you send a wreath to my brother. I'm a rich man with a wonderful wife and a big empty place in my heart. I never got the chance to go back and set things straight. All my people up and died on me. I love Alice, but sometimes I feel like a lonely bird sitting on a housetop. They died and left me holding the bag."

"OK, I guess I'm beginning to understand, but somehow I don't seem to see the problem. Mr. Luzadder, it's late. I've driven all day. My mind isn't soaking this in. I'm going to find a motel. I don't want to be rude, but could we sort this out tomorrow?"

"Oh, no, you stay with us!" Alice insisted.

William wasn't done. He had more to say. "I think Ray's alive. I think he's the one sending the flowers!"

The room was silent.

"William has been working up his courage to say that since the fourth of July, last year," Alice said. "Now you've said it, honey, but these people can't settle the question for you one way or another. Maybe you can talk some more tomorrow and it will put your mind at rest."

"Damnation, no!" he shouted. Tears came. "I hated Ray. Good riddance is what I said—him and his hotshot friends. Good riddance I said! The big man shuddered. Some people cry with grace, but not William Luzadder. His face grew beet red. He tried to talk but he just blubbered. He excused himself to the half-bath. We

The Hole in the Bottom of the Sea

looked awkwardly at each other as we listened to him blowing his nose—loudly. Soon he returned, struggling to regain composure.

"I didn't mean the things I said about Ray. It's just that we hardly ever saw each other. We didn't even write each other, but, oh God, I miss him so. I'm mad at him because he's not here for me to be mad at. Am I crazy, Winthorpe?"

"You're not crazy, Mr. Luzadder," Kitty said softly. "No crazier than I am. I understand that kind of anger."

I didn't understand anything.

Kitty took the big man in her arms. Alice was weeping softly. We talked long into the night. Years of anger and frustration came pouring out. We each had something to share.

"Life's a bitch!" William spat out.

"No," ventured Alice. "Life is difficult. How we handle it is the bitchin' part."

Luzadder studied his wife intently. He seemed taken aback at her use of the rough word. The quiet woman had contradicted her assertive husband. More than that, she had hit the nail on the head.

Luzadder produced a picture of Raymond. "I took that myself the day he graduated from the University of Louisville. He's looking at a check for five-thousand. It was my graduation present to him. He came out with a degree in law. Hell, I don't think he ever took the bar exam. I don't know. After he moved to Virginia, he got involved in computer software, or something like that. He always seemed to think that what he did was too technical for me to understand. We didn't talk about it."

"Could I have a more recent photo of Ray, Mr. Luzadder?"

"That's the most recent photo I have. He developed this weird thing about getting his picture taken."

I was looking at a photo of an extremely handsome blondish man. His features were fine to the point of having that movie star look. The hair, unlike William's, was straight. Raymond was looking down at the object in his hand. The hair nearest to his face had fallen free across his forehead, giving him a rakish air. William had captured the moment. Raymond was looking up as if about to speak.

"How long ago was this taken?"

"That's what twenty-five, twenty-six years ago—he was, maybe, twenty-two when I took that."

And, how old are you?" I continued.

"I'm almost fifty-eight," he replied. "Ray is, what, forty-nine?" He paused. "Ray would have been forty-nine."

"So what I have is a photo of a kid who, if living, would now be pushing fifty, This is a picture of a man who died in the Ohio River, but is suddenly putting flowers on his mother's grave?"

"It's a crock. Isn't it?" Luzadder responded.

"Oh, who knows?" I said. "Life doesn't surprise me much any more. What do you want me to do with this?"

"Winthorpe, I want you and your very fine looking wife to go back to Louisville. Every few weeks go visit my mother's grave. See if flowers are there. See what you can see. Ask questions. If you get any ideas, call me. That's all I ask."

I looked up from the photo, attempting to imitate the look on Raymond's face. "How much did you say this check was for?"

"Hell, you're wondering how you're going to get paid!" Luzadder exclaimed.

"Well, this is how I make my living."

"What's your fee?"

"Three-hundred a day plus expenses."

"I'm not about to pay you three-hundred every time you drive to St. Louis Cemetery."

"Oh, Will," Alice said.

Kitty took the picture from me—took a long look at it. "We'll ask for a fee after we get results!"

I looked at her with my mouth slightly agape.

"After we get results," she repeated—for my sake.

We had a task.

The Hole in the Bottom of the Sea

Chapter Six

The morning after our trip back to Louisville I fired up Plain Jane and took a short trip to see my friend, Maggie Branum. I knew her expertise would lead me right to the starting place. I parked near her flower shop in Old Louisville, popped a quarter in the meter and went inside.

"Maggie, I'm onto another odd one!"

"Aren't you always?" she replied.

Maggie gave me the once over. It was spring and I had dolled up with a shantung silk jacket of a color I would describe as raspberry. A yellow shirt, light tan slacks and pale blue silk tie worked together to make me quite the sight. Tan deck shoes finished off my outfit. From the look on Maggie's face, she was an inch away from snickering.

"You look like you're ready for Millionaire's Row on Derby Day!"

"That's the idea, Old Girl."

"So, what kind of an oddball quest are you on now?" she asked.

"Trying to resurrect a dead man, Maggie. A man, long time dead, is now putting flowers on his mother's grave."

"Oh brother," she said. "Don't you ever do anything like normal folks?"

The Hole in the Bottom of the Sea

"Too boring, Maggie. You remember the wreath I buy every Christmas?"

"Yeah," she answered. "That's the same one you never pay for until February."

"You got it. Well, it's the same guy. The brother of the deceased pays me to drop the wreath into the Ohio. Now, all of a sudden, someone is decorating the mother's grave. There's no other family and no suspects."

"Spooky," she said. "That's the guy that crashed his plane in the river, isn't it?"

"Right again."

"How do you plan to get me mixed up in this?" Maggie asked.

"I need some free information."

"No way, Davis. Somehow this is going to cost you," she teased.

"The brother has asked me to go check the grave from time to time. He want's me to look for a pattern, find a clue, figure out who's putting the flowers there. You know, stuff like that."

"You think the flowers come from my shop?"

"Maybe," I answered. "I wish it would be that easy. William, the brother, has found flowers two different times. Each time they looked like this."

I tried to sketch a picture of the flower that Kitty had called the bird-of-paradise. If this weird looking bit of flora was as rare as I thought, it would be a cinch to trace down its source and wrap up at least part of this mystery for William Luzadder.

"Oh, that's *Sterilitza*, bird-of-paradise," Maggie chirped. She cradled her chin in her interlaced fingers with elbows on the counter. She seemed amused at my artistic endeavor.

"Pretty rare, huh?" I concluded.

"Well," she said. "Let's go in the back."

I had never been *in the back* at Maggie's place. I was about to step into that never, never land where beautiful floral concoctions come from. *Whoops, what a mess.*

"There they are," Maggie said, pointing to a white five-gallon bucket packed full of the exotic beauties. It was my first time to see the bird-of-paradise fresh and in full color. The array left me wide-eyed.

"Where do they come from?" I asked.

"South Africa, supposedly," she said. "These are *Heliconia* from tropical America. I also have some Calypso. It's a hybrid. There are endless varieties in the tropical family."

Maggie just kept right on talking about several names of flowers that I couldn't begin to sort out. Most of it was Latin, or something. I did catch a few good sensible names that I could understand. I heard *ginger, pink mink,* and *heart of Hawaii.*

"Are most of these from Hawaii?" I interrupted, playing a hunch.

"Not many," she replied. "They do grow most of these in Hawaii, but the flowers originated someplace else."

That wasn't what I wanted to hear.

"Do you order yours from Hawaii?"

"Not at all, where I order depends on who has what. I get stuff from Knoxville, Indianapolis, or local wholesalers. Hawaiian grown tropicals are too pricey. Most of my stuff comes from Costa Rica, Mexico and Texas.

"Maggie, I'm confused. If I wanted to get flowers like this here in Louisville, could I just call any florist?"

"Just about," she replied. "Some specialize in tropical arrangements, but you can find them at Kroger's or Winn-Dixie."

My bubble was burst. Whoever it was who placed tropical flowers on the grave of the deceased Mrs. Luzadder could have picked them up in any neighborhood. The only connection left was the report that Raymond's mom took him to Hawaii when he was in his teens and the fact that flowers like this grow there. Otherwise, I was at a dead end. I wanted to stay with my hunch.

"Maggie, write some of those names down for me. I want to look them up on the Internet."

"You got it, Davis."

She immediately set to scribbling on the notepad she kept on her counter.

"Here," she continued, turning to the cooler behind her. She produced a beautiful arrangement in a brass dish. Spread elegantly in the midst of the lush green was a single bird-of-paradise. "Give this to that pretty new wife of yours. I'll put it on your tab."

"Uh, how much is that?" I asked.

"If you have to ask, you can't afford it, Davis. Consider it the cost of doing business."

Mike Bradford

I had the taste of adventure in my mouth as I made my way back to Peachtree Avenue. This wasn't going to be as easy as I thought, and that made it even better. I wanted to go home, get Kitty and go to the St. Louis Cemetery. I wanted to find the Old Gal's grave, get a feel for the action and savor the mystery. I felt life pouring back into me!

There was the most unusual feeling in the air as I stepped into our kitchen. I'm not really one of those *Honey, I'm home types*, but Kitty always seems to have some cute way to say hello. She's one of those in-the-door-with-a-smile types. Kitty was in the kitchen, sure enough. She seemed frozen in place, idly wiping her hands with a dishcloth. Her beautiful eyes seemed larger than ever. Her pouty lips were parted as halfway between speech and silence. She closed her eyes one time, slowly opening them again as she swallowed hard. The effect was haunting. This was not the Kitty I knew. I was at a loss. I chose to keep my silence. I walked to her. Taking her soft face into my hands I kissed her half-open lips. She gathered herself to me. I took her gently into my arms.

"I thought I would be ecstatic, Davis, but I feel half dead," she whispered into my ear.

The words riveted me into place. I still hadn't said a word. I stroked the back of her head.

"I got an e-mail from my friend, Jenny. My place and all my things in New York have been sold." That's all she said. The tears came—then the anger.

"Dammit. Damn, damn, damn," she repeated, pounding her fist into my shoulder. "I wanted to be happy about this! I wanted this to be such a new beginning for us. Instead, I feel broken and alone!" The sobs came again.

I found my voice. "Whatever happens, I will never let you be alone. I won't even try to replace the life you had. It isn't much, but all I have is yours. Homeless, penniless, or hopeless, I will be here for you."

"Oh, Davis," she said. "Don't get mushy on me. I just have to cry. Don't try to fix it. Just hold me."

That's what I did. We just gently swayed to the sound of oldies on the radio. It was an easy enough request to grant.

Kitty pulled away, wiping her tears with the dishcloth. "Can we go to Cincinnati? Jenny transferred the proceeds from the sale to a law firm there."

"A law firm? Cincinnati?" I questioned. This request was a bit hard to understand.

"Brawner, Spivey and Faust—I found them on the Internet, and made a call. They'll hold the funds in trust until I can transfer them back to me."

"Sorry, Kitty, I guess I'm still confused. Why are lawyers involved in this?"

"Jenny referred to it as a necessary precaution. It gives me a blind trust in a town away from Louisville. The firm will work directly with Jenny to receive the funds. Then they will work directly with me to move the funds into my name as Katherine Winthorpe. This way the money comes to me, not even Jenny knows my new name or location, and the firm provides a safe cushion."

Kitty's brief speech left my head spinning. In spite of all we'd been through together, the mystery of who she was and what was going on was still unsettled in my mind. It was a bit before noon. We'd driven nine hours the day before. It would be about two hours and a half each way to go to Cincinnati, assuming we could find the firm with little delay. My choice was obvious.

"You want to leave now?" I responded. "No, wait!" I had forgotten the bird-of-paradise. I made a quick dash out to Plain Jane. When I returned Kitty still stood where I had left her. She looked at me with a puzzled grin. I produced the bird-of-paradise from behind my back with a flourish.

"Oh, how beautiful! Where did you find that?"

"It was already made up and sitting in the cooler at Maggie Branum's shop. I was hoping to learn that this was some rare flower that would lead me straight to the heart of this mystery—but there it was, just like an everyday thing."

"And you bought it for me—you're so sweet."

"It was so pretty—the first thing I thought of was you. I just couldn't resist!" Well, at least the part about not being able to resist was true.

Kitty responded with an appropriate profusion of thanks, placing the arrangement on our kitchen table. At the same time, she made it clear that we needed to be on our way to Ohio.

We grabbed a quick bite at the DQ and hit the road. Kitty was regular chatterbox as we made our way up I-

The Hole in the Bottom of the Sea

71. I think it was nerves. She began to give quite an inventory of the things she and left for the auction block. I listened patiently. She used names for her furniture that I did not understand. It was the same for clothes. Her collection of first editions was gone. She said that she hated most was to lose her art. Not much of her chatter sunk in—and, what the heck, I had a couple of signed and numbered prints. Who doesn't?

The law firm of Brawner, Spivey and Faust was located in the urban sprawl east of Cincinnati in an area called Milford. We found the place easily enough. I took time before leaving Louisville to do a map search on the Internet. The map I downloaded pretty much led us straight to the place.

"Come in with me," she requested.

I sat patiently in the inner office making uneasy conversation with their all-to-pretty receptionist. Law offices always make me uneasy. Two times before I had sat waiting for lawyer's God-like pronouncements. The first time I was shedding a wife and unpleasant in-laws. The other time was to settle my mother's estate. So, there I sat. Kitty was the best thing that ever happened to me, but there I was—sitting uneasy and alone, waiting for her. One of the lawyers, Faust, I think, took her into his office alone. So, I wondered, about who knows what. *Oh, what the hell,* I thought. *Kitty knows what she's doing. I'm sure she does.*

After an infernal eternity, Kitty stepped out. By the time we reached the car the letter in her hands was open. She was read it slowly, weeping. Closing the door as she sat back down in Plain Jane, she sighed a long sigh.

"Jenny says that she refuses to sell the things she knows I love the most. *Precious items are in storage. Your irreplaceables are in the vault at Brenemann's. The jewelry is in there too...*" Kitty was quoting. *"Someday,"* she continued. *"It all will be yours again."* Kitty ended her reading with a flourish.

Yikes, I thought. *What does all this mean?*

"My place was pretty highly leveraged, but there was a fair amount of equity. My investments are still in my maiden name with dividends being reinvested. Jenny is keeping all the correspondence for me and will forward it through Brawner, Spivey and Faust. She's such a friend! Mr. Winthorpe, let's go back to Louisville and see how much of it we can buy!"

My clock stopped when she handed me the check. I saw the figure with just a glance. I had to read it slowly another time. My math skills suddenly disappeared.

"Is that millions?" I asked slowly.

She took the check back, studying it intently.

"Six-million four-hundred and eighty-three thousand, nine hundred forty two dollars and seventy-seven cents," she announced.

"For a studio apartment!"

"Oh, Davis, I guess I never actually told you. I owned most of the building. The auction of my things brought a few hundred thousand, but most of the check is equity. I've got to reinvest most of that to avoid capital gains."

Kitty began to chatter about the sale of her mother's business, the money her father had sent from Italy to set them up and all the deals she made to purchase various units in the building she called home. My wits drifted off to someplace up beyond the clouds over Milford, Ohio. I couldn't remember how to start the car.

I couldn't find a resting place for my mind as we drove back home. Kitty talked on and on, gesticulating rapidly with her hands. Her words were just a smudge. Nothing came into focus, well almost. I noticed a snow-white SUV standing out in traffic behind us. That was not usual, but the distance between Plain Jane and the white rig never changed. I slowed. The vehicle came close enough for me to make out that it was a Chevy Blazer, then the driver dropped back to resume a following distance. My suspicious nature came to the front. I wasn't hearing a word Kitty was saying. None of my instincts were working. Every reference point for knowing who I was and what I needed to do had turned to mush. *God, I'm dreaming!*

I eased off the interstate at the Glencoe exit. I slowed drastically on the ramp to watch the Blazer glide by. My imagination was at the boiling point. I didn't trust my eyes, but I was sure I saw a woman's face and a flash of red hair.

"Need a pit stop?" I heard Kitty's voice coming from far away.

"No," I muttered. "I've changed my mind."

I lingered at the stop sign until a car behind me prompted action. I eased across the road and drove slowly as I reentered the interstate traffic. The brief change of pace had altered Kitty's state of mind. By the time I was up to speed, she appeared to be fast asleep. We came quickly upon the next exit. I watched the rear view. A white blazer was coming down the on ramp. All the questions came to mind. *Who? What? Why? How? Is this real?* I had no answers.

"Kitty?"

"Hi, Babe," she responded.

"There's a state park at the next exit. I hear they have a good buffet. Are you ready to eat?"

"Always," she said, sleep still in her voice.

I had planned this little side trip at Carrollton. I have some special memories of the place. I also knew the state parks had dinner buffets to die for. Now, though, I was unsure. I was on unfamiliar ground, we had a check for a pile of bucks, and I was imagining that the Blazer was full of well-armed thugs. I also knew I didn't want to drive straight home. I needed time to think. I felt that I had to keep things looking normal. Kitty has this way of getting out of hand when the situation starts to heat up.

The meal was a winner, but my sense of enjoyment was all shot. I also forgot that Kitty does not take to what we in Kentucky think of as *country cooking*.

There was no sign of the Blazer as we sped off the ramp to join traffic. *Maybe it was all coincidence,* I wondered. Kitty was soon fast asleep. There's a rest area just north of Louisville. I hoped desperately for a big semi to hide behind as we passed, but I had the road

The Hole in the Bottom of the Sea

all to myself as we whizzed by the rest area. At the top of the on ramp I spotted the form of a female figure rushing to get back into her vehicle. The white Blazer was back. It was dark now, but the driver had spotted us. I was doing over eighty, but I couldn't hide. We were being followed, but I had a plan.

I stayed right on I-71 to the place where it ends just before the Third Street exit. I got off at Third Street. The retirement center where my Aunt Molly Garst lived during her latter years was on Fourth Street near downtown Louisville. Aunt Molly passed away a few years earlier, but the folks at the home remember me. I've done tasks for the Administrator and others. It was their new bus Win and I drove back from Dallas.

I eased Plain Jane into a parking space near the front of the high-rise. I knew that this building connected to its sister building on Fifth Street through an underground tunnel.

"Kitty, wake up!" I didn't mean to sound terse, but I knew that I had.

"What—what's happening?" she managed.

"My Aunt Molly used to live here. Let's go in for a minute."

"What time is it?" she mumbled.

I didn't answer. I closed my door and walked around to open hers. The Blazer had eased to the curb on the other side of the intersection. I made idle talk as we rang the bell to be admitted.

"Hi, Roger, I'm going to visit Mrs. Stokes," I announced.

Roger waved me through with a mumbled greeting.

Mike Bradford

We took the elevator down to the lower level. The halls were empty. I ushered Kitty along, heading for the tunnel.

"Davis, what's up!" she exclaimed. Kitty was wide-awake now.

"We're being followed. Someone's been on our tail ever since we left Milford."

"What, why didn't you tell me?"

"Wasn't sure, but I am now. It's a white Blazer. The driver parked a block south and watched us go in."

"Where are we going now?"

"Out," I responded.

She continued to ply me with questions as we rode the elevator back up to the entry level and headed across Fifth Street.

"Let's cut to the right. I don't think we'll be seen."

We rushed down the alley to the next street. We stood at the bus stop on the corner of Sixth Street for what seemed to be an eternity. My skin was crawling. I was sweating profusely. Kitty told me she was freezing. All I wanted was to see the lights of the bus.

We got off our TARC ride at the DQ and walked to the safety of home. Kitty was totally irritated. I had no answers for her questions. She had no answers for mine. We were only a few words from fighting. I trembled in the cold April air as I stood alone on the deck.

I called Winston Pence. It was two in the morning as Win drove slowly north on Fourth Street in his big red Chevy truck. I crouched in the floorboard as he circled the block.

The Hole in the Bottom of the Sea

"No sign of any Blazer," he said.

"Go around again," I demanded. I stayed out of sight as Win watched for Blazers and odd strangers.

"Looks clear," he announced.

Win pulled a long black flashlight out of the door pocket.

"I'm going to check this baby out," he stated as he slid out of the truck.

I kept my head down until curiosity got the best of me. I rose slowly to take a peek. Winston was looking under the fenders and bumpers of Plain Jane. He took on a casual air as he sauntered back to his truck.

"Don't raise up," he said. "Look at this."

He extended his hand to me. I couldn't make out the object in his dark fingers. He flashed the light on his prize for an instant.

"What the devil is that?" I asked. I was befuddled.

"Don't got no idea, but my best guess is that it is some kind of tracking device."

"The hell you say—a bug!"

"Davis, you done got yourself into a whole big bitchin' bunch of trouble this time. You got some kind of serious dudes messin' with you!"

I lacked the courage to tell my friend we'd been followed by a woman.

"What do we do?" I blurted.

"Watch this." Win flashed his compelling grin and walked casually across the street. The new bus was parked in the drive-through at the front of the retirement high rise. He walked around the bus as if he was checking out the good-looking rig. I saw him slip his hand under a wheel well in the process. Win walked back to the truck to stow his flashlight in the door. He tossed his keys on the seat and pressed the lock button.

"Come tomorrow morning I'd say your buddies will follow that tracking device right to the Cracker Barrel. I'll see you back on Peachtree."

Win slammed the door, got into Plain Jane and drove away. I laid low in the truck, watching to see if any vehicles followed. Win drove well north on Fourth Street before turning. Convinced I was safe, I powered up the Chevy and headed home.

I thanked Winston profusely as I swapped keys with him.

"Keep close on this one. I want to know what's goin' on," he said.

I muttered my agreement. I had no idea what sort of look was on my face.

"What you grinnin' about," he asked.

"Couldn't say, Just, glad to be home safe."

"Yeah, maybe," Win said, squinting as he cast a sidelong look at me. "You got more goin' on than I'm being told. I'll see you tomorrow, and you gonna come square with me. Get that silly-white-boy grin off your face."

"Tomorrow," I said.

"That's right," Win said as the truck door slammed.

I had no idea how I was going to tell Winston that I was married to woman who was filthy rich.

The Hole in the Bottom of the Sea

Chapter Seven

My name is Winston Pence. I'm not very good at putting down what I know about something. So, I'll say what I've got to say and quit.

This whole thing has to do with a friend of mine by the name of Davis Winthorpe. I say *friend*, but as of late Davis has been more like my employer. Maybe it's more like I work for that woman he married.

Several years ago I had a bit of a problem with a finance company. Their computer had my account messed up, so I got real smart and stopped paying my payments until they got me straightened out. That was a big mistake. I gave them lots of mouth and no money. Being the kind people that they are they sent this Winthorpe guy out to repossess my truck. To make a long story short, I caught Davis trying to take my rig and I beat him spitless.

"Hell, man—back off! I'm just doing my job!" is what he said.

"The hell you say!" is what I answered back. I was so mad I couldn't come up with anything a whole lot better to say.

Davis asked me what the deal was, and I told him. What he did next was the beginning of my respect for the man.

"Let me come inside. Show me the paper work. Maybe I can set things straight."

Some chance, I was thinking. I had called those people a dozen times and got nothing but messages telling me to press three for billing inquiries. When I did get a human I talked to some woman with a smart attitude and a voice like a sister with a big old butt. I took Davis inside my home and introduced him to my wife, Shannie. I gave him all the papers and letters from the company. The dude looked at the stuff for a long time then looked up at me.

"Let me make a couple of phone calls," he said. "I know some people inside the company. Maybe I can fix it."

Later I wished I could stand behind myself and kick real hard. I'd given all my paperwork to this white guy I didn't even know. I also knew he had a set of keys to my truck. I figured I had to go a bit to work my way up to stupid. Two days later I got a phone call from the manager of the local office.

"Mr. Pence," he said, "We have made a most regrettable mistake. I want to assure you that we have corrected your account and appreciate your excellent record of payment."

That took me by surprise. I had to sit down and stare. I don't know how he did it, but this Davis guy changed my fears to cheers. He had this gift. He knew how to talk to people and get what he wanted. It scared him to death though. I've seen him talk nose to nose with some uppity-up or some big shot and make the dude back down. Then Davis would find the nearest

The Hole in the Bottom of the Sea

john and throw up. Hell, I guess that's why I like him. He knows how to run a tough front, but underneath he's just as ordinary as I am.

Later that same day Davis was on my doorstep. He apologized for trying to take the truck and told me again that he was just trying to do a job.

"I do little odd jobs on the side to make ends meet," he told me. "I helped a woman at the finance company find work there. She gives me a job or two on the side every now and then. Most of the time I just verify information for them. Your truck was the first repossession I tried to do. I don't think that's a task I'm cut out for."

He stood there wearing this purple sport coat with a weird looking blue tie. He had this big grin on his face from ear to ear. I gave him my hand and a cup of coffee.

I figured that was the last I would ever see of him, and sometimes I wish that was true. Fact is, he called me a couple of weeks later.

"A woman I know in the east end wants me to drive her Mercedes to Charleston. I need someone to follow me down there and bring me back. In the spring she wants me to come down and drive the car back. You want in?"

"What's in it for me?" I answered.

"You drive that big red truck of yours. I'll pay for the gas, meals, motel and you get a hundred dollars a day."

"I'm cool with that," I said, and the deal was done.

Mike Bradford

Since then we've been in all sorts of gigs together. Most were straight up—nothing weird. For a while there I almost hated to see Davis coming. Then I started to get a kick out of those crazy thrift shop outfits of his and that crooked grin. Then one day I called him to see what we could get into next. I think that's the day I realized we were friends. I guess that's what friendship is. It's not a matter of who your friend is or how off center he gets. You're glad when you see him coming. So, that's the way it was—for a while.

I don't remember what I said, but I know it was stupid. He called me one day to tell me he had met this woman, and they were getting married. He asked me to stand up for him at the wedding, and, well—that's what I did.

"This can't be right!" I told Shannie, but she was all big-eyed over the notion of helping with the wedding. The whole thing sort of made my gut roll over.

The woman was a big gal from New York City. She had big old brown eyes, big boobs and a big mouth.

"She ought to do more thinking and less talking," I said to Shannie.

"Oh, Win," she answered, rolling her eyes at me. "Who are you to talk. People are different up there. You go to New York and you'll look like some wide-eyed hick of a black buck with hayseed in that nappy hair of yours. We all seem strange to people from other parts."

There's two things that Shannie enjoys most—being beautiful and being right. I saw no reason to argue the point, but this one thing I will say. This woman, Kitty, all at the same time, was the best thing and the worst thing that ever happened to Mr. Davis Winthorpe.

Most of the time Davis was humping around trying to turn up enough money to keep the wolf away. He would borrow money from me to get his laundry out. He always paid me back, mind you, and he paid me cash-in-hand every time I helped him with a job. *Then* he would borrow money for his laundry.

What happens is that this woman of his was made out of money. None of us knew that. All of a sudden she's buying this big house down in Old Louisville on Park Avenue. All of a sudden they are *the* Winthorpes of Louisville, Kentucky. She buys this big old Town Car, hires a chauffeur, and starts recreating Davis in her own image. Kitty was her name—Katherine Winthorpe to her *business associates*.

Long back, a couple of years before the lady showed up, Davis went after this notion of doing odd jobs for folks in a big way. Well—not so much in a big way as much as the only way he had left to make a buck. He walked off his job, put an ad in the paper and started doing God knows what for a living. That's when he and I became partners. Miss New York City came along and gets in the middle of it all. Davis used to call the stuff he did tasks. *I do tasks* was how he explained himself. The woman was the one who started calling him the *Taskmaster*. I was with Davis when she told him.

"Davis, sweetie," she said. "Our concern is no longer that of working for a living. We are now able to live for what we love to do."

That's it, I thought. *She'll cut me out and that will be the end of me and Davis.* I was wrong.

"We need to change the ad you have in the paper," she told him. "I don't want anymore of this business of driving cars around the country, or wiring up stereo sets on the weekend. Listen to this:

> ***Services performed.*** *When faced with circumstances of an unusual nature, or finding yourself in need of a creative problem solver, call the Taskmaster. Serious inquirys only, highly selective. Fees negotiable.*

What do you think?"

Well, we worked on *that* a bit. We changed the wording a little—more to Davis' liking, but what it came down to was that when folks called for help we would say no. That is, we would say no until something came along that sounded like an adventure to Mrs. Winthorpe. I say *we* because Kitty left me in on the deal. I was part of the team. On the other hand, it wasn't like friend helping friend any more. Kitty was in charge. Davis kept us all stable. He had the cool head when Kitty got excited. In a clinch, he was the man with the plan, but it was Mrs. Winthorpe that called the shots on what happened next.

The Hole in the Bottom of the Sea

Davis refused to drop his ad about driving cars around the country. That was one thing he loved to do. We would pile into the Town Car, take turns as we drove somebody's rig to wherever, have a blast for a few days, and head home by whatever route that seemed like fun. Kitty bought this beach house over on the Carolina coast. We would hole up there whenever it was not too far out of the way. Sometimes we would head up into east Tennessee to see her brother.

After a lifetime of making my living by blood and sweat I found myself in the company of the idle rich. Shannie traveled with us whenever she wanted. Davis always gave me a generous slice of the cash coming in. Kitty liked that, and that's what I liked best about her.

"It's only money, Davis," she would say. "Generosity is a greater pleasure than that of obtaining."

I liked her attitude about the money. I got my share. For the record, though, I want to say this. I sort of resented her use of the word *generosity*. I worked hard for every penny I got.

So, that's it. The Luzadder affair was the last of the old life. It was also the first of the new life.

I guess that's all I have to say—except for this. I would never say this to my friend Davis Winthorpe—actually, I love them both, but, in this man's opinion, the woman is a pain in the ass.

The Hole in the Bottom of the Sea

Chapter Eight

After the Cincinnati trip, the reality of or situation just didn't sink in. The next morning I went straight to the answering machine to see if I had any work. Kitty got the yellow pages out to look up a real estate agent.
"What's the deal?" I asked.
"House!"
The wheels in my mind stopped turning. I had developed the dream of being the conquering hero who buys some nice place for his lady fair. I had visions of working extra hard, making sacrifices and coming out on top. I even considered giving up my nutsey way of life and getting a real job—again. My first reaction was to question the wisdom of such a hasty move—then reality kicked in.
"Old Louisville is my primary target. I just love those old Victorian homes! I've got to put the equity into something sooner or later, and I would just as soon do it now."
I was silent. A pained look came on her face.
"Davis, I'm sorry. I've been sitting home dreaming and scheming. I've been just too afraid to talk it out. This has to be our decision. What do you think we should do?" She paused—then continued. "We can live in a castle, or we can live right here. I just want to be with you."

The Hole in the Bottom of the Sea

My mind was blank. A few weeks ago I was reasonably happy with my two bedrooms and a bath on Peachtree Avenue. I knew my home wasn't really a castle. I just wasn't ready to admit it. I took Kitty into my home during a rough time for her. It was very clear that she wasn't content with my little place. It was OK when I took her in—suddenly it wasn't good enough. The keys to Plain Jane were on the kitchen table. I reached for them.

"Davis?"

I looked long at her. My heart was tied up in a knot and I didn't know how to say why.

"Are you going out?"

"I told William Luzadder I would do a job for him and I'm going to do it!"

"Let me dress. I'll come too."

"No, *Kitty*," I said. "I'm going to the cemetery. I'll be back soon." There was an unfortunate edge to my voice.

"Davis!"

I listened for the back door to shut behind me. Actually, I was listening for a *goodbye* or *I love you*. I only heard the storm door hiss and slam.

I had hurt her feelings and I knew it. I guess my ego got the best of me. At the moment, I needed to be hurtful. It wasn't right, but I let anger rule my judgement. Kitty hadn't done anything wrong. Her only sin was excitement. Kitty had failed to think. I didn't know what my sin was. I just couldn't think. I headed for the car.

Mike Bradford

I had spent over forty years in Louisville without seeing the St. Louis Cemetery. I found it easily enough. I was an ancient place off Barrett Avenue. I was surprised at the amount and quality of the statuary. Ironically beautiful was this place for dead men's bones. I parked the car near a statue of an angel. The beautiful figure was high and lifted up. I stood there talking to a stone angel with moss on her wings. I think I talked for over an hour. I don't remember a word I said. What I did realize was that my problem was not due to anger at Kitty. My problem was my own feeling of guilt. It dawned on me that down inside I couldn't wait to start spending Kitty's money.

Mr. Luzadder had given me very precise directions. Finding his mother's grave was no problem. As I drove to the backside of the cemetery things began to change. The land flattened out a bit and grave markers became more like the headstones I was used to seeing. This is where Mable Luzadder was buried. I felt creepy staring at her grave. Flowers were there—dried and twisted. It was the same kind of stuff I had seen in William's home—and in Maggie's shop. *Whose hands have touched these?* My mind was abuzz. Was there any way this could be a tribute from a dead son? The compulsion came upon me to straighten the bouquet. It was a withered mess. I knew my inexperienced hands would be of little help, but I had to try. Something came over me as my fingers interacted with the ghostly flowers. Maybe it was a long dead mother calling from the grave. Maybe it was a long lost son calling from

The Hole in the Bottom of the Sea

the dark depths of the Ohio. I stood abruptly—with a shudder. I whirled around. It was as if I was not alone. Something came into me that I could not explain. I knew for sure that I would not rest until I had found some answers. I realized I was no longer working for William Luzadder. I needed to do this for myself—and I could afford it!

I made my way slowly back to Barrett Avenue. I guess it was out of respect for the dead. It was also a reaction to my own haste. I wished I had behaved differently toward Kitty. I wished she had been with me. I wanted to say, *Oh, look at that!* I wanted to see the look of wide-eyed wonder as she stood over the woman's grave. I wanted to see the sense of adventure bloom upon her face and take control.

She was on the deck when I returned.

"Did you find an agent?"

"No, I didn't look. I realized you probably already knew someone." She paused "And, we need to do this together. Come inside with me—*please*."

I held my ground. I was searching the back of my mind.

"Kitty, I don't think I know a single real estate agent. I bought this place as a fizzbo."

"Fizzbo?"

"Yeah, for sale by owner—F-S-B-O—fizzbo."

"So, what do we do?" she asked.

"Let's go down to Old Louisville and drive around. I want to play make believe and wonder *what if*. Let's get phone numbers from some for sale signs and work into the mood. At least that will be better for me. After we putz around for a while, we can go down to Tow Boat Annie's for dinner—no, wait, I've never taken you to Cunningham's. They make the best fish sandwich in the world, and it's cheap!"

"Thank you," she said. It was an unusually soft and sweet response. I think that maybe my terse reaction to her excitement had helped her to slow down a bit. I know my talk with the angel had put my senses back on the right track. The look of adventure was in her eyes. I couldn't wait to tell her about my moments at Mable Luzadder's grave.

Luck, or fate—or something had its way with us on that April day. There were homes with realtor's signs firmly planted in front yards, but nothing was right. Most had long since been converted to apartment homes. These were easy to spot. There would be a telltale row of mailboxes on the front porch wall. We ran the whole routine on the homes we saw.

"Look at the size of that place!"

"Too big."

"It's nice, but the homes around it are run down."

"Davis, it just lacks charm!"

I kept my mouth shut. I have been in a lot of Louisville homes. One never knows if a house is a home before the inside is seen. I have seen a lot of great looking homes—on the inside. My problem is that I can never picture my stuff in other houses. Kitty was full of excitement, and true to form she just kept chattering.

The Hole in the Bottom of the Sea

"Davis, this is a great old neighborhood. There is so much dignity. If the walls in these old homes could talk, what stories they might tell. I don't want a brand new place. Do you?

I started to speak.

"Look at that! I wish that was for sale. Davis, I don't really know what I'm looking for, but I'll know it when I see it. Don't you agree?"

I took a deep breath.

"Let's go to St. James court. That's my favorite place. Why didn't you take us there first? Davis, you haven't said a word."

The old stone lion at the entrance to St. James Court looked especially nice—unlike Kitty, he was quiet.

Then she saw it. I thought it was just a bit on the drab side. The brick work had been painted—many times. The color was a dull red. The wooden trim, that wasn't in need of replacement, was a dark olive. Someone, whom I assumed to have been sober, had painted the great wooden door purple. Leaded crystal in the entry door and side lights glistened in the evening sun. To phrase it, as I saw it—there was a tired elegance about the place.

"Davis, this may be it! Write down the number."

She read the number on the realtor's sign to me and made me repeat it. Then she took my notebook from me to see for herself.

"Find a phone!"

I supposed that someday I would carry a cell phone, but I was not ready for that yet.

Mike Bradford

We never made it to Cunningham's. I knew there was a phone in Central Park. We left Plain Jane in front of the old Victorian and took the short walk.

"You call, Davis. You call. I can't. You call!"

I stood quietly, looking into her big brown eyes.

"I never know what to say!" she exclaimed.

I mumbled, "Yeah, that'll be the day," and dialed the number—answering machine. A voice on the other end chirped, "To reach Julie quicker dial 555-1946!"

I hung up.

"Well!"

"Answering machine. Need to call another number." I retrieved my notebook and scribbled down the new number.

Kitty was expressing an irksome lack of confidence in my power to remember. I made dialing the digits into a laborious process just to nudge my pretty girl.

"Hello, this is Julie!"

The voice on the other end sounded all too perky. The agent made me remember a man I once knew who referred to realtors as *blondes with big hair and new Buicks*.

"Bingo!" I said to Kitty.

"I'm sorry," said the perky chirper.

"I was talking to my wife. Listen, I hate to trouble you at this late hour, but we're at a pay phone in Central Park. We got your number from a sign in front of a house on St. James Court—Uh—can you help us?"

My mind was blank. I had no idea what the lady might say next. I knew that whatever she said, I was unprepared. We had no plan.

Kitty rolled her eyes. "Ask if we can see inside!" she demanded.

"That house is pending," the agent said.

"Uh—pending what?"

Kitty was making beckoning motions with her hands, as if to say, *get on with it.*

"Pending financing—the house is sold. We have a clean contract and the deal should go through."

"It's sold," I said to Kitty.

"No big deal. Let's go eat."

I stared at her. I think my mouth was hanging open.

"Are you sure Old Louisville is for you?" the agent asked.

"We've just started looking. We really don't know."

"I have a pocket listing in Old Louisville. It belongs to an out of state friend of mine. The home is fully restored and will sell partially furnished. Since she's done so much work on the home, the owner is looking for a premium price."

"Well, what—I don't know. What's a pocket listing?"

"The house isn't really listed, listed. The owner doesn't have to sell, but says that if I find a buyer who's interested I should give her a call."

Listed, listed—I figured that was some sort of technical real estate talk.

"So, what do we do?" I asked.

"I can show you the home. The owners are away and I can meet you in about twenty minutes. I have to tell you. This seller will deal with serious offers only and this house will bring top dollar. If you are not pre-qualified and if you are not really serious, you'll be wasting your time and mine."

I started to ask her if six million dirty little George Washington's would make us pre-qualified or not, but I let better judgement rule the moment.

"Listen, Julie. Like I said, we just started looking. I'm sure we can manage the financing, but I just don't know. Where is this house?"

Kitty was doing something like the chicken dance and mouthing the word, *what!*

"The home is on Park Avenue. If you are in Central Park you should be able to see it."

"Park Avenue?" I repeated.

"Park Avenue!" Kitty exclaimed.

"Park Avenue," the agent said. She gave me the address.

"You said the owners are out of town. Have they moved?" I asked.

I heard a soft laugh. "They're wintering in Palm Beach. They're building a new place in Bardstown and don't plan on coming back to their house in Louisville."

"So what does that mean to us?"

"The house is available for immediate possession. Write me a contract tonight, we'll get the details worked out, you can move in—oh—probably by the end of the month!"

Her words made my head spin.

"Show us the house, Julie. We'll meet you in twenty minutes. My name is Davis Winthorpe. My wife is Katherine." I hung up the phone.

The Hole in the Bottom of the Sea

Kitty was silent—big eyes—blank look.

"I just bought a house. Did you bring the check book?"

I walked off toward Park Avenue. Kitty just sputtered as she followed close behind. I tried to tell all that I had heard. Everything seemed to click in her mind. She had dealt with real estate before. None of it seemed beyond her. I was unsettled. When I bought Plain Jane I spotted the car as I drove by a Ford dealership. I parked my car, asked how much and negotiated the deal. That was six years ago. When I bought my house I had to wait weeks for approval and jump through bunches of hoops. My financial deals had been few and far between. Besides that, what did agent Julie mean when she said the words, *the owner is looking for a premium price?*

As we waited for Julie to arrive, we tried to look behind the house on Park Avenue, but were prevented by dense hedges on one side and a steel gate on the other. Through the gate we could see only a narrow flag stone path along more hedge. The home was not as ornate as many in the area, but the paint looked fresh. Not a bit of decaying woodwork could be seen. It sat near the middle of the block. The porch was smallish, compared to some, but there was room for a swing and a couple of spring chairs. It went up two stories plus gables. To my right as I faced the house, was a turret which began at the second story level and rose above the peak of the roof. Three visible chimneys broke up the outline of the house. An ornate large door with natural finish and beautiful leaded crystal gave a classy look to the entryway. Sedate gray stonework was set off by elaborate carved stone trim at the windows. Each window on the first floor curved gracefully to a point at the top. Second story windows were rectangular in shape. The place was huge.

Julie took longer than twenty minutes and Kitty began to outline her strategies, "Davis, I want to put about thirty percent down and finance the rest. One does not just walk up and buy a house. Paying cash for a house is like waving a red flag in front of every money grabber in town. Besides, we can use the interest as a tax deduction. And, I don't really want to put too much capital into one property. We can pick up some apartments for rental. I also have some other things in mind. Let's just go slow and let this Julie person do most of the talking."

Yeah, right! I thought. Kitty continued to chatter.

Julie G. Patterson pulled up in a mini-van. She was a plump, sweet-faced brunette. Julie was wearing an outfit that Kitty described as being *cute as a button*. There went my theory on blondes and Buicks.

"Hi, I'm Julie! You will love this house!

She produced a key and made a beeline for the front door. I've been in Old Louisville homes before— enough that I never knew what to expect. These homes were designed in an age of opulence and indulgence of self-expression. Most have been redone through the years. I knew the place must have been worked over by several owners since the late 1900's—and Julie was right. I loved the house.

"When Alise bought this home the wood work inside was all painted with several coats of enamel. She found solid mahogany underneath. She had all the wood surfaces on the entry level stripped and refinished, and the floors redone. After Warren moved in he added the gazebo and redid the garden. Wait 'til you see that!"

Alise, I thought. *A few less bucks and she would be just plain Alice*—and I had no idea who *Warren* was. We stood talking in a large central hall. The hall was at least twelve feet wide. It went all the way through to a wide staircase at the rear of the house and was open to the ceiling of the second floor.

"Did you say Alise was in Palm Beach?" Kitty asked.

"Oh, yes. She purchased a nice place on Lake Worth several years ago. They go to Florida for the season. Usually they come back here before the Derby and stay through the St. James Art Fair. Alise refers to this as her summer cottage."

"My that does sound nice!" Kitty exclaimed. "Palm Beach is so lovely in the winter. Is her home near the Kennedy place?"

"I really don't know. I've never seen her home down south."

Lake Worth, summer cottage, Kennedy who? My mind was abuzz. All I wanted to do was see the house.

We moved to the right of the house through huge, double-hung pocket doors. The rich mahogany seemed to glow under the light from a large crystal chandelier that hung from the second floor ceiling above the stair well. The room to the right was bigger than my whole house—it seemed.

"This is the main salon. Alise uses it for entertaining. There's a wonderful sitting area to the front and dining toward the rear of the room. The kitchen is behind this room, and this window seat is wonderful!"

Yikes, three chandeliers dominated the room. They were smaller versions of the one in the central hall. The window seat was in a bow window in the center of the side wall. A stained glass window filled the center panel from the seat to the ceiling. The two side windows looked to me to be hand blown. The panes were filled with swirls and bubbles. The evening light was not on the window, but it was beautiful, never the less.

"The window is patterned after *Young David as a Shepherd Boy* by Louis Comfort Tiffany. It was done by local artists. The window had gotten into bad shape, but Alise had it releaded."

"Art Nouveau," Kitty stated.

"I'm really not sure," Julie responded.

Ching, ching! I was smart enough to know I was listening to one expensive conversation.

"Look over here!" Agent Julie dashed across the central hall, disappearing through another set of smaller pocket doors. "Isn't this a beautiful parlor!"

It was beautiful all right. A beautiful mantled fireplace dominated this room. A similar fireplace had graced the grand salon. The parlor was fully furnished, but appeared odd. It didn't fit.

The Hole in the Bottom of the Sea

"Alise has moved her furniture from this house to the new one in Bardstown. She brought these items up from Palm Beach. They are quite nice, but do look a bit like Florida."

"They look a lot like Florida," Kitty said.

I wandered on to the next room on that side of the hall.

"Look at this," I called out.

Julie described this as the library—duh. It was lined with shelves to the ceiling from wooden cabinets below. A rail circled the room, supporting two ladders that moved upon the rail. I wanted to jump on one and give it a shove. I figured this was not the time to let the kid in me get out. A huge desk backed up to a plain glass window—similar in shape to the one in the grand salon. Fine, leather easy chairs surrounded what appeared to be one nice oriental rug.

"Bingo—I'm home!" I announced.

"It is a very nice room," Julie stated. "The rug is a copy—but it's nice."

"Some of these are excellent volumes," Kitty said. "Do they stay?"

"If you wish. Alise doesn't really care about the books. Actually she would go to bookstores and buy whole shelves of used books just to fill these up. The next room down here is a small two-room suite with private bath. Maid's quarters. It's empty. Let's go upstairs."

"Kitchen first," Kitty requested.

"No, no, no," Julie said, shaking her finger. "That's special. Let's save it until last."

We ascended a wide set of stairs. The carved banisters swept down into curves at the very bottom of the staircase. We moved up to a landing, went to the right and ascended a more narrow flight to the second floor. A balcony was on three sides, looking down into the central hall. Several doors opened onto the sides of the rather plain balcony area. The wall toward the front of the house contained a series of nine pane glass doors. All the wood trim here was still painted white. Beyond the row of doors was a large solarium across much of the front of the house. The room was filled with wicker adorned with cushions of a tropical pattern and in pastel tones. It was also full of very dead and ugly plants. The glass doors appeared to open in such a way as to allow air to flow through the home freely. I got a chuckle as a picture formed in my mind of the former Lord of the House struggling to stay comfortable back before the days of air conditioning. In earlier years, before the trees of Central Park matured, this room would have enjoyed a great southern exposure. The Old Boy probably sat there in his white suit sipping on his mint julep.

Across the open stairwell on the other side of the balcony doors opened into three bedrooms. To the rear of the area and across the balcony there was another door. I couldn't begin to guess what was in there.

"Here are the rooms Alise and Warren used as a master suite," Julie said, motioning us through the door to the left at the head of the stairs.

A sea of white greeted us as we entered.

"This is Italian," Kitty said softly, into my ear.

"This furniture is French," said Julie.

"When pigs fly," Kitty whispered.

"I believe Alise must have had this imported," Julie continued.

"All the way from Grand Street in Brooklyn," Kitty whispered. "This is good stuff."

I ventured a small opinion. "Sure is pretty!"

"Oh, Davis! Kitty said as she took graceful strides across the room. The corner turret began in this room. The circular space looked to be about eight feet across. Richly brocaded upholstery covered a raised platform. Cushions were piled high. Inside the arched entryway the turret rose to a point above the upper level of the house. Windows with beveled glass filled the area. At the top one of the owners had installed a ceiling fan.

"I will live in this window!" Kitty announced. "We will make love in this window."

That's being noncommittal, I thought.

Agent Julie shuffled her feet.

Another bedroom adjoined this room toward the rear of the house. Kitty was into the room with a bound.

"And this can be the nursery!"

"I—what—whoa—what?" I sputtered. "Are you—uh—well—are we? Kitty, are you pregnant!"

"Oh, no, silly—but, Mr. Winthorpe, it is a thought."

"Do you to need to be alone?" Julie asked.

My mouth wouldn't work.

The long pause grew increasingly uncomfortable.

"I'm thinking about it," Kitty answered. "Show us the bath."

"This is both the strong point and the weak point of the second level."

"How's that?" I asked. I felt like I was better prepared for a discussion of toilets.

"It's the showplace of this level, but there is only one full bath on this floor. Two of the bedrooms across the way are joined by a half bath."

She opened a door into a room at least twelve feet wide and twenty feet long. A huge garden style tub was elevated beneath a large window wall overlooking a magnificent garden. It was a wonderful whirlpool tub with water jets and seats for two. A beautiful sink adorned the left wall. It was made to resemble a dresser, with elegant wood finish, beveled mirrors and sconce lighting were built into the piece. This, the commode and a bidet were all elegantly done in an old-world style. At the far end was a large glass enclosed shower. It was large enough for two people, or a small horse. At the far end of the room, near to the shower was the other side of the door that had aroused my curiosity earlier.

"Forget the window seat. I'll live here!" Kitty exclaimed. That look had come upon her face.

"Gonna make love here too?" I asked.

Kitty stared at me with an incredulous look. "Both!" she responded.

"This is all new. Alise describes it as an eclectic collection. Come, you must see the loft!"

We exited through the far door and made our way back to the solarium. From inside the solarium a door opened onto a narrow stairway that led to a large open room. This room appeared to be the neglected area of the house. Window seats were in each of six gables. The enclosed backside of the turret room could be seen. A few odd items and old looking paintings were propped up against the walls. Five or six neglected chairs and what appeared to be a hand carved headboard were here too. Assorted boxes, books and magazines were strewn about. The closed room was hot and stuffy.

"This room has not been touched in, oh my—decades. The wallpaper really looks bad, but it may be original. It's all hand painted!"

Kitty walked to the middle of the space—arms akimbo.

"Hmmmm," she said, looking about the room. She sighed a long sigh and turned to me with a strange look on her face.

Heaven help me, I thought. *What is on her mind?*

"Kitchen!" she said to Julie, and we trooped off to the lower level.

By the time we arrived in the kitchen I was fresh out of descriptive terms. I noticed an elegant but small powder room underneath the stairs and double doors behind the stairs that appeared to lead outside.

"This is also new!" Julie announced.

New and nice, I thought. Italian floor tile, double built in fridge, commercial oven, large island, cabinets everywhere and yet another fireplace.

"You could feed an army out of this!" I said.

"Yes, Alise did." Julie replied. "There's a large pantry through that door along with another full bath, laundry and a service entrance. Everything stays. Alise says that what she has here does not match the ambiance of her new place. All the cookware, utensils, silver, crystal—it all stays. There's service for twelve in standard dishware, and service for forty-eight in her formal service.

"Which is?" Kitty asked.

"Noritaki, nothing overly expensive", she replied.

Rats, I thought, *no Louisville Stoneware.*

"This is a nice place," Kitty said.

"Nice, and large—forty-two hundred square feet," Julie said.

I had counted fourteen rooms, six fireplaces, three full baths, two-half baths and one turret to make love in.

"We've not yet seen the best part," Julie said. "Let's go out back."

We stepped through the double doors under the stairs.

"Warren added this deck and built the garden area."

"Oh, holy cow!" I exclaimed.

A covered porch extended across the back of the entire house to a gazebo on the east end. Wicker and rocking chairs were abundant. And double hammock style swing was hung in the gazebo. Stairs led down to a large open sundeck that led to a stone walk to a beautiful lap pool. Elaborate stonework set off the pool area. On the left side of the pool a semi-circular area of stonework finished out the thing.

"The pool is not in service this time of year. When the pumps are turned on, a waterfall spills into the circle and there are water jets there! Lights are in the pool wall. At night, it is breathtaking!"

"Looks pretty good in the daytime," I replied.

Another large gazebo was to the right rear of the garden.

"In the gazebo, is that a—"

"Hot tub," Julie said, finishing my question.

The entire garden was surrounded by ivy-covered brickwork. I couldn't describe all the shrubs and rock gardens. To the very rear was another building. It was brick and did not match the house. One extra large door faced us from this building. A set of stairs was on either end. A second story featured window casements that appeared to be much newer than those on the main house.

"What's that to the rear?" I asked.

"Three car garage—there are two apartments over the garage."

"And the small building against the left wall?"

"A cabana—full bath, cabinets with towels for guests with his and hers dressing areas. There's a small sauna."

Kitty had grown silent. Abruptly she extended her hand.

"Thank you, Ms. Patterson. We have your number and can get back to you." She said flatly.

"Would you care to hear the price?"

"If you wish," Kitty answered.

"Seven twenty-four nine—as you see it. Alise does wish to remove a few items."

"Seven twenty-four what?" I said. "As in three quarters of a million?"

"Yes. That is a considerable sum, but the apartments over the garage could help with the monthly payment."

"Possibly," Kitty responded with a bit of an aloof tone. "I would prefer to use that space for servants."

Kitty took my hand as we made our way back toward Plain Jane. That's just as well. She kept me from bumping into things.

The Hole in the Bottom of the Sea

Chapter Nine

We bought the house on Park Avenue. That is to say, Kitty bought it. She was doing that I'm-so-excited-I can't-stand-it dance by the time we got back to the car.

"That's it, Davis. That's the house I want. Don't you think it's just grand? Tell me the truth. Isn't it perfect!"

I had a pretty good idea that expressing a negative opinion would get my heart ripped out. And, to tell the truth, in my wildest dreams I had never imagined that I would ever live in a place as fine as that. I responded with the absolute truth.

"God was smiling down on us today. How in the world is it possible that we walked out of the house, made one phone call and found—the perfect place?" I paused. Kitty was beaming. "Kitty?"

"What?"

"Well—it's not ours yet, and it *is* pretty pricey."

"Not to worry. We can get it for less than she's asking. Davis, stop and think. Be positive—we can afford it!

She got that last part right. Affording the house was the easiest part of the deal.

Agent Julie sent several offers and counters between Louisville and Palm Beach. The sellers and

Kitty were nowhere close to an agreement when my gal got stubborn and planted her feet.

"Call your friend, Alise, and tell her I'm making a firm and final offer at six-hundred and eighty five thousand. If I have to pay one penny more tell her she can rent a truck and come and get her tacky beach furniture out of the house and then we can talk!" she announced, slamming down the phone. Poor Julie didn't get a chance to respond.

That did it. In less than an hour the phone rang.

"Mr. Winthorpe, this is Julie Patterson. You just bought a house!"

I passed the message on to Kitty and watched her go ballistic. I never knew any one could emit a screech quite like the one she let out. She shouted, "Yes!" about twenty times, bolted out the door and ran all the way around our place on Peachtree Avenue before coming in to plant one huge kiss on me.

It was bittersweet for me. I'd wanted to do something wonderful for her. Now I was along for the ride, but what the heck. I figured if I got too frustrated I could go do a few laps in the pool and soak out my grief in the hot-tub.

In less than a month all the inspections were done, the paperwork was completed and the house was ours. That was the beginning of events in our lives that I could never have dreamed. I take that back. I could've dreamed some of them—nightmares.

I had a little trouble settling back down with the Luzadder affair. My plan was to make a trip to the St.

The Hole in the Bottom of the Sea

Louis Cemetery every six days. I thought that by doing that I could see if more flowers came. I hoped I could maybe find a pattern. My one best goal was to catch the mystery person red-handed. I also made it a point to mark the bundle of flowers each visit so that I could be sure when I was looking at a new batch.

The next fresh bouquet showed up around the first of May. I asked one of the caretakers to keep an eye on the grave and let me know if he saw any action of any kind. That cost me. I slipped the man a fifty-dollar bill every time I visited. I figured that a little money in the hand was the best way to keep my buddy in blue jeans from losing interest. He was a peculiar little man with stringy, shoulder-length brown hair, bright blue eyes and bad teeth. I had to fill him in a bit on what the deal was all about. The look of a frightened man came over his face as I told him of the drowning death in the Ohio and the mysterious appearance of flowers on the dead woman's grave.

"I don't want to upset no haints!" he informed me. "They's ghosts in this here cemetery. I get along with most of 'em, but you can't tell about a haint. Some folks, they don't believe, but I seen 'em—I seen 'em sure enough, Mr. Wenchert. How about you?"

"Yeah, right—who you gonna call?" I said that and let it go at that. I just hoped the little man in blue jeans was reliable enough to keep me informed. I didn't care what he believed in. He went on to inform me that shortly after Memorial Day they would remove all decorations from the graves for the mowing season.

After that, if any flowers showed up, they would be removed before the section was mowed.

"That's the rules," he drawled. "But mosta the time we sorta don't worry about it."

I called William Luzadder to let him know my plan and to tell him that a fresh bundle showed up in May.

"I was wishing this would just go away," William said.

I could sense weariness in his voice. I was dealing with a man who had his life settled. He liked living each day his way—the same way. He didn't like problems and he didn't like mysteries.

"You want me to let the matter drop?"

"No, I know it's a little bit of a dumb ass notion, but I want to know what's going on."

"William, I'll get back to you, if anything changes." I put the phone down. His words about this being a *dumb ass notion* kept scrambling around in my brain.

It cost me a couple more fifties to be sure, but, unless my grounds keeper at St. Louis Cemetery missed something, nothing showed up at the grave in June, July and August. I wondered if the affair was over. *Maybe that's it*, I thought. On the other hand, the situation made me think I was dealing with a person who knew what was what. That is to say—he (or she) knew the flowers might be taken away in the summer. My culprit could be a local who had learned from experience, or—what? I didn't know what. I didn't get too worried about it. I made a few trips to the graveyard, but, otherwise, I took the summer off from

The Hole in the Bottom of the Sea

the Luzadder affair. Winston Pence and I kept up my odd jobs on the side. He was too good a friend to let slip away. Besides, I hated to keep asking Kitty for fifty-dollar bills.

Kitty kept me, Winston and the big red truck on the run all summer. Shandalane and Kitty became constant companions. Kitty was on a mission. She wanted to get the new house completely ready before we moved. There was not a furniture store in Louisville and most of the Bluegrass that we didn't visit. Not a stick of our stuff from Peachtree Avenue got moved. We bundled up our *personal estate*, as Kitty called it, left all the furniture and rented the place to a young couple from Oregon. I did hate to leave the couch, though. Kitty and I had heated that thing up enough times to give it *sentimental value*. We took possession in late May, but didn't move in completely until early October.
"No need to rush," Kitty kept reminding me.
We didn't rush, but we did spend more than one night together in that window seat beneath the turret. Winston, Shannie, Kitty and I made the garden our own little paradise, enjoying steaks on the grill and late night swims. Kitty called this a warm up for good things to come. I knew a big party was in order once she had the house the way she wanted it.

Two days after Labor Day the phone awakened me. We were sleeping in the place on Peachtree.
"Mr. Wentley, you better get on over here. There's a woman at the grave!" It was my friend in blue jeans

from the St. Louis Cemetery. For some reason the man never did get my name right.

"I'm on my way!" I exclaimed. I checked to be sure I had a fifty in my billfold, threw on some clothes and headed out the door. I made a mad dash in Plain Jane down Taylor Boulevard. I connected up with Eastern Parkway at the University and put the accelerator on the floor. The lights and luck were with me—no cops in sight. I slowed to a respectable roar while going through the graveyard. My henchman was near the Luzadder grave, waving me on like my old third base coach. He shouted to me, excited and out of breath.

"She just left, Mr. Wentley—White Dodge minivan!

"Did you try to talk to her?"

"Skeered to, Mr. Wentley! Like, with what you been sayin' about dead men and these mystery flowers —I thought she might be a loony, or somethin'"

I laughed, then wondered—*he might be right*.

"What did she look like. Describe her!"

"Glasses, blonde, not young, sorta skinny, checked shirt with a denim vest and tan slacks."

"Middle aged—what?"

"Yeah, middle aged. That's it! Not pretty, but not bad lookin' either. She was white!"

He had just described maybe a third of the women in Louisville, but it was a start. He hastily led me to the grave. A fresh bouquet was there—no different from the others. I fingered the fresh flowers.

"I bet that's about the purtyest flowers I ever seen," he said.

"Pretty, and costly," I replied. "I've got to find out where these come from. I just wish we'd been able to stop her. I need more information."

"I wrote down her license number, and there was a sign on the van."

"What, why didn't you just say that!"

"You didn't ask."

"Com'on, man, out with it!"

He gave me a Kentucky license number.

"What'd the sign say?"

"Dee's Errand Service!"

Ouch—a gofer. This Dee, or whoever, was probably just a go between.

"Let's sit in the car. Tell me carefully everything you saw."

"I was over there runnin' the mower near the statue of the little boy. I saw this white van go by. I finished my run that way and turned around to come back and I see that the van is stoppin' near the Luzadder grave. So I watch. I see this woman I told you about gettin' out with a long box. She pulls out the vase that's on the grave. Opens the box and takes out these flowers and…"

"Wait a minute! What did she do with the box?"

"Beats me! I watched her maybe fifteen minutes. I rode my mower around and went right beside her, but I wasn't about to stop.

"What did she do for fifteen minutes?"

"Well, she got a milk jug out of the van and walked over to that hydrant there. She brought back water and put it in with the flowers. Then she sorta rearranged the flowers several times. Once she was satisfied with that, she put water in with some of them flowers on other graves and straightened on some of the others. Then she sat on that bench there for a while. Then she got in the van and left. It couldn't have been more than three or four minutes before you got here."

"Stupid!" I said out loud.

"I'm sorry!" Mr. Blue Jeans had a pained look on his face.

"No, not you—me! I saw a white van parked near the entrance as I came in—over next to Barrett. It didn't even cross my mind that it might be her."

"Wonder why she was stopped out at the front?" he said.

I thought for a moment. *That's it!* This lady couldn't stand to leave these flowers unattended and crooked. She was a compulsive neat nut. She didn't want the empty box cluttering up her van!

"Is there a trashcan or dumpster near the front?"

"Yeah, there's a big'un just before you go out."

"Take me there!"

We fired up Plain Jane and made a quick trip to the west side of the cemetery. The long slim box showed the abuse of shipping. It was still damp inside from the water someone had provided for the flowers during their journey. Something like wax paper and damp tissue were wadded up inside. UPS had delivered the box from a Sally Patton in Seattle to Dee's Errand Service. Dee's address was in the 40215 zip code.

"Well," I said. "From Sally in Seattle to someone in Shively. This is great! This may be the key to the whole mess!"

"How'd I do, Mr. Winthorpe?"

I knew that was my clue to pop for a fifty.

"Great! You did wonderful—uh. You know, you never have told me your name."

My stringy haired friend in blue jeans flashed a big grin. One front tooth was gone. "Danny," he said slowly. "My name is Danny Cutshaw."

"Thanks Danny!" I said, putting a fifty in his hand. "Can I take you back to your mower?"

"No thanks, Mr. Wentley. I think I'll walk."

I had a name, an address and a source. I figured I could wrap this thing up by the time day was done, have one less mystery to worry about and collect a few bucks from William Luzadder. I rushed home to report to Kitty. After receiving the phone call from Danny, I had just grabbed my pants and shirt and left. I was gone before Kitty was able to roll over.

"You took off like a shot. You didn't even wait for me!"

"No time. I drove like a crazy man, and still missed her. However—I got this!"

I held up the long box with pride.

"What is it?"

"The most recent bundle of tropical flowers came in this—and there's an address to a place here in town—and the address of the sender is on here too!"

Her eyes widened. "That's it! We've got it! Let me see!"

Kitty snatched the box from my hands.

"Dee's...Sally...Seattle...," she mumbled. "Let's go!"

"I thought you and Shannie were hanging pictures today."

"Forget pictures! Let's go! We can call Shannie from the car."

"How's that?" I asked.

"Cell phone—I got a cell phone yesterday."

Rats—the demonic machine had finally caught up with me.

Kitty searched a map for Kendall Lane while I made my way through the side streets to the area we refer to as Lively Shively.

"Here, here—here it is. Turn, look, no turn—here. Park, Davis, park!" Kitty was most helpful. She had caught the scent. There would be no stopping her now.

I parked two feet behind a white minivan with a sign on the back that said, "Dee's Errand Service."

A slim, white blonde with glasses, checkered shirt, denim vest and tan slacks answered the bell.

"Yes," she said.

"Are you Dee?"

"I'm Dee—Deanna Hopper. How may I help you."

The Hole in the Bottom of the Sea

"Ms Hopper you were observed placing flowers on a certain grave in the St. Louis Cemetery today," I tried to make my statement sound somewhat sinister.

"Is there a problem—uh, I didn't catch your name. You're not from the police are you?"

"I'm Davis Winthorpe, this is my wife Katherine. Sorry I didn't introduce myself. I'm not from the police, but I work for some people who are deeply troubled over the flowers that keep appearing at this gravesite." She took a breath to speak, but I continued. "Can you tell me whose grave that is—where you left the flowers?"

"Please come in, Mr. Winthorpe—and Katherine."

"Please call me Kitty."

"Yes, Kitty."

We entered the woman's house. It was typical of many of the older ranch style homes in Louisville. It was constructed from what people in our area refer to as Bedford Stone.

"Is there trouble of some sort, Mr. Winthorpe?"

"It depends on what you call trouble. Why do you ask?"

"I've had a strange feeling about this since I started delivering these flowers. I sort of run my own business. I do tasks for people. Most of the time I pick up ladies from the retirement homes around the town. I take them shopping or to the doctor's office. I do various things, but mostly it's transportation."

I just grinned at Dee as she spoke. I was fumbling to find one of my cards. I presented the card just as she finished talking.

"*I do tasks*—well I'll be. I need me a card like this. What's your angle in this, Mr. Winthorpe?"

"Who's buried there?" I asked, ignoring her question.

"All I know is what's on the stone."

"You don't know the lady or any of her family?"

"Not at all, Mr. Winthorpe. Why are you asking?"

Her last question was just a little terse. I have found that I can get more out of folks when a touch of anger is clouding their judgement. I was glad to hear her clipped tones. I wanted to nudge her just a bit more.

"I've been hired by a member of the family to find out where the flowers are coming from. It's her son, and he's not too happy with your activity."

"Well, I'll be, I can assure you—and the son that I have no improper intentions. I've been doing a job—and nothing more!"

"And you don't know anyone in the Luzadder Family?"

"Certainly not!"

I could see that the lady was getting irritated at me. It was time to shift gears and then get her to talk. "Dee, please call me Davis. Mr. Winthorpe—well that makes me sound stuffy. I've been a little pushy and I want to apologize. Let me start over. I work for a William Luzadder. He called me some years ago after reading an ad in the Courier Journal that says about the same thing as that business card I gave you. His brother died in a drowning accident in the Ohio. His plane crashed and they never found the body..."

"I remember that!" Dee exclaimed.

"OK, now we're on the same wavelength! The man that drowned was all the family William had. There's no one else. So, when flowers appeared on his mother's grave—well, he sort of had concerns."

"I can see why he's wondering who is putting them there!" she said.

"Bingo! What can you tell me?" I responded.

Dee pondered for a moment. "May I get you something to drink?"

"I'm parched!" Kitty replied.

Dee and Kitty went off toward the kitchen, leaving me to wonder why the woman was stalling for time to think.

"Tea or cola, honey," Kitty called.

"Cola suits me."

Dee soon returned with a tray. She placed coasters on the coffee table and methodically placed a glass on each. She took the tray back to the kitchen and returned to sit, carefully positioning herself.

"Mr. Winthorpe—Davis, I'm afraid that I have been sworn to secrecy."

"By whom?"

"I really don't know, and I don't think I should tell if I did know."

There was a look in her eye. Anticipation was there. It was sort of like the look on a kid's face during a game of Simon says. Or maybe—twenty questions. She wanted to tell me something, but wouldn't break a promise. I was going to have to play a game with her.

"Well, I guess that's it, then. Kitty and I should be going." I took a long sip from the cola and leaned back.

I said one thing while letting my body language give an opposite message.

"Yes, perhaps so. Please finish your drink." Dee leaned forward, placing both elbows on her knees.

"The flowers you placed today came in a box with a return address in Seattle and were mailed by a woman. Are you working for a woman?"

"Well, no. I mean the flowers usually come from Mailbox Express or some place like that. I've never noticed a name on the label before. Honestly, this time I didn't even look."

"Seattle?" Kitty asked.

"Sometimes. If the package doesn't come from the West Coast then it comes from Atlanta."

"West Coast?" I asked.

"Yes, L.A., San Francisco or Seattle, usually."

"Dee, I know that I don't work for free. How do you get paid?"

"There's always a money order enclosed. I assume that whoever packs the flowers puts the money order inside. It is always in a little plastic bag with one of those sticky back notes on it. The note always expresses a simple thank you. The plastic bag keeps it dry as a bone."

"Have you cashed the last one yet?" Kitty blurted, moving to the edge of her seat.

"Well, no, but—you want to see it, don't you?"

Kitty was nodding eagerly.

"I don't know. I could be saying too much. Wait a minute."

Dee left the room. In just seconds she returned, holding the money order.

"It doesn't tell anything. Here, you look at it."

The money order was from Western Union. It was made out to Deanna Hopper in the amount of fifty dollars. There was a serial or registration number in the corner. I memorized the number and handed the paper to Kitty. She returned it to Dee.

I spoke first. "The man I work for sends me two one-hundred dollar bills in a Christmas card in early December. How about the man you work for."

"Oh, no bills, he just sends these," she responded. Dee gave me a quick look. She realized I'd just tricked her.

"Let's cut the crap, Mr. Winthorpe. You know about as much as I do. I have an ad in the yellow pages. A man called me and gave me instructions. He wouldn't give his name. He said he was returning a favor to an old friend. He said it was a private matter and asked me to keep it to myself. That was four years and about eight hundred dollars ago. What are you getting out of this caper?"

"Oh—well, for me it's three years and about six hundred bucks."

"Gotcha beat, don't I?"

"That you do, Dee, that you do."

"What do you do for your two-hundred bucks?"

"I buy a wreath and drop it into the Ohio where the brother died."

"Then you buy the flowers. You've got overhead. I'm doing a lot better than you!"

Her comment struck Kitty in the funny bone. Her sudden laughter broke the tension between Dee and me. The three of us enjoyed a good guffaw at my expense.

"Davis, Kitty, that's all I know about this. Yes, I'm curious, but it's an easy enough job and I do it gladly. That's all I know."

We laughed and teased a bit, but no more information was forthcoming. I said an appropriate thank you and we headed for the car.

"If you learn more let me know," she called after us.

"You call me if something new turns up," I called back.

"No deals, Winthorpe. You know I can keep a secret."

As soon as the car door closed, Kitty was hooting with laughter.

"Davis, she is precious. You two should become partners!"

"What a team!" I responded. "She has the wheels and I have the deals."

It was one-thirty four in the afternoon. We finally went to get breakfast.

The Hole in the Bottom of the Sea

Chapter Ten

There was a restaurant down Dixie Highway a bit to the south of Kendall Lane where they would feed you breakfast twenty-four hours a day. Kitty had her mind fixed on a Belgian waffle. Her comments got me in the mood for eggs over medium with hash browns and sausage. We needed to get our heads together and this would provide us the break to do it.

"Davis, you simply have to start thinking progressively," she announced, whipping out her new cell phone.

Against my protests, Kitty was about to try to call Sally in Seattle from the front booth of the restaurant.

"That's got to be expensive!" I warned.

"Putting progress on hold is expensive. I may have this thing solved in the time it would take to drive back to the house!" She sort of whipped those words at me. She punched in the number for directory services. "Seattle, please—Sally Patton," she said, giving the street address as well. I watched as she punched more numbers into her keypad. Then she handed me the phone.

"Here, Mr. Winthorpe," she said. "First you decide what you want to say—then press the send key. You, my darling, must get with the times!"

I thought a bit then punched the key. I could feel money running right out through my finger, but what the heck.

"Sally!" I said as soon as I heard a woman's voice. "You're never going to guess who this is!"

"I'm sorry. Who are you calling?" The voice was young and silky—pretty nice.

"Sally, I'm on old friend of Ray Luzadder. I'm trying to get in touch."

"Are you sure you have the right number?" Ms. Silk replied.

"This *is* Sally Patton?"

"Yes, but I don't know anyone by the name of Luzadder.

"Oh, man!" I drew the words out, trying to sound disappointed. "I was hoping to find old Ray. Sally, I've kept you in the dark. You must think I'm nuts. You just mailed a package to Louisville, Kentucky. I bet you're wondering how I knew that."

Long pause.

"What about it?"

"Did you know what it was?" I asked, and waited.

"It was none of my business and probably none of yours. Who is this?" The silk was gone. An edge was in the tone of her voice—time to soften her up with another little lie.

"That package was delivered to the grave of Ray Luzadder's mother, rest her soul. It contained flowers. We were so close, Ray, his mother and I, and I—well— I just happened to be there when the flowers came. I

The Hole in the Bottom of the Sea

thought for a moment that they might be from Ray. You know—long lost buddies getting back together."

"Sorry," the silk was back. "I had no idea what was in the box. I was just doing a favor for a friend."

"A gentleman friend?"

"No, if that is any of your business. It was for a girlfriend."

"Why would your girlfriend send flowers for Ray's mother?"

"Cassie had to make a quick turnaround. She brought the box in with her. All she told me was that she didn't have time to mess with it. She asked me to mail it and I did."

"I'm sorry, Sally—wait a second. I need to ask my wife something."

I held the phone toward Kitty, "Honey, when do we need to be at the cook-out this afternoon?" I made a rolling motion with my hand. Kitty gave me one strange look.

"Four-thirty, why?" she responded.

"Nothing, I just didn't want to make us late—Sally, I'm sorry, I'm one of those who loses track of time. We're in Kentucky. It's a lot later here than in Seattle. Listen—uh, what did you mean when you said your friend had to make a quick turnaround?"

"Who are you?"

"Just an old Kentucky boy, looking for a friend. I don't mean to be offensive. I'm sorry."

"Cassie is a flight attendant. So am I. She was asked to pull a double. You know, fly both ways. She saw me at the airport and asked a favor. She's my roommate—we're always doing things for each other."

"Who gave her the flowers?"

"I really don't know. I didn't ask."

"Could you find out—when you see her, I mean?"

"Listen, I still don't know who you are. And, it's her business."

"Where did Cassie fly in from?"

"And that's none of your business. I don't mean to be rude, but goodbye."

"Sally, Sally!" The phone was silent.

"What was that 'ask my wife' bit?" Kitty asked.

"Oh, I don't know. She was starting to get more uptight. I thought that if she thought I was some married Joe, and my wife was nearby, she might feel less threatened."

"I guess you blew that!"

"No. We learned a few things. Her girlfriend—roommate is a go between. Her name is Cassie and she's a flight attendant. She flew in from somewhere and had to fly right back. She, the roommate, probably knows the person who's sending the flowers—that's my bet."

My eggs came.

"Look at this," Kitty said. "You got all that done before breakfast, thanks to my phone!"

I hate it when she's oh so right. I hate it when she's smarter. I'm still trying to get used to phone dials that don't go 'round in circles. I told her about the rest of the conversation.

The Hole in the Bottom of the Sea

"Where can you fly to from Seattle, L.A., San Francisco and Atlanta," I wondered, as I accelerated up the ramp onto the Watterson Expressway. I rolled down the window to flick my toothpick into traffic.

"The world," was her dry response.

"Get serious, Kitty."

"The tropical world."

"There's got to be a common thread here!" I said.

"Some place it takes a few hours to fly to."

"And, some place they would turn right around and go back too," I said.

"Japan, Alaska, Australia, Hawaii, Tahiti..." Kitty rolled of a few more exotic sounding destinations.

"Hawaii!" I almost shouted the word.

"Why Hawaii?"

"William said their mother took Raymond there several times. It all ties—tropical flowers, bird of paradise, trips to Hawaii, flight attendants."

"Too simple," she said.

"You probably can't fly from Atlanta to Hawaii," I said.

"Bet you can—you can fly from New York to Hawaii."

"You ever done it?"

"Nope, but I know one can."

"Let's call William. Ask him where in Hawaii they went," I said.

This time Kitty did all the work.

"Alice, Hello. This is Kitty Winthorpe—yes, I'm fine, and you? Yes, Davis is fine too. Listen, I'm on a cell phone and this is sort of expensive. Is Mr. Luzadder home? Yes, please."

I gouged her in the ribs during the long pause. She mouthed the words, "No foreplay in the car." I gave her a wild look and accelerated—hard.

"Mr. Luzadder, hello. This is Kitty. I'm with Davis and we are working on an idea about the flowers. Where did Raymond and your mother go in Hawaii— you know, when he was a boy? Do you know that?"

She listened for several seconds.

"And that's all you remember? No, no problem, I'm sure that will help. No, we don't have any answers. Right now we're full of questions. Fresh flowers were delivered just this morning. They were delivered by an errand service. We talked to the woman who did the delivery—and to the woman who shipped the flowers from Seattle. She said she was doing a favor for a friend. That's all we know. Yes—OK—yes, we'll keep in touch. Tell Alice I'm sorry we didn't get to talk, Bye, now."

She snapped the phone shut.

"William says he doesn't remember. It was always the same place—one island. He doesn't know the name, but remembers something about it being the Garden Island. He remembers something about a place that sounded like Honolulu, but wasn't Honolulu. That's it!"

I didn't waste any time getting back to our place on Peachtree Avenue. The computer was still set up in the corner of the dining room. I wanted to fire the thing up and show Kitty who's boss in this technology thing.

"What are you going to do?" she asked.

"Search the Internet."

"What do we have to look for?"

"Who knows," I said with flair. "Maybe we can turn up the next clue."

The computer came on line and I launched my Internet access program—then the web browser.

"So, here it is. What do we look for?"

"Hawaii, flowers, Garden Island..." she responded.

"Let's look for Garden Island." I typed in the two words and clicked on the search button.

The very first item read *Flower Arrangements ...Tropical Flowers...exotics from Kauai.*

"Kauai, where's that? I never heard of it," Kitty said.

"Me neither. Maybe we can map it." I pulled up the site.

"Lot's of pretty stuff, but nothing about the garden island. No bird of paradise, either," I said.

"This may take us nowhere, Davis. Let's go back and scroll down some more—look! There! 'Garden Island Plaza.' What's that?"

I pulled up the site.

"Look at that. *Kalapaki Bay*—how do you say that? And, look—'Kauai is nicknamed the Garden Island!' Davis, what do you think?"

"I think this is way too easy. It can't be this simple."

"Well, we haven't actually found the missing Mr. Luzadder yet," she reminded me.

"No, but we just entered two words and got this far."

"OK," she said. "Go back and let's search for flowers in Kauai."

I punched in a search for *Kauai and flowers*."

The same web site led the list. Others followed: B&B Exotic Tropical Gifts, Paradise Found Flowers of Hawaii, Hale Kai Tropical Shippers. There was enough to make a good starting point. I leaned back. My mind was blank.

"Kitty, what are we looking for? Will we know it if we see it?"

"Let's paint a picture in our minds," she replied. "The person sending the flowers buys from one of these places and gives it to Cassie to take to Seattle for shipping."

"Why not ship it himself?"

"I don't know. You think it's a he?" she asked.

"Why not? What if it's Ray? Besides, Dee let it slip that she works for a man."

"OK, let's say what if—he's hiding."

"Why?"

"No reason why," she said. A strange puzzled look crossed her face. I could tell she was playing the what-if game in her mind. "Well." Long pause "If he is alive, and the world thinks he's dead—then he's hiding."

"That's a stretch."

"If it's not Ray," she continued. "Then who on earth would send flowers to a dead woman's grave?"

"It's too screwed up. People saw Raymond Luzadder crash into the Ohio River."

"So what else we got?" she asked.

"We got zip!"

"Patience, Davis—have patience. How did the money order get inside the package?"

"The shippers put it there."

"That's pretty special—you know, sort of a personal favor. If the same people do the flowers for him each time, then they know him."

"Kitty, what if he packs the flowers himself?"

"Why do you wonder that?"

"Well, if I was hiding out, I wouldn't want the people that packed flowers for me to get suspicious by putting in these mysterious money orders. That could draw too much attention to what I was doing."

"So, how's the money order get inside?"

"He works at a flower place. Does it himself," I suggested.

"Or he runs one."

"Raymond Luzadder, former law student turned computer geek, fakes his own death in the Ohio River, goes to Hawaii…"

"Kauai, Hawaii," she added.

"Right—then he changes his name."

"Why's that?"

"Luzadder sticks out like a sore thumb. It's different. He'd change it."

"OK, then what?"

"He buys a flower shop, sends flowers to his mom…"

"And lives happily ever after."

"Until we show up," I added.

"Want to go to Hawaii?" she asked.

I'd been slumping in my task chair. I straightened up abruptly.

"Just on this? This is pretty a flimsy reason to go to Hawaii."

"Davis, we're self-employed and we have money. Why do we need a reason?"

"Too much going on, Sweetheart. I'm excited about the house, this Luzadder business is alluring, but I'm no go on Hawaii."

"So, what's next?" she said, giving in way too easily.

"I'm going to check the electronic Yellow Pages in some of these cities on Kauai. I want to make a few phone calls and see what turns up."

Searches of the towns of Kapaa and Lihue turned up a few more names and numbers: Flowers of the Garden Isle, Papalou's Fruit and Flower, Tutu's Floral Shop, and a few more.

"Can we do more on this tomorrow?" Kitty asked. "I really do want to hang a few pictures today."

I looked at the list I had just printed out. I reached to turn off the computer.

"Let's let this lay for a few days," I said. That's really what I thought we would do.

The Hole in the Bottom of the Sea

Two nights later I lay snoozing on the big leather couch in the library at the new place, Alise's summer cottage. I was half sleeping and half watching the news.

"Elsewhere in the news, flight attendants and flight crews on the West Coast threaten wide-spread strikes over what they refer to as unacceptable and dangerous conditions. One senior pilot was quoted as saying that many of their crews simply spend too much time in the air. Airline representatives say they are open to suggestions, but claim they are unable to find the staffing to give crews the ground time they desire.

Looking at an unrelated incident, it appears that staffing for the airlines will be just a little more difficult following the discovery of the bodies of two female flight attendants. In Seattle, the two flight attendants were found dead of a suspected drug overdose. A spokesperson for the airline workers stated that undue stress from overextended flight hours may have contributed to this tragedy. The authorities have offered no statements and have not released the names of the deceased. That's all for the news at this hour. Stay tuned for sports and weather after these messages."

Kitty was standing in the doorway.
"Davis, did you hear that?"

"Yeah, barely. Two stewardesses in Seattle, how'd they die?"

"Drugs—could that be Sally and Cassie? How can we find out?"

"I don't know, Kitty. It's just a coincidence. If it weren't for the airline problems we wouldn't even have heard about it."

"Could we find it on the Internet?"

"I doubt it. We could ask *is Sally dead*—it would be like a crystal ball."

"Be serious, Davis. Where can we buy a Seattle newspaper?"

"Oh, what—I don't know, Zimmerman's, maybe." I thought a few seconds. "Kitty let's go back down on Peachtree."

"Why? What?"

"Maybe we *can* find it on the net…"

As I drove Pain Jane south to our other place, I found myself hoping for the day we could get everything moved to our new home. This back and forth business was getting me down. I barged through the kitchen and cranked up the computer. Kitty set about making sandwiches for us. We still had all our food supply at the old place.

I guess I amazed myself. I asked the web for *newspapers and Seattle*. Within seconds I found the homepage of the *Seattle Times*.

"Kitty, you'd better see this."

"What is it?"

"I think everything in the Seattle newspaper is here, and there's a search feature."

"What do we do?"

I clicked on a link that offered local news, and scrolled down. News story after news story climbed the screen.

"Here, Look at this!"

"Visiting friend finds unexpected tragedy
A Seattle flight attendant paid a visit to fellow workers at their Normandy Park apartment last night. Expecting to find camaraderie, she found tragedy instead. Declared dead at the scene due to a drug overdose, were her two friends Sally Patton and Cassandra Bautista..."

I didn't read any farther.

"My dear Lord!" Kitty exclaimed. Her face was ashen. "They are the ones. Davis, what does this mean?"

"Sally and Cassie took too much goo."

"Don't be crass, Davis. Flight attendants are subject to drug testing. You can't be users and keep a job like that."

"Don't ask me. Maybe they didn't know what they were doing."

"And maybe they were murdered."

"Maybe you're nuts!"

"What if Luzadder did it!" Her eyes were wide—face more pale.

I felt a strange sensation coming over me, as well. "Kitty, it couldn't be. It's just one very bazaar coincidence."

"I don't know, Davis. If you ask me, we ought to call the Seattle police and tell what we know."

I stared at the web site for a moment. There was a link on the page to the local police.

"We don't know anything. Sally mailed a package to Louisville. Cassie brought it from Hawaii, maybe— we don't even know that for sure. As far as the authorities are concerned, Raymond Luzadder is at the bottom of the Ohio River."

"He's in the hole in the bottom of the sea. Now Sally and Cassie are there too. Davis, there's more to this than you will admit."

"Kitty, the odds are way against anything connecting all this stuff, and there's nothing we can do. Now let it go!"

There was an edge in my voice when I said that. Kitty was hurt by my sharp tone and I think she knew then that I was afraid. That's when I should have let it go. I should have called William Luzadder and told him we had run out of leads. That's what I should have done.

The Hole in the Bottom of the Sea

Chapter Eleven

The next morning found us at the house on Park Avenue—bright and early. The computer and all associated junk occupied the back seat of Plain Jane. I was in a rush to set up shop in the big library. I had claimed that as my world. By now I understood Kitty well enough to know that I had better get there first.

By mid-morning a committee from the Old Louisville Preservation League had shown up with a baked ham, a couple of casseroles, an apple pie and a jug of tea. The ringleader was one of those breastless women with too short hair. She was decked out in a well-worn denim shirt and way too big khaki shorts. Her-straight-as-an-arrow legs went down to some kind of clunky looking walking shoes. All in all, she was one of the sweetest people I had met in a long time. A strong blush peeked through her well-tanned cheeks, setting off dazzling, sky-blue eyes. I figured the committee was there to check out the new birds on the block. I was expecting subtle little questions that would reveal our pedigree.

"You've just got to let us see what you've done to the place!" the head-honcho said with a smile. She led the round of introductions. I learned that her name was Madison Wolfe. Sizing her up, I figured her for a

BMW—or a Jeep. I still couldn't figure out those shoes.

"Call me Maddie," she said, extending her hand.

I gave her my best grin as we shook hands. "I'm Davis Winthorpe, Louisville stock, and this is Kitty, my wife. Kitty came here from New York City."

"Oh, Mrs. Winthorpe," gushed one of our guests. "Some of us girls go to The City every other year or so for theatre, nightclubs and such. You must go with us! I bet you could show us a thing or two."

"That I could do!" Kitty responded. "That we will do!"

That was all it took. Immediately I was in the back seat. Kitty was driving the bus when it came to social relationships in Old Louisville. The friendships had begun.

They say the farther one goes into the south of Louisville the more red-necks one encounters per mile. Maybe that's so. As an old Southender, I had my share of attitudes and altitudes. I'd always found Old Louisville people to be wound a little differently from others I knew. Winston would say that some of the Old Louisville people were in a different orbit from regular folks. My mom had once told me that those in the Old Louisville crowd wobble a bit, being slightly off center. As time passed, I found all of this to be true, and I loved it. I came to believe I was a Southender by birth, but an Old Louisvillian by heart.

I was not at all surprised to learn that Maddie was planning to spend part of October in Colorado. *Hiking and camping by myself*, is the way she put it. Mrs. New

York Theatre was actually Dr. Estelle Kepple. She was a professor at the University with an earned doctorate in some sort of artsy field. Estelle, or Old Keppie, as the students called her, quickly became Kitty's heroine and best friend. Caller number three was the one who was way out there. Indigo Matthew, brown skinned and gorgeous, was from the Virgin Islands. She spoke with music in her voice. Eighteen karat gold graced her slender neck. Color and laughter always came alive whenever Indigo came around. A custom built, four-door Grand Marquis convertible was her means of transportation—black on black, white leather interior and a gold package made the car a sight to see. With her close cut tight curls, over stated bangle earrings and positively beautiful laughter, she was one to set fire to the moment.

Indigo slipped up close to me. She pointed gingerly toward the food we had just accepted. "Don't eat too much of dat stuff," she sang. "Indigo will bring some real food later."

Did she ever! Indigo was part of a family that operated a chain of restaurants around the West End. *Hot* was the word to use to describe the dishes she would bring us. Then she would produce a container of her special sauce.

"Dose who have courage will try dis." Her words would float to my ears. Her bewitching eyes would make me foolish enough to sample her hell-hot brew.

Indigo, and her people had a warm and wonderful outlook on life. They liked to enjoy and understood why.

"If we are to dine," she would announce. "Den we must feed both de body and de spirit. If we feed only de body, den we eat. If we feed both de body and de spirit den we *feast*. If all you kind people present will bow your head, we will pray."

No one argued when she spoke. As she expressed thanks with her dulcet tones, I would truly begin to believe that God was in the room.

"All de good things we have, dear Father," she would say. "Are as nothing when compared to all you have prepared for your children. And we are your children, oh Lord, coming with eyes wide and filled with wonder over de good things you give. Your blessing on dis great house, oh God, and dese who come here to live. Give, dem peace, give dem love and bless dese few simple things we have before us. For you, oh Lord, spread out de stars with de fingers of your hands. And you are de one who can make dis a happy home. We all say it—amen!"

Even the atheists in the crowd would say amen whenever Indigo was done.

Later in the afternoon on the same day as the visit from our three friends I struggled up the steps to our walk carrying a rainbow like arm load of blazers and slacks. I noticed the big, white Town Car sitting at the curb, but really paid it no mind. Shannie had gone home, and I was sure other guests had left. People who lived or visited on the block tended to park wherever a space could be found. *Must be a neighbor's car*, I thought. And, I didn't really pay much attention to the

The Hole in the Bottom of the Sea

hulk of a man clunking around the garage out back. Kitty had kept a solid stream of workmen coming and going for several days, at that time. I had all the clues I needed to anticipate the surprise. I just didn't see them.

"I guess I can't put this off any longer," Kitty announced abruptly.

"What's that?" My little here-she-goes-again alarms were sounding in my head.

"Davis, I've been wanting my own car. I still can't drive, but that's not a problem."

Yes, the alarms were definitely sounding.

"And—?"

"I uh—well, I sort of bought a car."

It clicked in my mind. No, it clunked in my mind.

"The Town Car?"

"Isn't grand!" she exclaimed. She was doing her little let's-go-see-it dance.

Grand, I thought, *at least forty-grand.*

Kitty was right on target. The car was grand. I settled in behind the wheel.

"Before you learn to drive this, I will teach you how to drive Plain Jane. This is way too nice for learner's mistakes. Want to go for a spin?"

"Well—Davis, there's more to the story." There was a funny tone in her voice. My mind definitely went clunk.

"How much more?"

"I sort of hired a driver too."

My mind went dead.

"Say again, I'm sorry..."

"Do you remember when we got married—how Harry Snapp loaned us his car and driver for the day?"

"I do," was my response. Some how that seemed appropriate.

"Davis, I knew Mr. Snapp's situation was about to change—and ours. I asked Garrett to call me in a few months. I had forgotten about it, but when he called. This whole idea just popped into my head!"

"Kitty, is this the thing to do?" I had started to ask if we could afford this. I knew better.

"Davis, it'll be a fun way to go. I told Garrett that we would pay him thirty thousand a year. He's to keep the car serviced, clean and tanked up twenty-four hours a day. He will eat when we eat, sleep when we sleep and vacation when we vacation. He agreed to that and is anxious to go to work"

"When do I get to meet him?"

"Well—he's here already. He's moving into the apartment on the west end of the garage."

I looked at Kitty and started laughing. I laughed uncontrollably. I didn't know why. The craziness hit her too. We laughed together until tears streamed down our faces.

A little impish look came on her face—the one she gets just before the fun starts. "Are you ready?" she said.

I took a deep breath. "I believe I am."

Kitty reached over and pressed a button on the wheel. A speaker-phone came to life from somewhere in the car. It dialed a number and began to ring.

"Madam?"

The Hole in the Bottom of the Sea

"Garrett, Mr. Winthorpe and I will be leaving."
"Yes, Madam."
"Well, Mr. Winthorpe," she said. "Let's get in the back."
"Where are we going?"
"Why don't we give Garrett the night off and have him take us to the Seelbach."
"Shouldn't we pack some clothes?"
"Davis," she said. "That won't be necessary."

Our man, Garrett, didn't stand a chance. The morning after our little night at the old hotel Kitty whipped out the cell phone from the depth of her purse. It seems that in addition to the phone wired into the Town Car she had another attached to the poor man's belt.

"Good morning, Garrett," She chimed. "Mr. Winthorpe and I are ready now."

I guess I have to admit that there was a certain pleasure seething down inside of me after the phone in our room rang. A smooth talker on the other end announced, "Mr. Winthorpe, your driver is here."

Grand old hotel—personal driver bringing our car to the front—It's a strange thing how little events signal the changes in our lives. I knew on that day—no, I knew in that moment that I was a different person. Life, when it's rough, can be a very satisfying proposition, but life, as I was living it then, was very, very good.

An urgent message was on the answering machine when we got home. It was from my buddy with the missing tooth, Danny Cutshaw.

"Mr. Wenchert, this is Danny. You better git over here. You need to see somethin' in the graveyard."

Kitty came into the library as I listened to the message.

"Do you need Garrett?"

"Nope, this is business. Better take Plain Jane."

"Take this too." She placed a box in my hand, wrapped with plain, white paper and a red bow. "And this." She also handed me a slip of paper.

I sat down at the big desk. The box contained one of those fold-up cellular phones. On the slip of paper was a list of all the numbers I simply couldn't do without.

"That will make things easier," she said.

"Wow, this is great!" I felt branded.

I cranked up the Toyota and backed out into the alley. I was out of sight now and feeling safe. I slipped the little phone from my shirt pocket and dialed Winston Pence.

"Win, I'm calling on my new cell phone. The damn thing works!"

"So..."

"Well, I had to try it out—you know."

"You done good, Davis. Now why you callin' me."

"We spent the night at the Seelbach."

Silence.

"We bought a new Lincoln Town Car!"

"Damn fool!"

The Hole in the Bottom of the Sea

The line went dead. I knew Winston hung up on me just for fun. He always showed this no-big-deal attitude when I came up with something. Then he would show up all excited wanting to see my new toys. I knew he was scratching his head and trying to figure out a way to get behind the wheel of the big Lincoln.

Danny flagged me down a section away from the Luzadder grave.

"Lookit over there. Under them Oak trees," he announced, pointing in the direction of the Oaks.

I was having visions of bodies in Seattle. "Don't point!" I said sharply.

"Yessir!" Danny quickly snapped his hand behind his back, holding them there like a child in trouble. I had spotted the dark green Ford van as I climbed out of Plain Jane.

"Not trying to boss you, Danny. I just don't want the folks in the van to know we've noticed them. What's going on?"

"There's one man in the van—big guy. He showed up yesterday and stayed 'til dark—back again this morning. I figgered you'd better know."

"You think he's watching the grave?"

"Don't know. He moves around. First he parked over yonder—then back up this way."

"Danny, you're pointing again."

"Yeah, right." Hands behind back again. "Ever time he stops he's settin' so's he can see the grave. You know, the one in question."

I talked small talk with Danny for some time. We both tried to keep from looking toward the van. I guess this is stupid, but I could feel eyes boring into me. I told Danny to let me know if anything at all happened. I wrote my cell number on the back of one of my business cards and gave it to him.

Back at the house on Park Avenue, I stood in my new library looking at the papers in the center of the desk. The parade of circumstances buzzed in my mind. The dead women in Seattle, the sharp words of rebuke I had laid on Kitty, that motionless green van, and the list of Hawaiian phone numbers from the Internet. Each took its turn. I could no longer resist. I spread the pages and picked up the phone. The words Kauai Fruit and Flower jumped out at me first. That seemed straightforward enough. As the phone began to ring I realized that, true to form, I had no plan whatsoever.

"*Aloha*, Kaua'i Fruit and Flower." A woman had answered. Her voice was sweet and inviting.

"Do you ship flowers to the United States?"

There was a long pause. "This is the United States, but we are always happy to ship to the mainland."

"Oh—yeah—I guess I see what you mean. I want to send my girlfriend some *Sterilitza* straight from Hawaii."

"Not many people call it dat. You want bird of paradise, right?

"That's it. She's nuts about the stuff, and—well I thought it would be a neat surprise to have it sent from Hawaii."

The Hole in the Bottom of the Sea

"Neat surprise?" It was Kitty. She came in and curled up in one of the big leather chairs. She mouthed the words, in a whisper, "What's going on?"

I covered the receiver. "Hawaii."

My Hawaiian friend continued, "We don't ship dat too often. It's hard to clean and pack. I can send you Ginger and Heliconia. Very beautiful and lasts long time. How about I pack that up and get it out on Wednesday?"

The thought popped up in my mind that I didn't want to give my name and address to the wrong person. If Luzadder was mixed up in this, I didn't want him to be tipped off by someone asking for the same sort of flowers and giving a Louisville address.

"I don't know. Maybe I better wait."

"Maybe you can buy bird of paradise where you are and put it in with the flowers I send you."

"That's a good idea. Let me call you back."

"No problem. *Aloha* and *mahalo*."

"Say, wait," I blurted. "I almost forgot. I had a buddy once who moved to Kauai, Ray Luzadder. You ever hear of him."

"No, dat's one new name to me. I don't know. Maybe long time ago. Kaua'i is a small island, but it's hard to know everybody. Na, don't know dat name. I would remember. Dat name sorta like—you know—odd."

"OK—well, thanks. What was it you said, *maha* something?"

"*Mahalo*. Means same thing. Thank you."

"Yes, *mahalo*."

"Aloha!"

"What are you up to, Davis?"

"Oh, Kitty, I just can't let this rest. Danny showed me a Ford van that's been parked near Mable Luzadder's grave since yesterday. It may be only a coincidence, but I have a gut feeling that something is going on.

"Learn anything?"

"Shipping bird of paradise to the mainland is a bit unusual, according to this person. What a voice that girl had. It was like listening to music. *No problem*, she said. I could almost hear the guitars in the background."

Kitty chuckled. "You going to make more calls?"

"Let me try a couple more. Tutu's Floral shop—that sounds cute."

I dialed the number.

"Aloha, Tutu's." It was an older voice, though it came to my ear with the same melodic sweetness.

"I need to have some Hawaiian type flowers shipped to the mainland," I announced, trying to sound as with it as I could.

"Oh, I don't do that," she sang. "But I can put you in touch with those who do. You need to call Kaua'i Fruit and Flower. They are so nice and do such a good job."

"I've already called them. They couldn't provide exactly what I wanted."

"Tell Tutu what you want."

"I was hoping to have bird of paradise sent to my girlfriend. Sort of special. You know."

The Hole in the Bottom of the Sea

"For you and your girlfriend, Tutu will make an exception. What do you want? I will send it."

I was taken aback. The sweet old lady had me in her spell. "Uh—something pretty—maybe a hundred bucks."

"Oh, that's too much. You give me your address. I will send a bill."

"Well, that's easy enough." I gave her my name and the Park Avenue address.

"I know your girlfriend is beautiful for you to do such a nice thing."

"She's a knockout, Tutu—a real knockout! Her name is Kitty."

Kitty gave me a screwy look and an insistant whisper. "What are you up to?"

"Uh, listen—Tutu, what is that. Uh—what does your name mean, I mean.

Tutu laughed. "In our language *tutu* means grandmother. I am Tutu."

"Oh, neat. You have many grandchildren?"

Her next few words were said with sweeping grandeur. I was caught up into the spirit of this special woman.

"All the children on the island are mine. Everyone knows Tutu. When you come to Kaua'i. You ask for me. Tell them you want Tutu who sells flowers in Hanamaulu Town. I will give you special bird of paradise."

"I doubt I'll ever make it there, Tutu. It's a long way from Kentucky."

"No it is only a short distance. The only long distance is the one between hearts that do not love. You will come. I know that. I can feel your spirit. You will come."

I was out of words. I hadn't even met the lady, and I missed her already.

"Tutu, I need one more favor."

"What is that, Davis?"

"Years ago I lost track of a friend of mine. I think he moved to Kaua'i (I tried to say the word the way Tutu said it). Maybe you know him. His name is Ray Luzadder."

"Raymond…" She said the name with a rounded fullness and delight. "Yes, his mother would bring him to the shop. He called me his little Tutu, but that was so long ago. Raymond's mother loved bird of paradise too. She came in here with him many times over the years, but it was long ago. No, Raymond is not on this island. I would know it."

"*Mahalo*, Tutu." I choked a bit.

"*Mahalo*, my Davis. When you come bring that pretty girl. *Aloha*."

In a whisper she was gone.

"Good grief!" I said, slumping back in my desk chair.

"What?" Kitty asked.

"What a woman! She knows Ray Luzadder, but says it was when he was a boy. She says he's not on the island."

"And?"

"I believe her—strange woman, my Tutu."

"You gonna make more calls?"

"Maybe one. I feel so close on this. God only knows."

"Here's one!" Kitty said. "Paradise Found!"

"Too tacky."

"Flowers of the Garden Isle?"

"Too flowery!"

"Papalou's Fruit and Flower?"

"Too fruity! No, let's call that one. Give me the number."

I was in a strange and silly mood. I was going to have fun and tease with this one.

"Papalou!" The voice was hard and straight on. This man was not an islander, at least not in the same way as the other two.

"Say, you guys ship to the United States?"

"This is the United States, pal. We ship to the mainland. What do you need?"

"Just a bunch of flowers for my girl. You know—stuff from paradise."

"Let me give you to Laura. She'll take care of you."

"Wait! Before I give her my order. I'm trying to find an old friend. His brother told me that he might have moved to Kaua'i."

"His brother doesn't know where he is? How's that?"

"Joined the Navy. Saw the world. Lost touch—you know how brothers can be."

"What's the name?"

"Ray Luzadder."

"Never heard of the guy! What's he look like?"

"Haven't seen him since college—blondish, six-feet, blue eyes. Ray had movie star good looks. Women fell at his feet."

"So—I guess we all should be so lucky. You say his brother thinks he may be in Hawaii?"

"That's the deal."

"You know the brother's name?"

"William—why do you ask?"

"No reason—curious. I don't know this Louwhathisname. Give your name and address to Laura. She'll help you get what you need."

Music started. I was on hold. My strange and silly mood came to a sudden end. A sickening knot in my stomach replaced it. My phone call to Sally in Seattle and the two dead women came to mind. Instantly I was in a cold sweat. I had called Sally and she was dead.

"*Aloha*, this is Laura."

I panicked. "Laura, I'm sorry. I'm on a cell phone and the battery is about to go. I'll have to call you back." I put the receiver on the cradle.

"Davis, strange way to end the call," Kitty said, but her voice seemed far away.

"I think I just said too much."

"Why?"

"Don't know—I started hearing the voice of Sally Patton in my head. I had to hang up."

"Who'd you talk to?"

"I guess I talked to Papalou himself. He doesn't know Raymond Luzadder."

"So, what's the big deal?"

"He wanted to know the brother's name. I think he was checking me out. He wanted to see if I'd say the magic word."

"And?"

"I gave him William's name. Kitty, if Luzadder is on the island and this guy knows him..." I looked at her and shrugged.

"What?"

"I told him I was an old friend and that William thinks Raymond is in Hawaii."

"Too many lies, Davis—too many lies."

I remembered my mama telling me that it isn't the first lie that gets you; it's usually the third. I tried to remember my lies. I had lost count.

The Hole in the Bottom of the Sea

Chapter Twelve

The next morning dawned dank and depressing. Low clouds seemed to spill their grayness just over the treetops. The breeze was warm and felt unusually humid. I stared into the strange sky. In Louisville a sky like that usually came before a storm.

I sat on the front steps of our new home on Park Avenue—I stared in the direction of the Fifth District Police Station. It was just a short walk across the park and I figured Detective Sergeant Curtis Cooper was there in his office. I knew Cooper from a previous scrape I had gotten myself into. I knew the man didn't particularly care for the sight of me, but he had this way of being straightforward about things. I'd told lies to Cooper too. I guess I resisted seeing him as much as he didn't care to see me. I was always uncomfortable in his presence, trying to keep my story straight.

I formed and reformed the words in my mind. I just couldn't seem to find the right way to tell Cooper about this Luzadder thing. I could see the snarl on his big black face. Every way I tried to line up the facts—the whole mess still sounded very unbelievable.

I was brought out of my doldrums by the ringing of my cell phone. The thing startled me. At first I didn't realize what I was hearing, never having experienced the sound of the new contraption.

The Hole in the Bottom of the Sea

"Hello!"
Silence.
"Hello?"
I could hear breathing and sounds of movement.
"Anybody there?"
A few more quiet seconds passed.
"Wrong number." Someone announced.

The phone went dead. The voice was male, deep and firm. I pictured a big man. White—I guessed, and maybe middle-aged. The strange call puzzled me. No one had my number—except Kitty, and Garrett—and Danny Cutshaw.

"That sure wasn't Danny," I mumbled.

I dialed Garrett's number.

"This is Garrett."
"This is Davis. Did you just call me?"
"No, Mr. Winthorpe."
"Thank you—just checking."
"Yes, Mr. Winthorpe."

I sat there. Once again, I was listening to a dead phone line. *I've got to find out the rest of that man's name, and get him to stop calling me Mr. Winthorpe!*

The caller hadn't been Garrett. There was no similarity between the two voices. Garrett always formed his words with an elegant manner of speech. There was a certain roughness in the two words I had heard a few moments ago. *Who was that?*

What the heck—it was just a chance wrong number. I know this sounds odd, but the silence of the unknown caller kept repeating in my mind. I wanted to go check on Danny Cutshaw. An uneasy mood settled over me.

I sat a while longer in the late summer gloom—then went inside.

"Kitty!"

I heard her answer from somewhere in the top of the house.

"Kitty, you want to go for a ride?"

"Right now?" She appeared at the top of the stairs. Was she ever a mess!

"What you been doing?" I asked.

"Trying to get all those dead plants and Alise crap out of the sunroom. I don't think she ever did anything to take care of this place."

"Well, it *was* just her *summer* cottage."

She grinned at my catty remark. "Where we going?"

"I want to go to St. Louis Cemetery and talk to Danny. Should I call Garrett?"

"Peter, James and John—No! Not the way I look. Let's sneak out and take the Toyota. I'll let Garrett know we're leaving.

"You know he pouts when we don't have him drive."

"Davis, either it's just you and me in the Toyota, or you wait while I clean up?"

"You win! Let's take Plain Jane," I declared. From the looks of Kitty, cleaning up would be a major project.

"Maybe I can give him a job to do so he won't feel left out," she said, punching in his number. "Garrett, Mr. Winthorpe has a few things in the cleaners. Could you pick them up for me? Davis and I will be out for a while."

She came bounding down the stairs, stuffing the phone into the pocket on her tight, little short shorts.

Little, tan short shorts, tight little yellow shell top, baby blue bandana holding up her hair—bandana tied in front. Sweat and dirt streaked her face—cute, little white running shoes. Yeah, she was right. Garrett shouldn't see her like that. She made a quick project of washing her face and applying fresh lipstick before we bundled into the old Toyota.

We made our way to the St. Louis Cemetery. My first pass through the place didn't turn up Danny. The low gray clouds had settled as a mist over the cemetery. I listened for the sound of his mower.

"Maybe he's off today," Kitty suggested.

"Maybe. I'm going to ask one of the other guys."

Across the cemetery I had spotted a crew of three. They were busy jacking up an old monument. I drove around to where I had seen them. The trio was shoveling and packing fresh dirt underneath the monument to level the thing.

"Hey, guys," I called. "Seen Danny today?" The three exchanged odd glances the tallest of the team pulled a sweatband from his head and started toward the car. He leaned down to speak through the open window.

"I'm sorry, sir, but, Danny, he ain't with us no more."

My heart sunk. "What'd Danny do—did he do some fool thing and get himself fired?"

"Oh, no sir—well, sort of, sir. Well, Danny got hisself killed yesterday."

"What! Killed?"

"Well, yessir. That Danny—I told him a dozen times he ort to be more careful. What he did was take loose all them safety switches on that mower of hizzen. He fixed it so's the dead-man-switch, pardon the phrase, didn't work. He would jump off and pick up flowers offen a grave. Then, like a fool, he'd get back on the mower with it still movin' so's to pass over the grave. I told him a dozen times he was a dern fool—but he would jump offen the mower, put the flowers back, and on and on like that. Hit was against the rules too."

"I'm sorry—I think you lost me. What happened to Danny?"

"Well, like I said, he was doin' this thing with the mower over on the back side there. The mower went crooked and hit a stone. Hit rolled and I guess Danny tries to catch on, or something. Anyhow, hit rolled over on Danny. Got him right in the gut too. I guess that's about the most awful thing I ever seen!"

"I can't believe it!" Kitty exclaimed.

I found myself without words.

"Hit's just downright sad too," the caretaker continued. "That Danny worked here for mosta twelve years. He loved the place, but they gonna bury him in that Potter's Field over offen that Manslick Road.

That's the shame—they ort to give him a space here were he loved to be."

I asked the man to show me the spot where Danny died. A light drizzle was falling now. Kitty peered through the rain-streaked window while I stared at the lines on the ground. The police had marked the place to show how he was positioned. Arms were out, one leg straight, one drawn up. I stared and I sought to memorize the scene. I wanted this moment to play over and over in my mind. I wanted to remember it precisely the same every time. I closed my eyes and shivered as rain dripped from my hair, under my collar and down along the thing I called a backbone.

Kitty was silent as we rolled slowly through the curves of the cemetery road. I eased to a stop at the foot of one of the stone angels. I had to say something —I just didn't know what. Neither of us spoke for a long time.

"Accident," Kitty said flatly.

"Could've been. I caught the front wheel of a riding mower in a chain link fence once. It climbed the fence and rolled over on me. I fell off and scrambled away. The mower rolled completely over, landed on its wheels and kept going. Just a few inches and it would have cut my foot off. I guess I'll never forget seeing those blades coming at me!"

Kitty still didn't speak. She just looked at me with an expression of incredulity on her face. I stared back.

"Davis?"

"What?"

"What's a dead-man-switch?"

"Well, it's a safety device. On a riding mower it can be under the seat. Sometimes, you push a pedal down with your foot. If you fall off, the dead-man-switch kills the motor."

"Did you tamper with the dead-man-switch on the mower that rolled over on you?"

"Well—yes, but I was careful. I would jump off to pick up sticks and stones in the path of the mower."

"You're dumber than Danny!"

"Not quite—Danny's dead!" I replied.

"So, the mower could have killed him—just like that?"

"Yes, just like that."

"I don't know, Davis. It seems like this *accident* was extremely timely."

"My thoughts exactly," I replied.

"What do we do?" she asked.

"I want to talk to Sergeant Cooper. You remember him?"

"Oh, yes!" she said. "It would be hard to forget that man!"

I made a quick trip back to Park Avenue and took the short walk to the Fifth District Substation. I had been dreading this, but now that another death had occurred I figured it was time to let the police know about my suspicions. I stopped at the front door and worked up my courage.

The Hole in the Bottom of the Sea

"Not my district not my problem," Cooper growled at me.

"Com'on, Coop. Just check it out for me!"

"Who you callin' Coop?"

"Sergeant—sir—Mister Cooper, ask a few questions for me, *please*." I don't like to put a whine in my voice, but, then again, it sometimes gets the job done.

"Go on Winthorpe. I owe you no favors—what part of *I don't like you* is it that you don't understand?"

Whining didn't work this time.

"You don't have to like me," I countered, raising my voice. "Frankly, I don't care if some dumb cop likes me or not. I think the man was murdered, but you don't want to hear it just because you don't like me. If it's not too much trouble maybe you or the lady at the front desk could tell me just whose jurisdiction it is and whose problem it is over on Barrett Avenue. I'll go talk to them."

Cooper had been sitting on the corner of a desk holding his knee up with both hands. He'd been leaning back, giving me that glaring stare of his. The station got quiet now. People were starting to listen. I didn't care how mad Cooper got. They couldn't arrest me for insulting the man.

"What you mean, *murdered*? Where you get off saying some dumb ass thing like that? What you know about this?" Cooper was on his feet now, coming right at me. He was right in my face when he said the last few words. I held my ground.

"I know enough to make me say it. You know I wouldn't come in here just to make conversation with a cop. Maybe there's some part of *I don't like you* that you don't understand."

"Get in my office—get in my office," Cooper commanded. The big man's breath reeked of onions and tobacco smoke. He breathed heavily in my face. I didn't have to nudge Detective Sergeant Curtis Cooper very hard to get action out of him. The door to his office slammed behind us.

"Talk to me, Winthorpe. If you don't catch my interest in about fifteen seconds, then you're out of here."

I started with the tale of the unrecovered body of Ray Luzadder after the crash in the Ohio. "Were you part of that search, Sergeant?" I wanted to be abrasive. I wanted to insult him one more time during the fifteen seconds he had given me. I've never seen any argument end in fifteen seconds. In my mind, I was buying time. He ignored the insult.

"Talk," he demanded.

I told the whole story of flowers appearing, my connection with Danny Cutshaw, the two flight attendants in Seattle and William's suspicions. Cooper kept listening.

"Flowers?" he asked.

"On his mother's grave."

"Flight attendants?"

"Yeah, dead—two of them."

"Danny what's his name?"

"Dead too."

The Hole in the Bottom of the Sea

"You talk to them—and they die?"
"Sounds like a crock doesn't it?"
"Yeah, except for one thing."
"How's that?"
"You're stupid enough to get in the middle of something like this."

Bingo, I was in. Cooper's insult was uttered in a softer voice. I knew his next words would let me know if help was forthcoming.

"Tell me exactly what the groundskeeper said about Cutshaw's death," Cooper said.

Yes, I had him going! I repeated the story one more time.

"Leave me alone for a minute. I'll make some phone calls. Wait outside," he commanded.

"Whoever you talk to, ask about flowers."

"Say what?"

"Ask about flowers," I repeated. "Ask if there were any flowers at the scene—on graves, scattered around, in his hand, whatever—ask!"

"Winthorpe, you're a fool."

"Ask!" I eased the door shut behind me—and waited. Several moments passed. I walked outside to watch dismal showers soaking the earth. I paced nervously—in and out of the substation.

"Mr. Winthorpe?" It was the lady at the front desk. "Sergeant Cooper asks that you step back into his office."

"Coroner says the death was an accident. He says the events are obvious with no indication of foul play—that's it."

"No investigation?"

"None."

"What about the flowers?"

"You don't think I asked, do you?"

"Did you?"

Cooper looked at his note pad, reading verbatim, "The body of the deceased was positioned near a bouquet of flattened plastic flowers, in the middle of a grave site. It appeared that the deceased had first fallen face down from the machine, flattening the flower bouquet. It then appeared that the mowing machine rolled over onto the deceased who had moved to a face up position. The circumstances indicate that the death was accidental and probably occurred instantaneously." Cooper looked at me, eyes wide. "Poor little man. What a way to go. Here's one fool that don't want to die in the middle of a graveyard."

"So, that's it?"

"That's it—accidental death. There'll be no further investigation."

"Well, Cooper, you've told me what I need to know."

"How's that?"

"Think about it. Cutshaw had this habit of jumping off the mower to pick up flowers. He would mow over the spot. Then he would put the flowers back and jump on again. If that's what he was doing, the plastic bouquet would not have been on the grave at the moment the mower hit the stone."

"So, what's the deal."

The Hole in the Bottom of the Sea

"It seems to me that the flowers on the grave should have been in Danny's hand—or scattered, but they were under Danny when he fell. That doesn't seem right. I think he was thrown to the ground—probably unconscious. Then the machine was flipped over on top of him—not accidentally. Someone did this to him!"

"Man, you are reachin' for it!"

"Sure I am, Sergeant, but the police in Seattle concluded the girls died from an overdose. Now the Louisville cops are satisfied that Danny Cutshaw died accidentally. The way I figure it, the connection with Ray Luzadder and my questions about him are just too much of a coincidence. Murder is the game, Cooper— I'm sure of it!"

Sergeant Cooper took his time lighting a cigarette. He rolled his big eyes toward me and spat a bit of tobacco off the end of his tongue. "What was the word you used—crock? *It sounds like a crock.* I believe that's what you said."

"Well—yes, I said that but I…"

You what," he interrupted. You were just trying to jive me, Winthorpe—booger jive and nothing more. You're one of those people who'll say whatever it takes to needle me into doin' what you want done. Just listen to yourself. I know you want to believe you are messed up in some big deal drama, but it don't fly. It takes too big a leap of faith to accept the connection between the dead man in the Ohio, the flowers on Ray somebody's mamma's grave, dead stewardesses in Seattle and a

Mike Bradford

lawn mower rollin' over in some cemetery. Our boys looked at it and it's done!"

"You go look at it," I said. "Go look at the grave. Check out the scene. Cooper, stand there with your eyes closed and see the action take place. Make the pieces fit. If they don't fit, and they won't, then ask why. Do it, Cooper. They do call you *Detective*, don't they?"

"Hell, Winthorpe, you're doin' it again. Don't try to con me into somethin' I don't want to do. If there's a problem, the boys over there will take care of it. Not my jurisdiction—not my problem."

"Just another dead, insignificant working slob. Cutshaw was a stupid, ignorant nobody—no big deal." I spat each word out. I was pushing the big cop too hard—the scary part was that I was enjoying it.

"Damn!" he roared. "Get on out of here. I made the call you wanted—I listened! Now leave me alone!"

I was halfway across the squad room before I turned and shouted, "Check it out, *Sergeant!*"

Detective Sergeant Curtis Cooper turned the air in the stationhouse blue as I made my exit. Never before had I made him that mad. *Mission accomplished*, I thought as I hurried across Central Park.

Later that evening my phone rang. The voice was deep, firm, black and straightforward. "There's tire marks on that grave stone. There's a gouge mark in the stone where the frame of the mower hit. It hit that stone hard before rolling over. If this was a deliberate act of homicide, then whoever did it did a damn good job of making it look accidental."

"Thank you, Sergeant," I responded, in a most respectful tone.

"There's somethin' else."

"What?"

"I did what you suggested. I sat there on the grass and made that scene repeat in my mind twenty times or more. I closed my eyes and rode that tractor into the stone. I visualized jumping off and back on again—over and over."

"And...?"

"No matter how I did it I couldn't land with my head pointed in the direction Cutshaw's head was pointed when the machine rolled onto him. More than that, there's not enough room. As close as the man was to the stone, there was not enough room for the blades to hit him. It should have broken his leg, or burned him with the exhaust—maybe even landed upside down on his chest. From the way I see it, he could have been crushed, but not cut up like that."

"So what's next?"

"Nothin's next. The case is closed."

"Well—thank you. I really do appreciate this. Thank you, Sergeant."

"Davis—" There was a tone in his voice, and the Sergeant never called me by my first name. "If this is murder, the assailant is smart—and big. He's smart enough to cold cock Cutshaw without leaving a mark. He's big enough to stand astride that tractor with both feet on the ground, ram it into the headstone and then pick up the front end while turning the machine to drop it on the body. If I saw this right, Cutshaw felt no pain."

"Wow, Cooper, I don't know what to say."

"Don't say nothin'. If I was you, I'd get out of this, but you won't. Be careful, Winthorpe. Be careful, and let me know if you learn anything."

"Thanks, Curtis," I said softly.

"Yeah, right, Davis—you're welcome."

I had to figure that Cooper would not let this rest. I knew that there had to be much more to this than either of us had managed to understand—so far. Yeah, I would be careful. I just wished I knew what the heck that meant.

The Hole in the Bottom of the Sea

Chapter Thirteen

It was sometime in the middle of the night when the thought struck me. My eyes popped open and I stared into the darkness. I'd awakened not knowing which house I was sleeping in. I oriented myself and became fully awake before I let the thoughts flood my mind. Dee Hopper was the next link in this chain of murders. If Ray Luzadder was somewhere alive and still on this planet, then he was the one sending the flowers. If that was so, and Luzadder had hired the man in the green van, then Luzadder would have to send his henchman after Dee Hopper next. Dee had seen the address on the box of flowers. I've got to warn Dee! *Oh, shut up,* a voice inside said to me. *Winthorpe, get off it. Next thing, you'll be seeing ghosts!*

I forced myself to a sitting position. Kitty was grinding away with that soft snore of hers. I made my way to the window seat and looked out through the lights in Central Park. The nagging parade of thoughts refused to go away. I debated calling Dee right then. I looked at the clock on the nightstand. "four-thirty," I whispered, softly. *Dee's asleep. No sense waking her.* A chill swept over me. *Dee could be dead already!* I hadn't even mentioned Dee when I told the story to Cooper. *No, that wouldn't have helped.* There's nothing the police could do to protect Dee. They didn't even believe Danny's death was a homicide.

I was wide-awake now. *No way I'll get back to sleep.* I decided to lie down beside Kitty. *In another two hours, I can make the call.* I figured I could just lie there and roll this whole scene over and over in my mind. I knew it was going to be a long two hours.

"Only a man with a pure conscience could sleep so sound." I heard the voice, coming from far away. It sounded like Kitty. *No, Kitty was asleep.* My eyes popped open. The room was full of light.

"Sleep well?" the voice purred. I felt a hand undoing the buttons on my PJ's. It was Kitty and she had morning glory on her mind.

"What—what time is it?" I sat up suddenly.

"It's seven-thirty, Davis." The purr was still there, but fading.

"Oh, Lord—oh, Lord!" I exclaimed.

"What?" Purr gone.

"I've got to call Dee Hopper!"

"Davis, you are the strangest man!" Yep, the purr was definitely gone.

I leaped out of bed, looking for my notebook. "I've got to find the number!" I blurted.

"What number, Davis—crime's sake, will you calm down!"

"Dee Hopper—no, wait!" I stopped in the middle of the bedroom floor—PJ's half unbuttoned. "What if I'm next—no, what if we're next!"

"Davis! Talk to me. Are you nuts?"

The Hole in the Bottom of the Sea

"Kitty, I've been so caught up in what's happened that I haven't even wondered what's next."

"What—what do you mean by what's next?"

"Who's next on Luzadder's list—that's what's next!"

The room was silent. Kitty was on her knees in the middle of the bed.

"Oh," she finally said.

I leaped into the window seat. I could see a good bit of Park Avenue and the other streets, but not all. "Rats," I exclaimed.

"What are you looking for?" she shouted.

"The green van. The killer is still out there, and he's watching someone. I think he will kill again!"

I had Kitty's full attention now. She made quick strides across the room, opened a dresser drawer and pulled out the big chrome forty-four. She checked the cylinder, snapped the gun shut and asked, "What do we do?"

I stopped in my tracks. The sight of my tall sweetie in her red satin nightgown with a double-handed grip on the big gun made me pause to wonder just who was in the most trouble right now.

"Get dressed. Keep the gun out of sight. We'll go out the back, check the alley and side streets and then the street in front. If we spot the green van, let's backtrack into the house and then decide on the next step!" I think I shouted every word.

Kitty and I checked the porches and grounds as best we could from inside the house. We stepped together onto the rear deck, each checking in opposite directions.

We eased down the steps into the garden, cautiously checking under the deck. I held Junior in one hand pointed down behind my back. Kitty carried her cannon with two hands—in front and pointed down. *Heavens, it's like a scene from the movies.*

The alley gate was bolted from the inside and showed no sign of attempted entry. I eased the bolt back and looked first into the alley. Kitty eased up beside me, checking the opposite direction. She was doing the cop thing I'd seen on TV, pointing the forty-four in each direction as she looked. I think that if a stray cat had moved in that alley one of us would have blasted it to kingdom come. The alley appeared clear.

"Keep that gun down, Kitty! We'll have neighbors calling the law on us."

"Let 'em call," she replied. The gun was still at eye level pointed down the alley.

My first impulse was to move toward Fourth Street together, so I could protect Kitty. Then I thought.

"Kitty, you check that way. I'll check this way!"

She moved off without a word.

The morning was crystal clear. A stiff wind had driven away the gloom of yesterday. The remaining breeze sent trash and tatters swirling down the alleyway.

As I made my way to Fourth Street I began to feel very alone and very scared. I, Davis Winthorpe, was armed with a thirty-eight and lying to myself about my ability to actually point the thing and pull the trigger. I think that I really believed I could actually defend myself. *Oh, God,* I prayed. *Keep that monster of a man away from us and protect me from myself!*

There was no green van parked on Fourth Street. Concealing the pistol under my jacket, I walked casually to Park Avenue. Sweat rolled off my brow. A peek down Park Avenue revealed no threat. At least there was no van in sight. Kitty waved from the other end of the block. *I must be nuts,* I thought. I stuck Junior in my belt and walked back to the alley gate. Kitty met me there.

"It's clear," was all she said.

We entered the garden and I slid the bolt on the big gate into the locked position.

"I'm sorry." The deep male voice came from behind us. I froze in my tracks, easing my hand to my belt. Kitty whirled, keeping her body between her gun and the speaker.

It was Garrett.

"May I inquire as to what is happening?"

"I—uh, well. I—we, I mean—." I was stammering —out of control.

"Morning walk?" Kitty said.

Garrett raised one eyebrow. It was plain to see that he had spotted the butt of the pistol underneath my hand.

"Hardly," he said. He held out his hand. "Mrs. Winthorpe, my I help you with that?" Kitty handed him the pistol. He snapped it open and stared at the loaded cylinder. He raised his eyes and fixed a flat stare upon me. My stomach rolled over. We hardly knew Garrett, *what if...?*

"I assume your weapon is also loaded," he said.

"Uh, yes." I took my hand away. Garrett handed the forty-four back to Kitty.

"Will you be needing the car today?" I guess that was his way of saying that what we were doing was our own business.

"Garrett, come inside with us, please. I have a phone call to make, and there's a few things we need to tell you."

"As you wish, sir," he replied.

The three of us marched inside.

We offered Garrett a seat in the kitchen. While Kitty went about making coffee, I gave Garrett the five-minute rundown on the Luzadder affair and made the call to Dee Hopper. I didn't want to go searching the house for the cordless, so I flipped open my cell phone. Impatiently, I waited for an answer. The phone rang forever. If I had gotten an answering machine, who knows what I might have done next.

"Good morning." The voice was cheerful and familiar.

"Dee?"

"Yes, who's this?"

"This is Davis Winthorpe. Remember me?"

"Davis, I could hardly forget you—and Kitty. I've had several good chuckles over our conversation and there is still a bit of a mystery about these flowers. Do you have any news?"

I paused for a long while. Again, I was caught in the middle of a situation with no idea what I should say first.

"Davis, you still there?"

"Uh—yes, yes I do have news, or at least, uh—some ideas. Dee this is going to sound strange, but you have to listen and take me very seriously."

"Oh my, what is it?"

I told her the story of the two women in Seattle and the story of Danny Cutshaw. She listened quietly, occasionally muttering some brief term of understanding.

"Davis, you make this sound like a very sinister situation, and, yes, you are right. This does sound strange. What does it have to do with me?"

"Dee, if there is something sinister here, then whoever is sending the flowers knows who you are and probably where you are. I believe you're the next link in this bazaar chain. Your life could be in danger."

"Oh, I don't think so. I'm sure this whole thing is all out of proportion."

"Do me one favor, Dee. Go to your front window and just peek out. Don't open the door and don't part the curtain. Just peek"

"And—?"

"You're looking for a dark green Ford van. It's a big van with no windows in the side. Look up and down the street. Come and tell me what you see."

I heard her lay the phone down. I was left with several long seconds of uneasy silence.

Kitty was pouring coffee now.

"Mr. Winthorpe, Davis, there is a van there—just as you described. I don't know if it's a Ford or not. I can't tell one from the other. Should I do anything?"

"Dee, you've got to believe me. The man in that truck is dangerous! You've got to get out of there. Could you see if the man was inside?"

"I don't know. I couldn't tell!"

"You need to slip out your back door and get away from the house for a few days. Is there someone you can go visit?"

"My sister lives in…"

"Don't tell me!" I interrupted. "No one needs to know where you are. Right now, Dee, get your purse. Don't even pack. Go out the back door and walk to a neighbor's house on the next block and call a cab. Don't go to your van. Don't let him see you leave! You've got to believe me."

"My back yard is fenced."

"Climb the damn fence, Dee. Get out of there!"

"Oh—I'm not sure. I think I would rather call the police and stay right here."

"Dee, the police already know about Danny Cutshaw. They think his death was an accident. They won't do squat about you until the man tries to hurt you! Chances are your death will look like an accident too."

"Maybe if I just hide in the basement."

"Dee!"

"Oh, OK—I just know I'm going to look so silly climbing that fence. Could I just have a cab come to my front door?"

"Think, Dee. Think!"

"Yes, yes—the man would follow. I still think one of us is crazy—maybe both, but I'll go climb the fence, call a cab and go see my sister. What should I tell her —my sister?"

"Tell her your plumbing broke. I don't care. Go on, Dee. Don't change clothes or anything—promise me."

"I promise! I promise!"

"Thank you, Dee. Now go!"

"Well, thank you—I think. Goodbye now."

I leaned back and stared with wide eyes at Kitty.

"Will she go?" Garrett asked.

"Who knows? Probably."

"What about us?" Kitty asked. If he's at Dee's place, then we're safe for a while."

"Yeah," I said. "Safe for a while—any suggestions?"

"Let's leave town. I've been hoping to take a road trip in that new car. This guy won't hang around forever. Let's get Winston to go with us and stay on the road for a few days. We can come back after things cool down."

"What about Shannie?"

"She's gone to a wedding in Chicago—friend's daughter—something like that."

"Garrett, you got an opinion?"

"I believe the lady has offered an acceptable plan. The car is ready. I have a bag packed."

Somehow that didn't surprise me. I leaned my forehead against the frame of the kitchen door. I think I banged my head against the frame a couple of times. What Kitty said about things cooling down was still rattling around in my noggin. I wondered if things would ever actually cool down. For some reason a picture of Humpty Dumpty came to mind.

"OK," I said. "Kitty, ten minutes to pack, no more. I'll call Winston. Where we going, anyhow?"

She was already to the stairs. "West," she shouted. "Let's go to Kansas City and take Winston and Garrett to that restaurant. We can take the Luzadders too."

Garrett was also out the door. I was alone in the kitchen. I flipped open the cell phone.

"Win, I got a situation. Can you hit the road on short notice?"

"You ever say hello first? What the hell kind of a situation?"

"A dangerous situation—and there's no time to talk. You still got that old forty-five automatic you showed me?"

There was a long silence. "Yeah, I got it. So what?"

"Bring it!"

"Say what?"

"I don't want to come to your house. Meet me at the old place in the Southend. Park around back. Pack enough for two or three days."

"Where we goin'?"

"Not sure—Kitty has some ideas—we'll talk it over in the car!"

"You crazy fool! What'll I tell Shannie?"

"Tell her it's me. She won't suspect a thing!"

"Yeah, got that right. When?"

"Now! Dress nice."

The Hole in the Bottom of the Sea

I snapped the phone shut. I knew that last phrase would get under his skin. He would hurry just to speed up his chance to get back at me. I headed for the bedroom.

The doorbell rang as I bounded up the stairs. It was the UPS guy with an early morning delivery—from Hawaii. I carried the small box upstairs to show it to Kitty.

"Let's open it now! Davis, please, we have time."

I pulled out my pocketknife and split the seams. Inside I found a mass of those Styrofoam peanuts protecting the items sent by Tutu. I guess I have to say I was pleased and surprised. The bird of paradise blossom was there all right—along with a bill for $73.62, but Tutu had sent more. I found a set of matched stones. They were gray in color, pitted and yet smoothed like Kentucky river rock. One had a circular opening carved or cut in the middle with a set of tiny plastic spikes in the bottom. Kitty understood immediately that this was designed to hold the flower. The other stone had been sliced into sections so as to allow one to take it apart and put a little tea candle inside. The candle was already there. That was so plain that even I could understand.

"Davis this is lovely. A flower and a candle for sweethearts—I think this will have to go in my suitcase!"

"Wait there's more!" Deep in the peanuts I found two coffee mugs and a small package of coffee. The mugs had the appearance of being typical tourist stuff—nothing special. The coffee was Kona brand. The bag said the beans were grown right on the Island of Kaua'i. "Neat!" I said. "Let's take this too!"

Kitty's cell phone rang. It was Garrett announcing that the car was ready. I threw a few things into a bag and we made our retreat.

I had Garrett head east to take I-65 to the Watterson Expressway. I wanted to avoid the city streets that led toward Shively. Once underway, I determined it was time for me to get a better understanding of the silent man who carried our safety in his two hands.

"Tell me about your name, Garrett. Is that a first or a last name?"

"He looked into the rearview. "My name is James Smith. Garrett is a middle name. While in the military, I got tired of being constantly confused with some other Jim Smith. After I retired, I set up all my situations under the name of J. Garrett Smith. I found that to be just a bit stuffy. When I took my first job as a driver, I chose to simply be called Garrett. That seemed to fill the bill—it beats being called Jimmy."

We both laughed at his candor and his attempt at humor. It was the first long statement I had ever heard him make. It also seemed to be the beginning of a more relaxed relationship.

"Garrett, I think I would prefer it if you just called me Davis—you know. Mr. Winthorpe is just a bit stuffy."

"I will make every attempt to avoid being stuffy, and will call you Davis as appropriate. Thank you, sir."

The Hole in the Bottom of the Sea

I felt that I had not even made a dent in his cool front. I wondered why the man didn't have an English accent. It was a start.

Once we had Winston in the front seat we headed for the bridge to New Albany, Indiana and points west. Kitty had a couple of paperbacks tucked away and was listening to one of those personal cassette players. She was slouching on the left side of the back seat—lost in her kingdom. As for me—I had time to think. Garrett and Winston were off into some conversation. I drifted away into my own little world.

"Davis?" she said. "Shouldn't we call the Luzadders? We can't just show up."

We were still on the Watterson and this would be a local call. It was silly, but I just couldn't seem to get over the notion of pinching every penny by avoiding long distance fees. I opened the cell phone and made the call. The call to William was brief. He asked for news. I gave him none. He said that he would decide about the Hereford House after we got there. Once again, I was patient as he gave me his address and detailed directions. It clicked in my mind after I hung up. It was just after nine-thirty in the morning and we had a nine-hour drive—or so. It would be around seven when we got to the Luzadder place. *No, wait—there's a one-hour time difference.* Six o'clock—that should work.

Mike Bradford

Kitty always had this way of dropping little bombshells when I least expected it. During the drive to Kansas City, she did it again.

"Davis, you remember the beach house were we spent our honeymoon?"

"Fancy Dancer—how could I forget that?"

"I got a call from the agent at the rental office. The house is for sale."

"Does that mean we won't be able to rent it again?"

"No, silly, it means I think we should buy it."

Winston shifted nervously in his seat. Garrett checked the rearview. I went blank.

"Uh, well, I guess that, uh—yeah, maybe. That's got to be a chunk of change."

"Not as bad as you think. I had her send me some figures. If I've done my *pro forma* correctly, we can put ten-percent down, leave it on the rental program most of the year and pick up a very nice asset for less than a thousand a month. And, Davis dear, we can then spend a couple of months on the island in October and November. It's still nice there that time of year."

Her little speech made my head spin. The very notion of owning the home we were in made me euphoric. The thought of a beach house made me simply nuts.

"How much is ten-percent?"

"About seventy-thousand."

"Kitty, that's three quarters of a million for the house!"

"They'll come down. I think it's a good deal, and it's smart. Davis, the equity will build rapidly. The expenses will enable us to show a loss and cut other taxable income—plus that, it's a whole new world of adventure. It'll be a blast."

We had Winston's full attention now.

"Honey, I just can't get used to this money stuff. It seems like we're spending a fortune, and, if you think about it, neither of us actually has a job."

"Davis, good grief, what we have is a life-style. You work. I work every day. We've put very little into our real estate. In fact, I need to invest more to avoid taxes. My investments have made money and the balance of the money from the New York sale is doing pretty good in some short-term bonds. Honey, I've made as much in the last few months as I've spent. We can do it!"

I gave her a long stare. "You're serious, aren't you?"

"Yeah, serious is the word. I'm serious, and I'm good."

"What you gonna do all that time down there at the beach without me along. Davis, you know you're helpless without me. Now, shut up and let that woman buy that house. You and me—we goin' fishin'." Winston had put in his two-cents worth.

I laughed and asked Kitty to let me think on it for a day or two.

She said she didn't think there was a rush. The agent had told her that most people buy in the spring so they could take advantage of the upcoming summer income. "From our position it works better to buy now while the market is down," Kitty said.

I guess I felt the need to change the subject. Kitty had made her point and there were a few things I wanted to ask her in private—before we made the big decision. I let some time pass before I spoke.

"Garrett, you said you were in the military. What did you do?"

"I was in for fifteen years, sir—Master Sergeant, retired."

"Ever want to go back?" Winston asked.

"I've done my share—had enough."

Winston said, "I'm a former Marine—three stripes —five years—done my time."

"Yeah, I figured you were a jarhead."

"Shows, huh?"

"Once a Marine, always a Marine." Garrett looked at me in the rearview and grinned.

I continued, "What did, uh—what did you do in the military?"

Garrett looked at me in the mirror for several seconds before speaking. "After basic, I was assigned to the Diplomatic Corps. I worked in the Diplomatic Escort Service. Later, I was assigned to the Department of State—my activities there were classified."

His comments seemed cryptic and were completely beyond my understanding. "Does that mean that if you tell me, you have to kill me?" I asked.

"Those aren't the words I would use. I'm just not at liberty to discuss my former activity. I can boil it down into a simple idea."

"Please, if you don't mind."

"I drove cars and delivered messages."

"Oh—yeah—OK. I get it." Actually I didn't. For a moment there I had visions of special operations, secret missions, blood, guts and spy stuff. I kept quiet for a while. I figured I had best let the matter drop. Kitty was propped up again with a paperback. She was off into her world of unrealistic fiction. *I wonder if she takes that stuff she reads in those paperbacks seriously.*

"Davis—sir?" There was something threatening about the calm in Garrett's voice. I looked up without speaking and caught his glance in the rearview.

"There's a green van on our tail. It's been closing on us for the last few minutes."

I took a quick glance at the vehicle behind us. It appeared to be more than a quarter of a mile behind. "Closing?" I responded.

"I don't think we are being followed. The driver would have matched our speed by now. He's been passing other vehicles. This is the first time there have been no vehicles between us."

Winston rolled his thick body around to get a look at the big van. Then he looked at me. "OK, Mr. Winthorpe," he said. "I brought this forty-five like you said. Now what is it I need to know about guns and green vans? I've waited long enough."

I looked back one more time. The van was just yards behind us now. It seemed like just seconds passed before the van pulled left and passed us at high speed. I got glimpse of the driver. The man was big, white. Curly blonde hair was pulled back into a little bob of a ponytail. I saw an earring. The driver never gave us a glance. The van was plain enough. It bore

Virginia tags—no other markings. I wrote the tag number down in my notebook and let the matter pass. *It's probably some working stiff on his way to his next job.* I figured that only a fool would be spooked by every green van he saw.

"Match his speed?" Garrett asked.

"No—no, let him go."

"Talk!" Winston's word was a terse command.

I spent the next couple of hours telling all I knew about the Luzadder affair and discussing the matter with Winston. Kitty came back to life and joined the fray. Garrett tended to his business. His occasional glances in the mirror assured me that he had a clear understanding of the situation and was taking it all in. The tangle of expressways in St. Louis and the rolling countryside of Missouri fell behind us. We were approaching Kansas City.

The Hole in the Bottom of the Sea

Chapter Fourteen

Our reception at the Luzadder home seemed cool. I got the feeling that our whole relationship was one of those situations in which William needed someone to hear his troubles. He needed a sense of being proactive over a bizarre concern. Now that he had confided in me and I was on the job, perhaps I knew too much. Being uncomfortable with me was now part of his ongoing uncertainty. I had become a liability to this very private man.

"It seems, Mr. Winthorpe, that your station in life has changed a bit since we last visited." He cast a critical eye toward the big white car, the large man who climbed from behind the wheel and the heavy black man who stood beside the driver. I knew that I didn't fully understand what was on his mind, but we were inside William Luzadder's comfort zone.

"I came into some money," Kitty supplied. Additional comment didn't seem necessary.

"Nice work, if you can get it," Luzadder responded.

William and Alice turned down our invitation to go to the Hereford House. They had some leftovers that would go to waste and besides that William said it appeared to him that *the Lincoln was comfortably full*. In my opinion, he was rude to us and to our friends. I guess that's OK. I was not straightforward with him about the deaths in Seattle and Louisville, or my suspicions. I really didn't have any solid facts to give the man—I was willing to leave it at that. William uttered an appropriate insult and we parted company. In the end of the matter, I never did tell him all I would come to know about his brother.

Garrett declined our plan to have him sit with us at the Hereford House.

"I will ask for a seat near the entry. That will be better procedure," he said.

His peculiar choice and his use of the word procedure didn't make much sense to me at the time, but I was going to receive a better understanding of our driver/protector before the evening was over—several things changed for me that night.

After we placed our order I made a polite excuse and headed for the men's room. Winston followed close behind.

"Davis, did you hear what that man said about his time with the Diplomatic Corps?"

"Yeah, what's the deal? He was a driver or something."

"Driver my fat you-know-what! When I was in the Marines I wasn't no fightin' man. I went through basic —you know weapons trainin' and all, but I was assigned to motor pool. I worked on trucks and cars."

"Mechanic?"

"Yeah, grease monkey. I drove trucks too, but mostly worked on them. For a while I was assigned to a motor pool that maintained vehicles for the

Diplomatic Corps. I seen those spit and polish Marine Sergeants come down in their dress uniforms. Man, those dudes would check the car out from one end to the other—all quiet and mechanical like. I seen them get behind the wheel and make a car do things I didn't know was possible. Those guys were specialists assigned to embassy duty and stuff like that. They were amazin'!"

"So what's the deal?"

"Those dudes had one rule, *death before dishonor*. They meant it exactly the way it sounds."

"Maybe I'm dumb, Winston. Why am I not catching on?"

"Hell, stupid, you got a trained killer working for you. He's a trained professional, genuine U.S.M.C bodyguard—meaner than a bulldog. That man will lay down his life for his passenger and kill anything or anyone that gets in the way. Why do you think he's over there at the door watchin' everything that moves, man?"

"Clue me in."

"He's on the job, Davis. Right now he's as nervous as a cat. He can't see us, and if he comes to check on us, he will lose sight of Kitty. He's on guard and his responsibility is conflicted."

"He's protecting us, you mean?"

"With his life! Her, at least, he may stick his nose in to check on us, but she's his primary responsibility."

"Damn! Wait 'til I tell Kitty!"

"Fool, you think she don't know that already? You got yourself a New York City woman there with tons of dough. She done told you she came to Louisville on the run. That woman done hired her a bodyguard and never even told you! You can bet this ain't the first *professional* she's had workin' for her!"

I thought that one over for a while. I punched the electric hand dryer took a little extra time getting the job done.

"Win, you are a suspicious man," I said.

"Yeah, you'll see. Sooner or later that dude will save your life—or take it. He's workin' for the woman. Look inside yourself. You know that. Com'on get outa my way. I want to get to work on that steak."

I grinned as I walked out the door. Winston hadn't seen anything yet. I'd bribed the server to ignore Winston's order and bring him the thirty-two ounce special with all the trimmings. I was going to make my wide-bodied buddy say uncle! I stepped into the dining area. Garrett's gaze was fixed on the men's room door. He was working on a large salad. He made eye contact without any acknowledgement. I gave a slight nod. Yes, I was feeling a little weird. I made the turn toward our table—then I glanced back. From Garrett's location he had a clear view of our table, the front door and the entry from the kitchen. Was he ready for trouble? Who could say? Winston Pence had a way of exaggerating when excited.

"Fool! What you do to me?" Winston shouted. "Man that much red meat's gonna kill me. Pass the salt! Hang with a fool—be a fool!"

He thanked me later.

Kitty made out with *escargot* and lobster tail. I went for the prime rib—twelve-ounce variety. Well—that sounded smaller than Winston's cut, but I was among the walking wounded by the time we were ready to head for the parking lot. Garrett had demolished the big salad plus a full slab of baby-back ribs. They served the ribs with something they called cowboy beans.

I settled with the waitress while Garrett went to get the Town Car. Winston followed him, waddling close behind.

The next several seconds are engraved into my mind. I remain amazed at the clarity with which I remember what happened. As the events unfolded, it took me a few seconds to get tuned in. I think I was experiencing what Kitty calls *food coma*. Once my mind caught up with the action, things stuck like crisp images in a photograph!

I was watching for the Town Car, stowing the receipt and congratulating myself on my good fortune. Kitty had taken a quick trip to the ladies' room. Perhaps Garrett had let his guard down—I don't know and no blame needs to be fixed. It's just that all hell broke loose. Whatever the case, I somehow didn't see the big green van approaching. It slid to the curb about three feet from me, coming to an abrupt halt. The driver was a monster of a man. He faced me eye to eye as he slid open the cargo door. He was on me in an instant. I saw him clearly and will never forget. My assailant stood well over six-feet. A wide rough looking face with scruffy dull brownish beard was set off by pale blue ice-like eyes. A teardrop was tattooed near the corner of his right eye. Bleached, Golden yellow curly hair was pulled back into a bob of a ponytail. There was an earring in his right ear. I had seen this dude before. It was the same guy who passed us on the Interstate. He was dressed in faded blue jeans and a sleeveless black shirt. On his left shoulder was a tattoo of a straight flush—spades to the Jack. A death's head represented the Jack of Spades. There were other tattoos. That's the one I remembered.

First he shoved me backward—fist full in my chest. As I lost balance, he kept coming at me. Catching me, he spun me around. From behind, he locked a beefy arm under my chin. He was dragging me into the cavern of the van. Strangely enough, I remember the fragrance of some familiar cologne.

I saw Kitty coming out the door of the restaurant—mouth opening into a shout. I heard the roar of the big engine in the Town Car. I was starting to see bursting sparks of light before my eyes. I think his hold was designed to make me pass out. As we left the curb, the Town Car slammed into the rear of the van. The man spun around and slammed me hard into the rocker panel beneath the van door. He produced a gun from somewhere. I bounced off the van and scrambled onto the sidewalk. It was like slow motion as the gunman swung his weapon toward the Town Car. I definitely heard metal wrinkle as Garrett came sliding feet first across the hood. The big man, the assailant, fired his gun. Garrett was down and rolling toward him. That's the last I saw.

The Hole in the Bottom of the Sea

I heard a piercing scream and the giant of a man came tumbling down on top of me. I had heard the impact, but had no idea what had happened. Later I learned that Kitty had screamed at the man as she swung that big purse—cannon and all. She caught him full in the face just as Garrett took his legs out from under him. He about killed me when he fell. My face plowed into concrete and all my air went away. If I could have taken a breath—I would have. Strength failed me.

It was Garrett who pulled the hulk off me. Somehow I staggered to my feet. I don't even remember drawing my gun, but as my wits came back to me I found myself standing over the downed man—gun in hand, shouting obscenities. They came from inside me somewhere. I didn't even know that I knew how to say such things.

"Sir—Davis?" Garrett said, calmly. "Please." He was holding out his hand. I gave him the gun. "Yours too." He held his hand out to Kitty.

Garrett sprinted quickly to a trashcan about ten yards down the side of the building. The weapons disappeared inside. People were coming out of the restaurant now. Garrett pointed at Winston—still in the front seat of the car. He hooked his thumb toward the can. Winston scrambled out. I lost sight of him, but I knew he was ditching the forty-five. In moments the police were on the scene.

It took a while, but the police concluded that the incident was an attempted armed-robbery. They carted the man and the big van away. We received profuse apologies from the officers on the scene and the manager of the Hereford House. They assured me that this was not the kind of experience that visitor's usually received. The police inquired as to our safety and took our statements. I told the officers that I had never seen the man before, which—in a sense of the word, was true.

The grill was crushed on the new Town Car. The hood was caved in from the impact of Garrett's big backside. There was also an ugly hole in the right front fender. The gunman had missed our man, Garrett.

"I'm so glad you're alright," Kitty exclaimed.

"Why you worried about him?" Winston interrupted. "Look at this!"

Winston yanked open the door of the car, leaned over and placed his pinkey into a bullet hole just under the edge of the front seat where he'd been sitting. "Man, I felt that thing plow in there. Scared me so bad I'm still all puckered up!"

We laughed—and we cried. Kitty cried. I trembled.

I had a rip in my light blue slacks and a definite bruise on my cheek, but the car seemed to be in good running order. We took our places and Garrett eased into traffic.

"Where we going?" Kitty asked.

"Ten out—ten back," Garrett replied.

"Meaning?" I said.

"Give the police time to clear the area," he answered.

The Hole in the Bottom of the Sea

About twenty minutes later the Town Car slid to the curb next to the trash can at the Hereford House. Garrett exited the car, reached into the can and returned.

"Mrs. Winthorpe," he said, presenting her forty-four to her. "Sir," he said to me. Junior had been rescued. He laid the old forty-five on the seat beside Winston and nudged the gun toward him.

"Thanks, man."

We were quiet for a long time.

Garrett elected to head east—back toward home. It was after ten at night. I knew we were all completely frayed and well past exhaustion.

"Find us a motel," I said softly. Garrett glided off the Interstate at the next exit.

I got our room assignments while Garrett removed all bags from the trunk. As we came together back at the car, Kitty was face to face with Garrett.

"Thanks, Jim," she said softly.

"And to you," he said.

She hugged the big man. It looked awkward at first, but then he returned the gesture. It was strange. Somehow my tall doll looked like a little girl in his arms.

I reached out and shook his hand.

Winston said, "Yeah!" He worked his shoulders and neck. Hitched up his pants and said, "Yeah! We done good!"

Kitty shut the motel door behind her and stood there. I threw our bags on the bed.

"Davis, I'm not moving another inch until we decide some things!"

I didn't understand my own mind—at the moment. I was sure that I didn't want to talk. There was deep-seated anger—and fear churning down inside me. I didn't want to misdirect any of this at my Kitty. I announced, "I'm going to the bathroom. You can start without me." I don't know where *that* came from.

"Davis, don't get cute. Do what you have to do and get back here. We've got to settle this."

"I'm Ok, Kitty. I don't know why I said that. I guess, well, I guess I just don't know what to say. Maybe this settles the Luzadder business. Maybe this is the last of it. What do you think?" Put the ball in her court—that seemed like a plan.

"Why can't we tell the police who he is?"

"Who is he?"

"He killed Danny Cutshaw—maybe the girls too!"

"No evidence, no investigation, no jurisdiction—I told you what Cooper said. They've got him here for attempted robbery, or assault, or something. He was armed and he fired his gun. That's probably pretty serious. The Kansas City cops can do whatever they will with him, but Kentucky isn't going to make the first move to extradite a man when there isn't even a crime—in their eyes. Kitty, I got mugged! That's it! There's no more we can do."

"I want to find Luzadder. I want to go where he is and find the truth!"

The Hole in the Bottom of the Sea

"Kitty, are you nuts? Listen to yourself. Go where? If any of this is real, then the man's a killer. We go where he is and let him know who we are—and we're dead."

"I think you were almost dead tonight," she replied. I also think that Luzadder is alive and isn't done with us. We either disappear, or we go after him."

Her tone and determination was unsettling. Nausea swept over me. I was in a cold sweat. I could see my assailant's face before me—in flashes. I could even smell his breath. The terror inside me was real. I was afraid.

"Damn it, Kitty, aren't you afraid!" I shouted.

"Yes, I'm afraid! I was afraid when I met you. I was afraid when I came to Louisville. Davis, I've been afraid for years. I thought I had escaped my fears when I dropped out and came to Louisville—to you, but, hell, I—I..." Kitty broke down in tears.

I held her, stroked her hair, kissed a tear from her cheek. "What do you want to do, doll?"

"I want it to go away." Her voice was thin and weak.

"What if it won't go away?"

"Then maybe we will. Maybe we can go to Sal in Johnson City and start over."

"Wow—you really are serious!"

"Davis, it sounds crazy, but I would rather face the madman than go hide. I sure don't want to live constantly wondering when he will come for us."

"Kitty, surely it's not like that!"

"Yes it is. I have lived in the shadow of people like him all my life. They, and the people they associate with, never give up."

Her statement glued me to the spot. I had no ideas —no resources. I couldn't begin to comprehend the kind of a former existence she had just revealed, but, at the Hereford House, I had gotten a very good glimpse.

"Kitty, who was your bodyguard before Garrett?"

"What!" She took her head from my shoulder and pushed me back to an arm's length. Her look was one of disbelief. "He's not a bodyguard! I just wanted a car, and a driver. I never thought of such a thing!"

"You may not have thought it, that's what he is. He's a trained professional—and probably would kill, if needed. You saw him in action tonight."

"Yeah, I saw him, and I saw me. Davis, do you think my actions tonight were just those of a panicked woman?"

"Well, I—No! I hadn't even thought about it. It was instinct!"

"Instinct my big behind! I could take you off your feet in the blink of an eye. In the time it takes to think about it I could disable you. If life was at stake, I could kill you—without drawing the gun!"

"You're nuts! You can't..." That was as far as I got. I don't know what she did. I felt a finger slam into my chest and I was flat on the bed. Kitty had a twisting grip on my thumb that was excruciating. She rammed a thumb into the side of my neck.

"In an instant," she growled. There was something in this woman's voice that came from a world I did not know. At the moment—I wasn't sure I knew her.

"Is this foreplay," I squeaked.

She laughed and tumbled down on top of me.

"No, my wonderful Davis, I detest violence, and for me sex and violence don't mix. Any passion I might feel tonight is all anger and upset. Sex ain't on my mind tonight, baby! And, yes. I saw what Garrett did. You're right. He is a bodyguard—probably a good one. I guess I've known that and wanted that all along. I guess I'm trying to protect myself and hide from my past all at the same time. Someday—well, someday." Her speech ended there. I was smart for once. I let the matter drop. We both had other things on our mind. To be honest, I don't think I really wanted to know where she had learned that kind of stuff.

"What are we going to do?" I asked. "About Luzadder, I mean."

"Davis, I was teasing about that martial arts stuff. I did take some lessons, but it was no big deal—did I scare you?"

"You startled me—that's all. Every time I think I'm getting to know you—there's another surprise. You're a complicated gal, Kitty."

"Not really—well, I guess—no, not really."

I waited for a moment. "Answer my question."

"About what?"

"Luzadder—what are we going to do?"

"Let's go to Hawaii—to Kaua'i. That's where all our leads point. Let's go, have some fun—if we can, ask a few questions. And, Mr. Winthorpe, you should be remembering that this next Sunday is our first anniversary. I would like to spend it with you in paradise."

"Kitty, you're crazy, and I like it! When do we leave?"

"Let's go to the airport tomorrow. We can leave from here. Garrett and Winston can go on to Louisville. We can schedule a flight that will take us back to Louisville when we're done."

"Just like that?"

"Just like that!" she said. We've got credit cards. Anything we need we can buy over there."

"Just like that?"

"No, darn, there's some things I just have to take. Let's go home tomorrow and fly out on Tuesday. We might as well do it up right!"

Kitty was wrong. She did have sex on her mind that night. She was passionate and forceful. I think that down inside anger was driving her emotional state. Aside from a very sore cheek, I was in heaven.

I asked Garrett to let us out in front when we arrived back on Park Avenue. Somehow the open spaces there seemed more assuring that the close confines of the alley behind our house.

"Shall I carry the bags in?" he asked.

"No, we're OK," I replied. "Take Winston on home, please. Winston, Luzadder doesn't know about you. I think you're OK. I'm not so sure about you, Garrett. Why don't you take the car and take some time off while we're away. Get out of town for a while. We'll cover your expenses."

"That's very generous, sir, and not necessary."

"I know that, but I'd feel better."

"As you wish—where is this island and house the Mrs. mentioned? I may go check that out."

"Maramassee Island—North Carolina," I told him. "It's your call."

"Find the agent in the office to the right as you come off the bridge," Kitty said. "Tell her you work for me. She'll show you the place."

"An' don't think you're doin' this alone, big man," Winston said. "Unless you got some objection, I'm goin' with you. Davis here will cover my expenses too. The dude owes me!"

We all laughed a good hearty laugh at Winston's invitation of self. Yes, he was right. I owed him, and would continue to owe him for years to come.

"Sir, before we go over to Winston's, I need to get an item or two from my quarters. Would you mind to wait here with Winston and Mrs. Winthorpe until I return?"

"No, no problem," I replied. Garrett bounded up the steps.

"You know he's checkin' out the house, before you and Kitty go in, don't you.

"Yeah, Win, I know that. I believe he's going to be a good man to have around."

I scanned the area nervously. I was anxious. By this time tomorrow we would be in Hawaii—almost, facing who knows what. I gazed out across Central

Park. Nothing was out of the ordinary. Two guys were tossing a football. A middle-aged gentleman sat on a bench reading a book. Nothing was out of the ordinary.

Once inside the house, we packed immediately. I mention that only because of something I did. I stood for the longest time at the edge of our bed. My suitcase was open. I looked at the gun I held in my hand. Two times I had pulled it on another man. This last time—I almost fired it. I shoved the gun into a sock and put it in its place in my dresser drawer. I turned and closed the suitcase.

The Hole in the Bottom of the Sea

Chapter Fifteen

The man leaned heavily on the counter in front of him. Blue eyes twinkled and a grin spread across his big face as we approached. He'd strolled about the restaurant while we dined. He would chat with patrons and inquire as to their satisfaction. I was obviously looking at the proud owner of the Paradise Pacific Restaurant. I couldn't keep from nudging a conversation from the fellow.

"So, how's it going?"

"Aw, just another day in Paradise."

His grin broadened. A little touch of the blue of daylight lingered in the sky. Across the road still rosy clouds were peeking over the azure sea. Light trade winds whipped around the corner of the building, sending a gust of air through the open door—air that felt like velvet.

"Life gets rough, doesn't it?" I quipped.

It was only our second day on the Island of Kaua'i, but I understood the smile on the handsome man's face. I had already seen enough to know he was one of those mainlanders who had started a life of renewal on the island. He had the look, but he didn't yet walk the walk.

Mike Bradford

We arrived on the island at dusk on Tuesday and holed up in an oceanfront hotel called The Beachboy in the little town of Kapa'a. It wasn't the fanciest around, but I couldn't resist the name. Light of day was just fading as we left our room to find a meal, but in my head it was one o'clock in the morning. This was a new experience to me. Somehow my mind was still on the sidewalk in Kansas City. I figured it was what they call jet lag.

"Don't worry about it. Ignore it!" Kitty said. "Just keep putting one foot in front of the other. When your eyes cross, we'll go to bed. By tomorrow afternoon your body will adjust."

My body was starving.

"Let's try this place," I said. We wandered into a restaurant with the catchy name of Mr. Z's Ono Café. The café was at the far end of a shopping center called the Coconut Marketplace. A huge man with an enormous smile and tattoos covering both arms served our table. The place had no air conditioning, no screens and no doors. The breeze whipping through the restaurant caressed me with soothing comfort. I felt as if I could gather up the wind in my hands and rub it on like a soothing lotion.

Predictably, Kitty ordered something that sounded Italian. It contained mahi-mahi, and grilled baby shrimp over fettuccini with an Alfredo sauce. I ordered what the menu called Ahi—fish, sort of like tuna. The waiter took our order, flashed his big smile and announced, "You gonna like dis! Firs' day on de island?"

The Hole in the Bottom of the Sea

"Longest day of my life!" I responded.

The big man sort of cruised off. There was a beauty to his easy gait. I heard him chuckle after his back was to us. I think he was taking delight in my misery.

"Davis, there's a lizard on the wall behind you," Kitty whispered across the table.

Let him eat me, I thought. I was too tired to care.

"Aren't you going to tell the waiter?"

I just wanted to sit and let the wonderful air soak through to my insides. *What the heck?* I motioned for the man to come over.

I turned and found the little green monster. I pointed toward it.

"Sir, there's a lizard on the wall behind me."

He leaned to look—quizzical expression.

"No, dat's no lizard. Dat's a gecko."

He turned to leave.

"Shouldn't you remove it?"

"No way, man. Can't do dat. Dat's his wall. He live dere. He take care of de place. Anudder live on dat wall and annuder over dere. Dey don't get along so good. So dey each have deir own wall. Dey eat bugs. Dat keeps de gecko happy—keeps me happy, no problem."

"No problem!" I said, with an edge in my voice.

Mr. No-big-deal leaned toward the gecko again—same quizzical look.

"De gecko looks OK. Him got no problem." He leaned back. I glanced at Kitty. Her eyes were dancing with delight. He continued, "I got no problem—soon you have no problem. Listen," he said softly. "We had a famous actor in here las' week. At firs' he didn't like de gecko. But later—he had big time. He name de geckos Curley, Moe and Larry. You can name dem too, if you like. De gecko, he don't care."

He headed for the kitchen, walking that easy walk. This was a strange encounter with a wonderful man. I got the feeling he was a talker. I knew I would come back to Mr. Z's. I wanted to see how much information I could nudge out of the big fellow.

The food arrived shortly. The presentation was so wonderful. It was almost too pretty to eat. After a lot of reaching across the table to sample from each other, I had to admit that Kitty's dish was better than mine.

Later the server told us we should try the mud pie. The dessert looked like pie. It was on what I took to be a graham cracker crumb crust topped with layers of vanilla, peanut butter and coffee flavored ice cream. It was smothered in hot fudge and whipped cream.

I pushed back from the table. "Are my eyes crossed yet?"

"Not yet," Kitty responded. "Let's walk around this place a bit."

I was good for about three shops. I waited until I caught Kitty looking at me. I stared at the end of my nose and tried to put on a dazed expression.

"Let me take my baby home," she responded, snuggling up to me. "Too bad you're so tired. They say that paradise does wonderful things to one's libido."

"Don't give up on me," I said. "I may have a little steam left."

The Hole in the Bottom of the Sea

Wrong—I slept like a dead man. I don't think my libido had caught up with me yet.

The next morning we went looking for a woman who called herself Tutu. The little shop in Hanamaulu Town was a quaint mixture of floral displays, Hawaiian and oriental art, gift items and wonderful odors. We stood at the door taking it all in. An elegant older lady stood in front of the counter. Her cream colored ankle length dress seemed to glow against her bronze skin. Her hair was white as snow. Strands of tiny shells were about her neck. She studied us with the same quizzical look we had seen on the big Hawaiian at Mr. Z's.

"This is Davis and Kitty. I knew you would come!" She almost sang the words—with a grand tone.

"Tutu, how did you know?"

"I have watched every day for beautiful lovers with stars in their eyes. Very few tourists come into this shop. It is sort of a place out of the way for the locals. I told you before—I knew you would come. You came to see Tutu and you are still looking for Raymond."

I'm sure I was slack-jawed. Her off-handed statement caught me by surprise. Yeah, I was looking for Ray Luzadder, but the real reason I was in her shop was to meet a woman who was already captivating in my mind. I didn't answer for a long time. I stared and I smiled. I couldn't begin to guess the age of this ancient beauty. She was still standing straight with head high. Her tiny frame simply seemed to flow with grace and elegance. Her comment about Raymond made me think she saw right through to my ulterior motives. For a moment, as the morning sunlight streamed through the door, I felt naked in her presence.

"Actually, Tutu, I had to meet you."

"And," Kitty interrupted. "I had to thank you for the wonderful things you sent!"

"Yes," she said, with one precise little word. She looked fetchingly at me. "Kitty, you brought them with you, didn't you?"

"Well—uh—yes. I did."

"The stones bear the spirit of love in them. They came from the volcano, from the heart of the earth. The spirit of the island and the mighty Pélé is in them. They were smoothed by the waters that flow to the sea from Mount Waialeale and crafted by the hands of those who love this island. The candle will warm your spirits to release the spirit of *aloha* into you. My lovers will have a very good week. The coffee—well—I just threw that in extra."

We must have talked for over an hour with Tutu. It seemed like minutes. Much of what she said she would say first in Hawaiian and then repeat in English. Always speaking with that same musical softness. At least I think she was speaking in her native tongue and then repeating for us. At no time did I ever understand how she knew the things she knew. It all seemed so obvious to her. I was befuddled. She told us of the *aloha* spirit, and the people of the islands. She told us about the language they spoke and how to pronounce the words. She was sad over how so many things had changed. She also told us about a great place to get breakfast. We'd left the hotel without eating. My animal nature was getting the best of me—hunger was taking control. I told her we would save the breakfast spot for tomorrow. I wanted to go back to Mr. Z's, mostly for information. We wished her a happy goodbye, heading for the door.

"I was wrong about Raymond," she announced. Her tone was different. "He may be on the Island. If he is here, he is not looking to see old friends. There is more to his story that one can speak. It would be best if true friends would remember him fondly from days that are long ago—and forgotten. If you must find him, be patient. We never hurry on this Island. Things we need to know come to us—if they are needed—when they are needed."

I didn't know what to say. My hand was on the doorknob. "Thank you Tutu," I said softly.

"*Aloha*, Davis," she said.

"*Mahalo*," I replied.

Kitty was silent as I pointed our little red convertible back toward the Coconut Marketplace. I was looking forward to a long lazy early lunch at Mr. Z's and conversation with the big man with no problem.

Kitty finally spoke. "That was a warning Tutu gave us. She's protecting him. I think she's protecting us too."

For a moment I could find no words, then I said, "What should we do?"

"Have a second honey moon, enjoy paradise and keep our eyes open. Tutu will open doors for us, if they need opening. I think that's what she was telling us."

Mike Bradford

We took a table nearest to the Marketplace to watch the world go by. Many of the locals would park in the street behind the Marketplace and enter near Mr. Z's. This gave us a chance to do some first rate people watching. That is when we began to play our little game.

"Look at her. She's a local," Kitty said.

"He's a tourist."

"Got that right—socks, white legs."

The game was simple to play. There was a great diversity among the people walking before us. Sounds of many languages floated in with the breeze. Regardless of the color of the skin or the manner of the dress, there was a certain easygoing nature about the people who had enjoyed island life for some time. We puzzled over this, picking out tourists and locals.

Kitty said, "The locals never window shop.".

"The look on their face is different," I said.

"Yes, but—what is it that makes them look so different?"

"It's the walk!"

"That's it!" she agreed.

We started watching the way people walked, and we studied their feet. Most locals were shod with well-worn sandals of some sort. Most had their feet protected with little thong sandals made of straw, rubber bound with velvet like straps. Their feet were dark from the sun, callused and often dirty.

"Yes, that *is* it," I said. "Tourists, like us, mostly wear some sort of athletic shoe…"

The Hole in the Bottom of the Sea

"And socks!" Kitty added with disdain.

Some tourists and short timers had caught onto the comfort of the island style, but they didn't yet walk the walk. The graceful walk of the island people, we figured, came from years of slowly striding along while trying to keep the loose fitting gear on their feet. That's why I said the owner of the Paradise Pacific Restaurant did not yet walk the walk.

"Hey, It's de gecko man!" Our big Hawaiian friend came strolling over. We both looked at his feet and stifled a grin.

"So you name dem yet?"

"Huey, Dewey and Louie," I replied.

Kitty said, "Babe, Hank and Stan."

"Hey, I like dis lady. She know what's what! So, what to eat?"

I told him we wanted salads, a sandwich to split, sweet tea and some time.

"Surprise us," I said. "We'll finish with more of that ice cream pie."

"And Kona Coffee!" Kitty added.

He smiled his big smile and winked at Kitty, "I get something pretty for you and de gecko man."

He went his way as elegantly as he came.

A couple breezed by us. They turned right just as they passed our table and walked away.

"Locals!" Kitty asserted.

"She's gorgeous!" I blurted.

The woman stood patiently on the walkway just a few feet from us, waiting for the man. He had uttered a few quick words to her and entered a shop. She looked like a mixture of all the races of the Pacific—so slim she seemed unreal. Jet-black, long, straight hair, coffee with cream complexion, large, dark, jewel like eyes. She was small busted and wearing a silken, floral dress of azure blue. The garment covered her from neck to ankles, revealing every curve of her lithe frame. That's all I noticed.

"She's OK," Kitty said.

The man lingered on my mind. I figured him to be a mainlander for sure, but he had the look of the locals. He also walked the walk. In just a few minutes he was back. He continued to talk to the beauty as he sorted through a stack of mail. His thong sandals were worn to the point of looking mangled. Long awkward looking, well bronzed legs showed beneath his khaki shorts. He wore a faded floral shirt in shades of blue, pink and green. He was topped with a sky-blue ball cap. It was embroidered with a sea turtle and the word *Kauai*. The face was average—wide lines about his nose with full, almost paunchy, cheeks. A close-cropped grisly beard covered his face. Pale blue eyes twinkled.

Our server came to place our tea on the table. The couple walked toward us a few steps. The man paused to open one of the letters. He renewed his conversation with the woman.

"Who is that man—in the cap—beard?" Kitty asked abruptly.

"Lady, you're lookin' at Papalou. He's da man! Hey, Papalou, howzit? Some day, yeah?"

"*Aloha*, Big Jim, just like yesterday!" Papalou called back.

The man made eye contact with me. He looked up from the mail in his hand, giving me a half-smile. The impish look on his face was the same as I had studied so many times in the photo William Luzadder had given me, but the face was different. I tried to roll back the years and see the boy that used to be, but the face was different. I watched as Kitty slipped her hand to our camcorder as it lay on the table. The machine was on its side, but she turned the lens toward the couple and pushed the record button.

"Who's the girl?" she asked, speaking softly, as the couple passed.

"Don't know her. She's a new one. Dat Papalou—always with de girls. She look like an island girl for sure, but not dis island. Don't know her—probably a flight attendant. Papalou flies a lot—Honolulu, Big Island, mainland. Lotsa time he bring a girl home. Dat's his vice, yeah.

"Who is Papalou?" I asked.

"Oh, Papalou—he's alright! He's one mainlander who learn what's right about de *aloha* spirit—you know." Big Jim said the words almost reverently. "He's got several businesses on de island, but he's more dan dat. He takes care of people. Lots of kids on de island sort of get lost—you know. Kids from mainland come here—dey almost homeless. Papalou owns a fruit and flower shop—and gardens. He puts dem to work, gets dem straight, sends dem home. He owns dat coffee shop he went in, owns a kayak place on the Wialua

River, has a fishin' boat—you know—private party boat. Everywhere, he keeps people at work—takes care of dem—you know."

"What's under the hat?" Kitty asked.

"Don'know, he probably bolohead, yeah.

That got completely by me. In the few hours I knew Papalou, Lou Addison, I never saw him without a cap on his head.

"How do you know Papalou?" I asked.

Big Jim's voice got husky. "He took care of me. I got stupid and walked in front of a truck up near Auntie Ono's—got me broke up pretty bad. Papalou went to my house wit' groceries, brought my wife down to Wilcox Hospital, had his girl stay with our two kids. He didn't even know me. He came here and told Mr. Zazzi to hold my job until I was well. He argued with de man. Papalou took care of Big Jim. I told you—he's da man."

He turned abruptly and walked away. Then he called back over his shoulder, "I get your food now. I talk story way too long, yeah!"

Big Jim brought us a chicken salad sandwich, loaded with pineapple and nuts. Tender slices of fruit were arranged, almost making a picture. A beautiful day and beautiful food all blended together—just another day in paradise. Tiny little doves came across the walkway and right into the restaurant, walking in their jerk-neck way. They parked themselves near our feet, waiting for crumbs to fall.

"I wonder if dey own de floor," Kitty said with a grin.

The Hole in the Bottom of the Sea

Doves at my feet—geckos on the wall—my sweet Kitty near to me—Papalou on my mind. Yeah, just another day in paradise.

"Want dat pie now?" Big Jim was back.

Kitty looked at me with big, wide eyes. Slowly, she shook her head.

"I think we've had enough, Jim—sorry about that."

"Don be sorry, man. Dat pie it's da kine way too much!"

"Tell me, Jim." I wanted to nudge him a bit. "I guess this is dumb, but he called you Big Jim. Is that just because of your size."

"You got eyeballs dat work good! Yeah you got it, but it's more. We are many people on dis island—not always get along. We don't use las' name all de time. Las' name—well, it point out our differences. Hawaiian, Filipino, Japanese, Portuguese—all different. Some island people all mix together, but maybe las' name still Japanese, or what, see? After a while you get a nickname, yeah. I'm Big Jim, but den dere's Heavy Jim and Too Small Jim. Dat way people know who dey talkin' about, yeah."

"So, I guess Too Small Jim is a little guy?"

"No way, Dave. He's one big dude. He move here, and already, over in Hilo, he was Big Jim, yeah. So, dey bring him right here one Saturday and stand him up with me, OK? Dey look and him and look at me den somebody say, 'Nope, he's too small.' So dat's it—Too Small Jim. Den you come here—you de Gecko Man!"

Kitty was laughing at me. I could feel the heat creeping up the back of my neck. Kitty rubbed a bare foot up against my calf and knee.

"Hey there, Gecko Dave," she cooed.

"Yeah, I like dat!" Big Jim said. "Yeah, you Gecko Dave!"

The place wasn't busy, so I pressed my luck.

"OK, Big Jim, why is he Papalou?"

Jim laughed a laugh—a huge laugh, matching his great frame.

"When he first come here Lou wanted to get in good with this Hawaiian. You know—important guy. So the guy has dis birthday and Lou gets dis cake made to impress de Hawaiian. Lou wanted to say on the birthday cake, 'Happy Birthday to the Big *Kahuna*.' That's like to say the 'Big Chief.' Lou don't know from nuthin', so he tells de baker to put on de cake 'To the Big *Kahona*.' Well, de baker he say, 'what de hell. Dis *haole* don't know from nuthin', yeah!' So he does it. Big *Kahona*, dat means *big stink*. So, den everybody call him Big Stink Lou. Dat's his name, but dis Lou, he's OK, yeah. He enjoys de fun.

"And?"

"Well—Bigstink Lou, he has this thing when he talks to you. He listens to what you say. Den he will say, 'You listen to me. I'm gonna talk to you like a daddy.' Dem kids dat he helps, dey stay up on his place next to Sleeping Giant. He's got cabins up dere and dey work for him. De kids start calling him Papalou 'cause of what he say 'bout talkin' like a daddy—and dat's it. Nobody call him Big Stink Lou anymore.

The Hole in the Bottom of the Sea

"What's his real name?"

"Lou Addison. Mos' people don't know his las' name, but I know. Without Mr. Lou Addison dis one Big Jim would be sunk, to da max, brah."

"I'd like to meet him," Kitty said.

"He's in here every day. Jus' say '*Aloha*, Papalou.' Dat's all it takes."

"What about Ray? Anybody around named Ray?" I asked.

"Not many—dere's Crazy Ray up at Anahola Town, but he's out there—sorta strange."

"Hawaiian?"

"He's a local—not Hawaiian, yeah."

"Any Caucasians named Ray?"

"Naw." He paused. "Yeah, dere's Sunstroke Ray. When he firs' come he got too hot playing tennis and pass out. So, it stuck, Sunstroke Ray. Dere's a haole kid called Noplace Ray. His family has a house up in Princeville, but Noplace Ray—well he jus' don't care where he sleeps. People here don't lock things up. Sometimes his friends get up and Noplace Ray is on their couch or lanai. I found him in my truck one time. He's OK though—no problem. His folks live for money. I think he just likes to show dem he don't care."

"What about Raymond?"

"Some—not many. Mr. Bautista, Raymond Bautista, he jus' lost his daughter. She died on de mainland."

"What happened?"

"I don't know—some bad scene. Cassie was one sweet island girl. Her father, Mr. Bautista, runs a hardware store in Lihue, you know. She was all the family he had. Dat's sad, yeah.

"He must be heartbroken," Kitty said softly.

"Oh, yeah. We all are. It's a small island. Papalou too. He and Cassie were real tight there for a while. He took her in when she get mad and run off. Papalou got her a job with de airline. Den day sorta get together —you know. Mr. Bautista, he didn't like that too good, but it didn't last too long. Papalou's OK, but too many girlfriends.

"You know anyone by the name of Luzadder on the island."

"Gecko Dave—you ask too many questions. And, nope, dat's not a name I know."

Big Jim was abrupt. I knew the conversation was over.

"Sorry, man, I had an Navy buddy named Luzadder. He used to talk about moving to Hawaii when he got out. We sort of lost touch."

"Don't be sorry, brah. I like to talk. Beside dat, you gonna leave a big tip."

I laughed as the big man strolled away, walking the walk.

"Jim," I called. "If I wanted to take a pretty woman to some exotic tropical beach, where would I go?"

"Dis is gonna cost you bigger tip, Gecko Dave."

He told me how to find a hotel on the north shore. He said we should go to the west parking lot, climb a fence and go down a cliff.

"Yeah, right," Kitty chimed.

"Oh, dis mo bettah," Big Jim insisted. "Not many people dere. Good snorkelin', feel good sand and de right shade. Take water. And stop at de bakery in Kilauea. Jus'watch de signs and ask for it. It's late, but dey may still have bread left. Get some bread. Go aroun' de corner and get wine and cheese. You go to dat place and lay in de sun, drink your wine, eat good bread. You come back and make love to dis pretty lady all night!"

It was Kitty's turn for the color to come up to her face.

"Thank's Jim!"

"No problem, brah—*Shaka!*"

Jim made a fist, leaving his stubby pinkie and thumb protruding. He shook his hand at us gently as he said the word. Grinning his big grin and walking his easy walk, he went his way.

"*Mahalo*," Kitty called softly.

I left a fifty on the table for Big Jim.

"Davis, I feel like I've been bought and paid for!"

"Nobody said paradise was cheap," I replied.

We talked as we drove toward the north shore. Tutu had told us that the Tradewinds had returned two days ago, bringing the soft, soothing breezes with them. Great white clouds rolled up against green mountain and azure sea. The sky was a special blue that I simply cannot describe. It was hard to keep our minds on anything besides the constant vista unfolding before us, but reality forced its way into the act.

"Papalou, Lou Addison, Luzadder," Kitty said.
"Yeah, but the face doesn't fit."
"He's about the right age."
"I know, but things aren't right."
"He knew Cassandra Bautista!" Her tone was angry.
"Strange coincidence," I responded.
"Too many coincidences, Gecko Dave!" she said sharply.
"Not enough facts—you need a nickname, don't you?"
The wind whisking through the Pontiac swept her laughter away.
"Lord, look at that mountain!"
"Look at the sea!"

The beach Big Jim directed us to was spectacular. He had called it by some name I could neither understand nor pronounce.

Kitty gasped at the splendor. "I've seen beaches around the world, but this takes the prize!"

Oh, the sun was so great. The ocean breeze washed my soul clean. Tropical fish sparkled in the dancing waters as we snorkeled hand in hand. The wine, the bread—we lay together on the sand. Later the young Hawaiian at the front desk at the Beachboy told us that most folks called the place *Hideaways*.

It was that night that we had stopped at the Paradise Pacific Restaurant.

"Just another day in paradise," the owner had said.

Yeah, I thought. *And, I feel new and clean inside.*

The sea breeze kissed my face.

When we entered our room back at the Beachboy we saw that a single bird of paradise bloom had been placed in the small stone vase. The vase was placed side by side with the stone candleholder. It sort of gave me a mixed feeling. I was warm and wary at the same time. Tutu had found us.

Kitty and I took a long sweet shower together. We slipped on our robes and I walked her out onto the lanai, the balcony. A nearly full moon was creeping up over the sea. My heart was filled.

"I say this to you softly, my sweet Kit, is this not paradise?"

"Paradise, my love, and truly it is, but not for sky nor sun nor sea, but because I share it here with thee."

"More poetry?" I replied.

"First verses only, remember?" she said. "That's as far as I can get."

"Then that's far enough," I whispered into the sweet spot behind her ear.

Kitty was in my arms. My libido was back. I wanted to say something equally poetic, but all I could think of were the words, *Paradise Lost*. I kept my mouth shut. I walked with her back into the room and together we lit Tutu's candle.

The Hole in the Bottom of the Sea

Chapter Sixteen

Dawn on Thursday came with me standing alone on the lanai at the Beachboy. I had stood for several moments, watching Kitty as she slept. I wondered why we couldn't just take life as it came to us. Everything was too complicated. I had no idea how far from home I was. A trip of a lifetime—that's what it was, but there we were, chasing ghosts. A trail of deaths had led me to this place and to this moment. I wanted to wake her up, gather her into my arms and say firmly, *Let's forget this Luzadder thing. Let's go find another secluded beach, climb a mountain or sail on this crystal sea.* I wanted to, but I waited. *Wait 'til she wakes up*, that's what I said to myself.

An old Japanese gentleman was already padding about, cleaning up the grounds. Soon the sun set fire to the sea. Its warmth crept up across my face. That's the way that day began and that's the way that day ended—with warmth creeping over me.

"Davis."

"Hi, Doll. Look at this sunrise!"

She came to my arms.

"It's a beautiful day," I said.

"Yes, just like yesterday."

The sun climbed above the low clouds and let the blue sky come to life.

"Davis, we may have come onto something yesterday. Maybe Papalou is Raymond Luzadder."

"Say some more."

"Well—I was wondering, what if we mention him to Tutu. Maybe she will tell us if he's him or if he's not him. Does that make sense?"

That was my chance. *End it now! Say it. End this now!* I was too stupid. I wanted the action. I wanted the intrigue. I also wanted to keep on living. *End it!* I thought.

"Let's go see Tutu," she said.

"Not before breakfast." *Coward!* A voice down inside spoke to me. *Fool!* It continued. *Can't resist, can you?* The sun was getting hot. "Let's get dressed," I said.

I left her side and walked into our room.

We took earlier advice from Tutu and found Auntie Ono's. Many things on the island were called *ono*. Loosely translated I think the word meant *the best*, or *tops*. Big Jim would have said, "*Ono*, dat's number one, yeah!" I knew for sure that anything called *ono* was always delicious.

A beautiful, bright-eyed girl of mixed heritage showed us to a seat in the open air, beside the main drag. With typical grace she served us another wonderful meal. I watched as men on the way to work drove by, calling her name. She ignored them, of course, but a tiny smile played on her lips with every call.

Calling out the name of friends seemed to be a major pastime for the locals, and they all knew each other.

An unseen voice came from a passing car, "Gecko Dave!"

"Some one's been talking," Kitty teased—broad grin on her face.

I pulled my collar back and scratched my neck. Too much sun, or a little embarrassed—one or the other.

I watched Kitty as we ate. Something was happening to her. She wore a constant smile. She was not smiling at me, or at any particular thing. Her smile had simply taken control. She gazed up across the jade-colored, sun-washed slopes of Sleeping Giant. She stopped eating and took a long breath of the silky air. She was drifting away. Kitty was starting to look like a local.

"Where were you?" I asked.

"What, I—What?"

"Just now—where were you?"

"I was up there with that white bird. I was flying up along that mountain ridge. I could feel the wind against my face as the bird flew through the mist."

A truck driver honked at the pretty waitress.

"God, I'm hungry!" Kitty bolted down the remainder of rather wonderful looking banana pancakes.

I laughed—to myself—inside myself.

She seemed proud of her empty plate. She gave me that look, *now what?*

The Hole in the Bottom of the Sea

I had learned about a place called Secret Beach. I wanted to go hike through the lush Kaua'i forest and find it. I wanted to know what was so secret about Secret Beach. We were in paradise and in love. If I had possessed just a little bit of good sense, I would have taken Kitty by the hand and gone off to do what it is that lovers do. It was time to decide. As does the gambler, I gave in to that little demon inside me that prodded me to risk it all. I had the juice and it was pounding its way through my brain. I guess that I just wimped out. I suppose that I was hoping Kitty would be wise enough to let good sense prevail. I put the ball in her court.

"Tutu?" I said.

"Yeah," she answered. "Let's go see Tutu."

The morning sun streamed through the big windows in the front of Tutu's shop when we entered. The matriarch greeted us with a knowing glance.

"There are my sweethearts. Did you get the gift I send to you?"

"Tutu, that was lovely," Kitty said. But, how did you find us?"

"Oh, it's a small island. Besides everyone knows—Gecko Dave."

"Oh, man!" I exclaimed. "Tutu, who's talking about me?"

"Nobody—everybody. It's a slow week. We have time to talk. Did you get my message?"

"No. We've been up at Auntie Ono's. What's going on?"

"I left a message at your hotel to call me. There is a luau tonight at the home of Mr. Lou Addison, a gentleman most of us call Papalou. I think it would be a good thing if you and Kitty would attend."

"Well—sure, Tutu, but, well—are we invited? Will we, uh—be welcome?"

I hate it when I stammer.

"It is like this, Davis, dear. If you know about the luau, then you are welcome. You just go. You will be treated well."

"Why?" Kitty's question was too abrupt—too brief. It drew a look from Tutu.

"Because you have asked questions about the people of this island. You are drawn by spirit of this island. You want to know us. Perhaps there is something you can learn—that is why."

"Should we buy something special to wear?" Kitty's soft-voiced question was more acceptable to Tutu.

"This is lesson one. Please remember. Wear what you wish. This is not a place for a lot of pretending." Tutu looked directly at me as she answered Kitty's question. "Wear whatever you want."

"Tutu, we'll do it," I said. "This will be great."

"Then you need to go. You have things to do. Take some fruit, or a bottle of wine. It will not be needed, but it is a symbol of good will. That's in the *aloha* spirit."

"May I ask you one question?" I asked.

"You are going to ask me if Papalou is Raymond Luzadder."

The Hole in the Bottom of the Sea

"Uh—well, uh—yeah, sorta. I mean that's—yeah," I stammered, completely out of words.

"Davis, you lack patience. You must learn to wait, and understand. You wonder about the spirit of the island, but you will not slow down so it can find you. You will never be more than a *haole* tourist, and I am afraid that you will never hear the spirit of this place calling you to return. Davis, you ask too many questions, and never hear the answers. Do you understand?"

I nodded my head yes. I had no idea what she was talking about.

"This island changes people. Who a man is now is not who he was. Papalou is not Raymond. You must understand. When I said Raymond is here, it was maybe only the spirit of a man who used to be. Some people go away, but their body remains. Those who wish to bring back the old person will only kill the new. Papalou is Lou Addison—no more. I say no more. I am *pau*!"

"Yes, but…"

"No more! *Pau!*"

"But, I…"

Davis, Gecko Dave, enjoy the Luau. In two, tree, days you come to dis island and you are given a name. Dat is special. Now don't ask questions. Just go enjoy. Enjoy the man you meet and forget about the man you think you are looking for. Go!"

It puzzled me that she had slipped into a little bit of *Pidgen* for a few seconds. Her gracious calm had remained, but, somewhere deep inside, Tutu was very agitated.

"Manicure and hair—in that order!" Kitty announced.

We were back in the Pontiac, returning to Kapa'a Town.

"Kitty, you look great. Your hair is great. Your hands are great, and Tutu said no pretending."

"Davis, you don't know anything at all! It's not a matter of how I look. It's a matter of how I want to feel. Besides, Tutu said it is a slow week and people are talking. I want to go where the talking gets done."

"You just lost me! What do you mean by that?"

"Nails! Hair! Davis, do you remember that brick you threw into the Ohio River."

"Well, yes I do."

"I think it was your brother."

I drove on in silence. I think I had just been insulted. I was too miffed to ask her to explain. We found a nail salon.

The salon was in a small shopping center. I wandered about a bit. The shops were sort of touristy and I lost interest. I figured it was time to enter the enclave of the female soul—the innermost part of the womanly mystique. I went to the salon.

The young woman working on Kitty's nails was an absolute beauty. Her exotic charm matched that of the woman I had seen with Lou Addison. No—she was better—younger, more refined. Strangely enough the two of them had the place to themselves—until I arrived.

Kitty greeted me with a warm smile. "Davis, this is Lili. She knows Papalou."

I noticed that the girl stiffened a bit. I sensed that Kitty had abruptly revealed a little more than she should.

"We all do," Lili said softly, tersely.

"Does that mean—like, you're friends?" I realized that I was inside some sort of comfort zone. I wanted to nudge her a bit.

"I'm twenty-three, now. A few years ago things weren't good at home." She leaned back from her work, stretching her back and neck. "Well—I should say that things weren't good with *me*. I got mixed up—all attitude. Left home. I slept with friends for a while. I kept moving so my dad would have trouble finding me. Told lots of lies. It was hard. This is a small island, you know."

"Then what?"

"You're Gecko Dave aren't you?"

Floored, trapped, caught again—I confessed. "It's true! How did you know?"

"Big Jim, he's off today. Got nuthin' to do. He talk big story 'bout dat, yeah!"

She mimicked the big man's manner of speech—got a good laugh.

"So, this friend told me that my dad had already been looking for me up at Papalou's place. She say, 'why don't you go up there?' so I did. My friend and I thought that since my dad had already checked out

Papalou's then he wouldn't go back there for a while. I was like, eighteen. I knew who Papalou was, but—you know. He was an old guy."

"Like me?"

"Papalou's better looking." A grin spread across Lili's face. She enjoyed nudging me back. "He told me I could hang around there for a while. Sent me to a cabin and said he would be up to see me. I was upset at that. I figured he would be trying to jump on me. He's always got these good-looking girls with him—ladies' man. It's not like I hadn't—you know—been around, but I thought—well—yuck!"

"Not what you had in mind?"

"No way, Brah! So, Papalou comes down to see me. He makes me sit at the table and listen. 'This island is your life, Lili,' he say. 'If you stay on Kaua'i, you will always be running from the people who love you the most. If you leave the island, people will only use you. You're not ready for the world—maybe someday, but not now. What you need is for someone to talk to you like a daddy, and I'm telling you now. You've got three days here—then you go home. Get yourself sorted out. Figure out what you're going to say to your mother and father!' And that's Papalou. I don't know. I might be dead now—or worse. He may have saved my life."

"Wow," Kitty whispered. "That's some story."

"I'm only one. Many have stories to tell about Papalou."

"Did you know there's a luau at his place tonight?" I asked.

"Oh yeah, I'm dancing."

"What, the Hula? Are you a Hula Hula Girl?"

Lili gave me a look.

"Some Polynesian, some Tahitian—and some Hula. Please don't call me a Hula Hula girl. Dat's one ting make me geevum one big kick in de *okole*, yeah!"

Mischief danced in her pale gray eyes. I wasn't sure what she had just said, but I got the message. I could see a fabulous person in this young woman before me.

"We'll be there. I'll watch you dance."

"If you come…"

"If?"

"I will give you a hula lesson, Gecko Dave."

Laugher filled the room. Lili was a delight.

"How do you know about Papalou's luau?" she asked.

Kitty answered, "A lady who runs a flower shop over near Lihue Town told us—told us to come."

"Oh, you've been over in Hanamalu, talking to Tutu."

"Right! You know her?"

"It's a small island. Tutu has been an old woman ever since I was a little girl. She's very respected."

"She seems to already know everything before it happens," I said.

"She is different," Lili replied. "Some people think she's crazy."

"What do you think?"

"I think she's Tutu. If she *is* crazy or if she's not, she's still Tutu."

"I love the way you Hawaiians think!" I said.
Another look.
I'm not Hawaiian. I'm an Island Girl."
"What's the difference?"
"On my father's side Portuguese and Filipino—on my mother's side Japanese and English. My great grandmother was Hawaiian. My family has been on this island for five generations, but my blood is not pure. The Hawaiians will never let me forget that. They think they are special because their blood is pure, or if they are descended from the Polynesians. I think I am special because I work hard and make something of myself. Most of us always treat the other person right. That's the *aloha* spirit, but some still turn to hate. This is true on both sides. Here—we get along. In Honolulu and some of the other cities there are gangs and fighting. I'm a friend to everyone who will let me be a friend, but I will never be Hawaiian. Neither will you, *haole* man."

"I guess I've been told!" I responded.

"Oh, I'm so sorry. You hit a nerve, somehow. I'm a little more strong headed than most. That's what got me all mixed up when I was eighteen. Have I offended you?"

"No, not at all," I said softly. "You have taught me."

"All done, Kitty. You do have beautiful hands," Lili said.

"And you have a beautiful spirit, Lili. You did a wonderful job on my nails!"

The Hole in the Bottom of the Sea

We went back to the Beachboy so I could take a dip in the pool while Kitty went to get her hair done. She walked to a nearby salon. I guess I had taken her hair for granted during the year I'd known her. It was jet-black, worn natural and straight. Enough silver streaked through her hair to give her a gangbusters appearance. When I met her, she had her hair sort of layered up high in the back with longer strands to the front along with bangs that were cut to the shape of her face. That New York do had knocked my eyes out. As I sat on the edge of the pool I realized that her hair was longer now—maybe shoulder length—maybe. *Lord, I thought. I'm so dull. I can't even describe what her hair looks like right now. I stared at her over breakfast—but I can't describe her. Winthorpe, you have too much on your mind!*

"Daaaaaavis!" I heard her calling to me. Three—four times she called before I could get out of the water.

"I hope you like this!" She had spotted me and was heading for the pool. I was transfixed. Wispy black and silver bangs came down straight, almost to her eyes. A thin peacock blue band of silk-like scarf crossed her head just in back of her bangs. Behind the thin scarf, and covering the back of her head appeared an unruly mound of tight, tiny curls, glittering with black and silver. The cascade ended at the nape of her sunburned neck. "The girl said that dis is de right kine, yeah!"

"It's beautiful!" I exclaimed. "You are the peacock—I look like—the turkey."

She ran her fingers through the hair on my chest. "You—" she said softly. "Are the eagle. I am the swan."

I didn't know what she meant, but, what the hell—she looked beautiful.

Tutu had told us to wear what we wished, without any pretending. I wondered what it was that I wished to wear. I was crashing a party. The party, luau, was being thrown by a man I had never met. I, we, were strangers on an island in paradise about three million miles from home. The only person I might know was a manicurist who would be there to dance the hula—with me. And I was Gecko Dave. I walked over to the Coconut Marketplace and bought the loudest aloha shirt I could find. I picked up a pair of white shorts, with pleats and a pair of thong sandals. I didn't look the look or walk the walk, but I knew I would be seen.

With the beginning of a good tan and the flush of sunburn on her cheek, Kitty went without makeup. She'd used a light coral lipstick. I'd never seen that shade on her—with the new colors and the new hairdo, it was almost like I was seeing an all-new woman. She wore a long sleeveless one-piece dress that hung loose and straight. It was plain and black. The dress had a deeply scooped neckline and a hem that came almost to her ankles. It was split on one side to the middle of her thigh. She'd found a black and white sarong that she had somehow draped from shoulder to hip. Her little blue scarf had been exchanged for black. I noticed that with just a little shifting she could go from displaying somewhat of an elegant and modest look to showing a heck of a lot of cleavage. She spent most of the evening doing the latter.

Finding Lou Addison's place wasn't much of a problem—once we found Kahuna Road. We crept along looking for the proper left turn. Watching closely was not necessary. Tiki torches flamed brightly at the entrance to his place. The first few yards into his drive went easy enough. Then we plunged into what seemed like the depths of the jungle. Huge leaves dipped gently into the open Pontiac as we eased through. The dense foliage opened suddenly into a large open area that appeared to be surrounded by more jungle. To the left, in front of a house, I spotted tiki torches arranged in a large circle. At the far side a young man in a faded floral shirt motioned to us and directed us to a parking spot. The beautiful island girl we had seen with Papalou at the Marketplace greeted us almost instantly with leis of carnation and sweet little white flowers that she identified as plumeria.

"*Aloha*, Gecko Dave," she said sweetly as she placed the lei around my neck. "*Aloha*, Kitty." She kissed us each on the cheek.

"*Aloha* and *mahalo*," Kitty replied softly.

Typically, I was without the proper words, "You bet," I responded.

The beauty was also clad in a sarong, bright red with flowers of many colors. It was tied low and directly across her hips. If she wore anything underneath, only God knew—and maybe Papalou. She wore a most scanty top over her smallish breasts. The tiny thing matched her skin color giving the appearance of wearing nothing at all under her lei of tiny orchids. Her black hair glistened and fell straight down her back to below her waist. She was crowned with a wreath of bright-green, pointed leaves set off by little flowers that looked like puffs of flame. At her wrists and ankles were circlets of the same stuff. We learned later that her name was Mary Mott.

"Mary, James and John," Kitty whispered. "What a body! She makes me look like a Holstein!"

For once my mind remained with me. I knew that death or beating awaited me if I dared to make any comment about the girl's appearance—or Kitty's for that matter. I knew that there had to be the right thing to say. I was sure I would not find it.

"I sure hope they have something good to eat!" I exclaimed.

Mary led us up small rise to an impressive though small house. It appeared to me to be oriental in design. It set up off the ground slightly with a short set of steps going up to a long, spacious lanai. The front of the house and half of each side appeared to be completely open to the Hawaiian air. As we approached the crowd within the circle of lamps, two robust young Hawaiian men raised a whole pig from a steaming pit in front of the house. Papalou, dressed in what appeared to be jet-black pajamas and velvet slippahs, supervised the event.

"Look at that!" Kitty exclaimed.

I'd just been saved by a pig. *Better he be roasted than me*, I thought.

At least thirty people were gathered about the pit. They gave up a big shout as the roasted pig was raised into the air. Faces of all color and kindred wore happy smiles and warm greetings.

"Well, Gecko Dave," Papalou said. "Glad you could make it. Tutu said she thought you would come."

"I—well, I, uh—well, I guess I feel embarrassed. I feel like we're crashing the party. Uh—*aloha*," I stammered.

"Nonsense, I don't make guest lists. *Aloha*, my friend. *Maholo*, thank you for coming!"

Mary Mott placed a glass in my hand.

"What's this?"

"Mai-tai," she answered. A perfect white smile graced her dark face.

Yes, you might, I thought as I stared into mystic eyes.

Papalou brought me to my senses. "I'm glad to have you as a guest, but I am somewhat insulted," he said.

"I'm sorry—what?" I was sipping from the sweet tasting Mai-tai.

"You haven't introduced me to your beautiful lady."

"Oh, yes—gracious! Forgive me. I could feel Kitty's eyes boring into the back of my neck. I think I had looked too long at Mary Mott.

"This is Kitty, my wife. We will be married one year—Sunday, actually"

"Katherine, actually," she said. "Katherine Winthorpe. The gentleman is my husband, Davis, and I do enjoy being called Kitty."

"Kitty and Gecko Dave—on a second honeymoon," Papalou said. His smile was contagious.

The crowd gave a big hurrah and started to applaud.

"*Mahalo*, thank you. *Mahalo* to all of you. And I do really prefer to be called Davis.

"Anyting you say, Gecko Dave," called out a big Hawaiian man whom I had never seen before. Lou Addison laughed a great laugh.

"Looks like you're stuck with that name!" he shouted for all to hear.

Cold chills swept over me as a strange rhythm fell on my ears. Drums sounded from the jungle on the far side of the clearing. What appeared to be flames suspended in mid-air came floating out of the darkness as the sound of the drums grew louder.

"Man! Dat kine give me chicken skin every time," someone nearby mumbled.

The two young men who had presented the pig moved slowly into the circle of light, each carrying a flaming lamp in the palms of their hands. The men were bare-chested, wearing similar apparel to that of Mary Mott. More flames came floating from the jungle as three young beauties joined them. Each carried the same type of flaming lamps and were also dressed much like Mary. The effect, indeed, was spooky. I knew exactly what the man meant by *chicken skin*—goose bumps.

"So sorry." Mary Mott was at my elbow. She gave me a second Mai-tai.

The five dancers shouted, "*Pele!*"

The Hole in the Bottom of the Sea

They were in the middle of the crowd now, near to the pit. Each stooped gracefully, placing their lamps on the ground, in a circle about them. The drums stopped. Quietly Mary Mott joined the other dancers. She handed each a pair of split bamboo rods. The men jumped from the circle, stamping madly and shouting what sounded to me to be a war chant. They stamped their bare feet, moving in front of the circling crowd as if to intimidate us with their ferocity. The crowd slowly moved back as the young men beat the bamboo rods together and continued shouting ferociously into the faces of Papalou's guests. "*Pele!*" The four women shouted, with a musical lilt, and began marching out toward the guests. They moved the bamboo rods in rapid rhythm, slapping one rod against the other as they moved, and shouting Hawaiian words with each beat. The men joined the women as the drums took up a frantic rhythm. The crowd had fallen back now, forming a much larger circle. Suddenly all six dancers shouted a single word together and fell on their knees with faces to the ground, placing the rods in front of them. The rods formed a second perfect circle. The drums stopped immediately. The Hawaiian night was silent.

A trio had slipped onto the lanai above us during the show—two guitars and a keyboard. A woman played lead guitar. A man played a string bass. Another woman was on the keyboard. I figured this all out later. At the moment I was breathless and all chicken skinned, watching the dancers. The trio started to sing music with sweet Hawaiian sounds. The men went back to carving the pig and the four women began to dance the dance I always thought of as the hula.

The four women moved into the crowd—each choosing a partner. Lili came straight to me. Mai tai in hand, I watched her as she showed me the moves. The young woman had a body to die for, but, somehow, in the circle of light, I could look only into her beautiful exotic eyes. I was a long way from Peachtree Avenue.

"If you enjoy this," Lili told me. "Come tomorrow afternoon to the Coconut Marketplace. The children will put on a show. You will enjoy that too."

Maybe, I thought. *But not nearly as much.*

"*Mahalo,*" I said, as Mary Mott handed me another Mai-tai.

As the evening wore on, Kitty got into the act. Actually, the dance movements came easily to her. The elegance of her stature and grace of movement drew my attention from the island girls to her. She was the beauty. I was the Holstein stamping about. Papalou handed me another Mai-tai and invited me up onto the lanai. From here I could see a dramatic great room with much bamboo, rattan and a wash of pastel colors. A collection of ceremonial masks adorned the far wall. Tiki torches were placed every few feet along the front of the lanai and a sea of light washed from the beautiful living space.

"Wow, Lou. You have a fabulous home!"

"Two bed rooms and two baths in the back; hot tub and sauna in the space between them—kitchen off to the side there. There's another small covered lanai off

The Hole in the Bottom of the Sea

the kitchen. It's great when the rains come." He described his home with a careless indifference as if to say, *what, this old place.*

"You're showning us a wonderful evening," I said.

"And you've shown me a beautiful woman. She from New York?"

"Jersey, actually. She was living in New York before she came to be with me in Louisville."

"Kentucky?"

"Yeah, right. You been there?" *Oh, stupid,* I thought. *If this is Luzadder, he's from Louisville. Where's your head, Winthorpe?*

"Drove through there three or four times. I worked in Memphis for a while—had a girlfriend in Cincinnati. I drove up a few times, but that didn't last. Too much distance. I always wanted to stop and check out Louisville, but I never did. I hear they have a great minor-league ball club." Lou Addison said that very convincingly.

I wonder if his girl friend could be the red-head who followed us from Cincinnati, I thought. *Naw, too unlikely.*

I didn't respond to Papalou. I wanted to speak, but seemed to be thinking in slow motion. Mary joined us, taking a chair next to mine. She had changed into a long loose fitting silk caftan. It was dark blue with white hibiscus. Suddenly she jumped to her feet.

"How silly," she said. "You must think I'm neglecting you!"

Mary brought me another Mai-tai.

The crowd was thinning now. I could see Kitty hugging on people like they were old friends. Lili came up onto the Lanai to collect from Papalou and tell me what a good dancer I was. She spoke with a twinkle in her eye. I knew I was graceless.

"I think I'll keep my day job," I replied.

Mahalo, Howzit, Aloha—they all said good-bye to Papalou, da man.

Soon Kitty was beside me. There were four of us now—Lou, Mary, Kitty and Gekco Dave.

"Papalou," Kitty said. "This evening is like *déjà vu*. It reminds me of a scene from a book I read last year."

"What was the book?"

"I'm trying to remember—*Princess of Paradise*, I think.

He responded, "*Princess of Paradise*, eighty seven hundred words, by Louise Addler. The dance tonight was a recreation of one portrayed in that book."

"You've read that!" she exclaimed, eyes wide, hand to her heart.

"I'm familiar with it," Lou said.

"I just love Louise Addler. I think I've read all her books!"

"They're mostly trash," he responded in a soft tone.

"What are we talking about here?" I asked. My voice had returned.

"The writings of Louise Addler. Papalou is familiar with them."

"Is that what you've been reading all the time—those paperbacks?" I asked.

"Yes. I'm a great fan!"

"What are these books about?" I continued.

"Love, romance, adventure," Kitty answered.

"Sex," Lou said.

"No, they're classics," Kitty said.

"They're trash!" Lou said.

My interest was starting to peak.

She asked, "Have you read *Savage Sand?*"

"That's the one where the heroine is trapped for three days in a sand storm with a Bedouin Prince," he responded.

"How about *Passion and Ice?*"

"Isn't that the one where the heroine is trapped for three days in a survival tent, on a glacier, in a snowstorm, with a mountain climber?"

"Well, yes—but"

"But nothing! They all have the same plot!"

"*Tropical Embrace?*"

"Three days, wrecked sailboat, hidden lagoon with a smuggler."

"How do you know so much about it!" she snapped.

"I'm Louise Addler. I wrote those books."

"And I'm the Princess of Paradise," said Mary Mott, batting her exotic eyes.

Kitty leaped to her feet. "Oh, dear Lord!" she exclaimed. She sat back down. "Oh—I—Oh, my. It—I—well, I don't know what to say."

"It's like we've been intimate?" Lou asked.

Suddenly, I was all ears.

"Well—no. It's just that I thought you were a woman and all this time I've been sharing these things written by a man."

"It's not like I was in the room, you know. Ever put any of that stuff into practice?" Papalou grinned. He looked at me as he spoke.

Suddenly a light came on. "This ish the way you make love to an exhausted man," I quoted, shakily. My mouth wouldn't work right.

"Oh, no—Oh, dear!" Kitty said.

"Davis, you heard that line before?" Addison asked. "Shower—baby oil—old quilt?"

Kitty wailed.

My mouth was moving. I don't think sounds were coming out. I knocked back the rest of the Mai-tai.

"Another?" Mary asked.

"No," I said. "Two's enough."

"That line is from my first book, *Seek the Dragon*. The title is taken from the Chinese Zodiac where the monkey should always seek the dragon to find true happiness. It was supposed to be a spy thriller, but everyone went wild over the romance. That's all I've written since."

"Kitty?"

"What!"

"Hash our love life been coming from hish novels?" The words still wouldn't come out right.

"Well—sometimes, sorta." The look on her face was beyond description. "Davis, you could call it research!"

"You, been unhappy with your love life, Davis?" Lou, Louise, asked.

"No—ish great!"

"Then get off it. Where do you get your ideas? Don't you bring a fresh idea to the bedroom from time to time—from a movie, or a book—magazine?"

"I gesh I do," I managed.

Mary started to giggle.

"Are you a besh-seller?" I asked.

"Nope—they sell my stuff at super market checkouts and convenience stores—mass media paperbacks!"

"Why do you write? Are you driven by the passion?" Kitty asked.

"Hell, no. After the first book, I moved here. It takes money to live in paradise. I make a few bucks, put it into businesses, give some away. I really live a simple life, but it ain't cheap. People want to read my stories, so I write. I only have one plot. When they get tired of that, I'll find another."

My mind was reeling. I wanted to say, *what about murder and deception? What about Sally, Cassie and Danny. Who the hell are you?* That's what I wanted to say.

"Why the *nom de plume—Papalou*," I asked. I think too much sarcasm showed in my voice.

"I like my privacy. The people on the island don't know that I write. I'm just Papalou here, and that's the way I like it."

"Lesh hope no one finds out who you really are, then," I replied.

Papalou sensed the tension. He started telling a joke about a Hawaiian with a dog that had three legs and one eye. The Hawaiian named the dog *Lucky*. I laughed like a fool at the old joke. I told one about a gorilla that escaped from a zoo. The gorilla was handcuffed when he reached down to protect his private parts. I think that's the one I told. Kitty started in on a story. I looked closely at her. I could see her mouth moving. I could hear the clicking sounds her tongue and lips were making. I couldn't understand the words. I leaned my head back against the chair. The stars were moving toward me. The heat from the tiki lamps was warm against my face.

The Hole in the Bottom of the Sea

Chapter Seventeen

Ray Luzzader sat at his kitchen table in the half-light of the Hawaiian dawn. He picked up his cordless phone and punched in a familiar number. He entered a second code number to tell a repeater device in New Mexico what mainland number to dial. Luzadder activated a signal scrambler and flipped a switch that would modify the sound of his voice.

"Yeah."

"Pearl," Luzadder said flatly.

"Who's callin'?"

"This is Ray, Pearl. I haven't heard from you for a while."

"Oh, wow—sorry, man. I hit a snag in Kansas City."

"Talk to me. What's happening?"

"I picked up the trail of our friend—thought I would snatch him and pump him to see just how much he knew. I got careless. Some jerk plowed into the back of my van. I looked away and the dame that was with the mark cold cocked me. Would you believe it? I got knocked out by a woman and then got arrested!"

"Arrested—in Kansas City? How'd you get out so quick?"

"No problem. I had a friend that owed me a favor. He put the money up, then I skipped bail."

"That must have been a good friend. Was my brother involved?"

"No, no sign of your brother."

"So, where are we on this?"

"Ray, I watched the grave, like you asked. The flower girl, she comes and goes—no big deal. Everything is happening like you said it would. Then this sappy looking grounds keeper starts hanging around my truck. It's like, he never comes to me, but he's always in sight. Then this guy shows up. I see them taking. The sappy one points at my truck. So, I put two and two together and make the connection that this is the guy causing your problems. I also figure the sappy one had caught on to it that I'm watching the grave and he called our friend so's to fill him in."

"And?"

"Well, I'm cool on this. I'm going to follow our friend, find out who he is and where he is. I figure maybe I can just do him and your problems will go away."

"I didn't tell you to kill the man, not before we know how many are in on this."

"That's why I tried to snatch him, Ray! I was going to beat some information out of him, then take care of business."

"Pearl, I'm not sure you've handled this very well."

"It's cool, you're all right, Ray. Just take it easy. I'll get back on the guy."

"Why do you say that?"

The Hole in the Bottom of the Sea

"I got his cell number and matched his frequency. Next time he makes a call, I'll be on the line. He'll tell where he's at and I'll be back on him."

"So you lost the guy?"

"Ray, it's temporary!"

"How did you get our friend's cell number?"

"I saw him write something on a business card and give it to the groundskeeper. I tried to follow our friend but—what? I don't know how he did it—he disappeared."

"That was sloppy, Pearl."

"I know, Ray. It's not like me to lose a mark. That graveyard is weird. It all looks the same—and that part of Louisville—the streets go off in strange directions. I don't know what happened.

"Yeah, I know, Pearl. I've been there. So, what did you do?"

"I went back and took the card from the sappy groundskeeper. The cell number was on the back. I called the number and, you know, he was, like—hello—hello—hello. I used one of my gadgets to get a fix on the frequency. I've been listening to his calls since then.

"Did the groundskeeper get a make on you? Can he identify you?"

Long pause.

"The groundskeeper had an accident. His mower rolled over on him. He's dead."

"I've told you more than once, Pearl—no hits that I do not approve."

"I said he had an accident!"

"Before or after you took the guy's card?"

"Com'on Ray! I had to. He was just a nobody—a grubby little groundskeeper. Don't give me grief over this!"

"No hits without a reason, Pearl!"

"OK, I had a reason! Gimme a little damn room here!"

The phone was silent. "What came next?" Ray finally asked.

"I staked out the flower girl. I wanted to put a tight box on her so I'd know her patterns and where to find her. You know—*just in case you felt you had a reason*." There was sarcasm in his voice.

"Did you do her too?"

"No, Ray—our friend tipped her. He called her from his cell phone. I heard him tell her! He's cool, man, he told her to look out her front window for a green van, like he already knew I was there. She opens the curtain and looks right at me. I'm sitting there in the van, listening to the conversation!"

"Then what?"

"He tells her to skip. I just let her go. She's an every day Jane. She'll be easy to pick up on, if we need to."

"Too many loose ends, Pearl. I'm not sure I can depend on you like I used to."

"Nothing I can't handle, Ray baby. You've got to keep your confidence."

"How did this whole thing move to Kansas City?"

"The guy made a call. He called your brother and told him they were coming to see him. I monitored the

The Hole in the Bottom of the Sea

call and was at your brother's when our friend made contact."

"They, Pearl. Who's they?"

"They, them—his lady." Pearl paused. "There was a driver with them too."

"Oh, hell, Pearl. This is getting too messy!"

"Ray, I can handle it. It's all quiet now. The guy's out of town or something."

"Th*e guy* is where I am, Pearl!"

"What!"

"He's here. I went to a party last night. He was there—him and the woman."

"Want me to come and take care of it?"

"You know better than that, Pearl. I'd have to tell you where I am and that would be bad for your health."

"Unfriendly words, Ray—unfriendly words."

"Remember those words, Pearl. You mess this thing up too bad and…"

"And, what?"

"You'll never hear the shot that kills you. Pearl, you mess me up and someday you'll be sitting wondering where I am, and the next minute you'll be staring into the face of God!"

"Your tone is not necessary, Mr. *Luzadder!* What are you going to do about our friend?"

"I'll take care of him and the woman myself. I've been watching them. I know where to find them. Don't worry about it."

"Maybe you can make it look like an accident."

"Yeah, something."

"Good luck, Ray baby. Don't forget to write."

"Yeah, cute. Say, Pearl…"

"Yeah?"

"I want to thank you for keeping things neat in Seattle. That was very efficient."

"It's what I do best, Ray."

"How'd you pull that off—I mean, well—no one suspected anything."

"You know I can't tell you that—professional secret, you know. Are you still flying, Ray."

"I have a job next week."

"Where?"

"You know I can't tell you that, Pearl—professional secret, you know. This one will make the news. Read your paper."

"An accident?"

"No accident. The man with the money wants certain people to know that the mark was put away for a reason."

"Bullet?"

"No, a bomb—maximum impact! The man wants it messy."

"Don't get any on you."

"I'll call you, Pearl—down the line. I don't think I'll have anything more for you to do in our current situation."

"Sorry about that, man. You win a few. You loose a few. I guess I'll…"

Ray Luzadder broke the connection. The conversation was over. He took a deep drag from his cigarette and a sip of warm Kona Coffee. He stared for several moments across his lanai toward the quiet cottage on the edge of the jungle. He put on his ball cap and walked to the edge of the lanai and slid his feet into his slippers. He had just enough time to make his morning rounds before he took Mary to the airport.

The Hole in the Bottom of the Sea

Chapter Eighteen

I awoke staring into unfamiliar space. A ceiling fan slowly rotated above my head. I was flat of my back. I knew I was in a bed, but my arms and legs were heavy. I couldn't seem to get awake enough to move. A gecko chirped loudly somewhere in the room. The sound of the little critter sent echoes booming through my head. *Oh, my head*—pain is not the word to use to describe it. I felt like my scalp was expanding with every beat of my heart. The horrible taste in my mouth reminded me of something from the bottom of a cage at the zoo. I forced my eyes open for a second time.

"Hey," a voice said softly. The sound sliced through my brain. I turned to look. It was Kitty. She was curled up in a big papasan chair near the side of the bed. I tried to raise my head, but the room swam about me. I flopped back onto the pillow. It was like thunder.

"Do I get to die now?"

"No such luck. It's your punishment. You have to live."

"Is this a hangover?"

"Something like it," she said.

"I didn't think a couple of Mai-tai's would do this. What was in those things?"

The Hole in the Bottom of the Sea

"Rum—and other poison. Davis, you had three on an empty stomach. Then you ate like a fool. You had two more while you danced the hula, and maybe two more while we sat on the deck. That adds up to about two." She was showing no sympathy.

Slowly I felt myself. I was wearing something that felt like a pair of silk drawers.

"Where are my clothes?"

"Mary washed them. You threw up on yourself while we were dragging you to the cabin. I would be just as happy if she threw away that ugly shirt."

I struggled for my senses to come. I couldn't remember my shirt.

"Cabin? Where are we?"

"We're in one of Papalou's little cottages. You were in no shape to drive last night and he insisted we stay. We drug you in here, took off your clothes and put some of Lou's sleep shorts on you."

"You and Lou Addison undressed me?"

"Papalou and Mary—she's quite helpful."

Oh, Lord, I thought. *Please, let me die."*

"What time is it?"

"Friday—maybe Thursday. I've lost track." I knew she was teasing me. *Tormenting me* would be a better way to say it. We'd been joking about how people of the island worry so little about the passing of time.

"Don't be cute! What time is it?" I raised my voice—wished I hadn't.

"It's daylight. Sun's not up yet. I really don't know what time it is. Does it make any difference?"

I gathered my courage and sat up. All my weight seemed to go to my fanny. I looked at Kitty. She was wearing a jade caftan similar to the one I'd seen on Mary Mott the night before. I felt as if my mind was starting to come back.

"Did Papalou undress you too?" I asked. OOPS, that was the wrong thing to ask. My mind wasn't back yet.

Kitty didn't answer for a long time. I waited for her to yell. I just knew my head would split.

"I suppose you're going to offer to take that back." She said softly.

"Yeah, sorry. I didn't even think that. It just came out. I think I was trying to make a joke."

"I'm laughing—can't you tell?" she said.

I laughed—I hurt. "Please don't make me laugh," I said, and laughed again. I hurt again. Nature was calling in the most ferocious way. I struggled to my feet.

"Where's my shoes?"

"Outside—on the lanai. *Hawaiian style,* Papalou said. They never wear their shoes into the house. They want to keep the red dirt outside."

"Where is it?"

"What?"

"The john!" I raised my voice again—another mistake.

The act of moving around seemed to settle me a bit. I started to have the first inkling that I might survive. I heard the musical voice of Mary Mott.

The Hole in the Bottom of the Sea

"Davis, Mr. Winthorpe. I've brought your clothes. I'll leave them here on the lanai. As soon as Papalou gets back I'll leave for the airport. I must get to Honolulu for a flight to Atlanta. I'm working today—hello, *aloha*."

I heard Kitty go out onto the lanai and express a proper thank you. I finished my business and wandered back into the light. Kitty handed me my neatly folded clothes.

"You up to driving?" she asked.

"I'll have to manage. Got coffee?"

"None here. Lou's gone. Mary's getting ready for her flight."

"OK—OK, let me think. I can do this. Let's go to the little café in the Marketplace—the one Lou owns."

We got into the red Pontiac and roared down Kahuna Road.

"Davis, shouldn't you go a little faster?" Kitty asked.

I squeezed my eyes tightly shut and then looked at the speedometer. We were doing about twenty-five.

The young man at Papalou's coffee shop was named Wayne. He looked as if he bore all the blood of the nations—all charm and sympathy. He supplied me with a cure, or at least the beginning of a cure.

"Here, man. You drink this. Drink it down all at one time!"

The mixture he set before me was disgusting. It was a sick looking brown, foaming over onto the tray.

"What is this?"

"That's my special volcano. That'll fix you up good. Drink it now!"

"What's in it?"

"Little cola, little coffee, two aspirin and chopped up Alka-Seltzer. Drink it now—all at one time."

I drank the brew—one long drag after another. Papalou's manager looked all too proud as plunked down the empty glass.

"You feel better now, yeah. You drink too many Mai-tai's. Mai-tai's taste sweet, but the way Papalou makes 'em—you got one kickass drink."

I just stared. Whatever that concoction was, it was still growing—inside me. I felt a belch coming on that would blow my head off.

"You need food with that too, brah. Let me fix you something."

"Oh, no, not food!"

"Yeah, brah—you got to. Got to get food in there to fight off all that booze—help get things going. I'll fix something nice for the lady too."

Dry toast and tomato juice was the fare set before me. He brought Kitty a plate that looked absolutely gorgeous. As long as I didn't think about it, I could look at the beautiful offering.

"You'd better tell me about this!" she exclaimed.

"Oh, that's something I made up for me and my girl. We fix that and sit on the lanai—watch sun up. You got sunrise papaya. I take him and cut in two. Then scoop out and use for bowl. Put in Kashi—that's a cereal you can get at supermarket. Any grain or granola will do. Then I cut up what we call custard apple into little slices and make like flower petals. You got wedges of fresh pineapple and some Mandrin orange yogurt. I would put on some banana, but don't got. I arrange it all to make pretty. At last minute I put half and half over the cereal. Dat's *ono*, sistah, broke de mouf."

Kitty laughed at the way he broke into pidgin. She began to delicately pick through her special breakfast.

"So?" the manager asked.

"It's too pretty to eat—and too good not to. I love it! Broke de mouf kine, yeah!"

His smile radiated. "'Ass right—now you talk like sistah—almos!"

I was choking down my dry toast, and it was helping.

"You OK, brah?"

I took a swig of tomato juice as I made my fist with pinkie and thumb protruding. I shook my fist at him. I had learned to enjoy this form of greeting and good wishes.

"Yeah, *shaka*, man—you get much better now, yeah."

"I was wondering where I would find you two." It was Papalou. He was back to his khaki shorts, faded floral shirt and ball cap. He had a twinkle in his eye that made me figure he'd come to torment me.

"I'm starting to feel human again," I said.

Papalou looked at Kitty's plate.

"Wayne, you giving away your breakfast special again?"

"Not on the menu—can't charge 'em."

"He's the reason I can't make any money here."

"Aw, go easy on him. He's OK—*Louise*," I said.

"Careful..." Papalou responded.

"Lou, I want to tell you I'm sorry. I made a fool of myself last night, and you have been way too kind."

"Nonsense. Life has too many wonderful situations to go around being sorry for the few times we mess up. Now, if you do that again tonight, I'm going to have to sit you down and talk to you like a daddy!"

I laughed out loud *and* without pain. Lou Addison was patronizing me, but it was pleasant. In spite of all the wonder in my mind, I liked the man. I liked him very much.

"Think you'll have your sea legs back by this afternoon?" Lou asked.

"How's that?" I replied.

"I own a fishing boat—catamaran. I'm going to take her out this afternoon. You two want to come along. I can show you the *Na Pali* Coast."

"That would be wonderful!" Kitty exclaimed.

"I know where to find some world class deep water snorkling. There's a couple of places the Captain's never take the tourists—some of the best in the world!"

"Hope you two are good in the water. Papalou don't swim so good," Wayne interrupted.

"Nonsense, Wayne, with the mask and snorkel on, I'm as safe as anybody."

"Yeah, just be careful. Don't get too far from the boat. Currents are tricky where you're talkin' and there's a big swell comin' in. Mos' places *haoles* swim

The Hole in the Bottom of the Sea

OK. If you get in trouble, you jus' stand up—maybe scrape knees or get mouf full of water. Not so where Papalou go."

I gave Kitty a glance. She gave me a little nod. Kitty, typically, was an excellent swimmer. As for me —I could manage. The pool at the house on Park Avenue had helped me to get in pretty good shape for a swim.

"Papalou, I can't say no! I'm just not sure I can find the words to thank you!"

"Then don't. Accept my hospitality and enjoy— besides you're going to buy me supper at Gaylord's tonight. We'll both get our money's worth before the day is done."

With those words Lou Addison slipped through the curtain and into the back room.

"You be here about two. I'll get you to the boat," Wayne said.

"*Mahalo*, Wayne, you've done wonders for me!" I answered.

"*Aloha* and *mahalo* to you too. Good to meet you, and especially you, Mrs. Winthorpe—you one pretty lady, and you got that *aloha* spirit."

"Thank you very much, *mahalo*, these few days here have taught me what a great compliment that is. Your special breakfast is marvelous!"

Wayne gasped and struggled for presence as Kitty scooped him up into a big hug, kissing him on the cheek.

"Oooo," Wayne responded, rubbing his forearm. "I get one chicken skin from that!"

I expressed my thanks again and we made our way back to the car. I had parked along the street behind the Marketplace instead of parking at the Beachboy.

"I think I'll pull the car into the lot and then try to lay down for a while." I said to Kitty.

"Suits me. I'll just walk on over and meet you at the room."

We met at the front of the car for a kiss before parting. Suddenly the strangest sound just seemed to zip right through my ears. Kitty abruptly pulled away.

"What was that!"

"Bullet!" she whispered hoarsely. She dropped to one knee, pulling me with her.

We crouched as several seconds of silence passed.

"Papalou, Papalou!" We heard a shout. Out of the corner of my eye, I saw a woman in white running toward the old blue Toyota truck that Lou Addison tooled around in. Now she was looking in the window and shouting. "Papalou, you OK?"

"Don't touch anything," another voice said.

We leaped to our feet and ran to the truck.

"Stand back!" commanded the Japanese gardener from the Beachboy.

I could only stand and gape. Papalou was slumped against his steering wheel. His ice blue eyes were wide open and motionless. Behind his left ear was a small round dark red mark—almost like a tiny bruise. A thin trickle of blood ran down his jaw line. At the time, I'd never seen anyone die, but I knew instantly that he was gone—Papalou was a dead man.

The Hole in the Bottom of the Sea

People came from all directions. With stunned looks on their faces they came, moving as if in slow motion. Low whispers of unbelief came from all around us.

"I saw it happen. I saw it happen," the lady in white kept repeating.

In just moments the whoop of a police siren parted the crowd. Two uniformed officers took charge of the scene.

"Stand back and nobody leaves!" shouted one.

Big Jim from Mr. Z's shoved his way through the crowd. The huge Hawaiian pounded on the hood of the truck. "Dis not so, man. Dis not so!"

One of the officers shouldered his way between Jim and the truck, ordering him to move back. Soon both officers were face to face with the angry Jim. Tears streaked down his face. The heartbroken Jim blubbered as he called out his words.

"Dis not right! Why, man—Why? Dis not happen here!"

The murmuring of the crowd was turning into shouts and demands.

"What you got to do with dis?" Jim shouted at me.

I shook my head and gave a look. I had no words for the gentle giant.

Another whoop of a siren and the crowd parted for a second car. The appearance of a short beefy man in the typical faded floral shirt and blue jeans seemed to quiet the crowd in an instant. Round faced and balding, the man appeared to me to be mostly Japanese. He took control with authority.

"What's happened here," he demanded in a loud voice. He looked directly at the nearer of the two officers. "You first on the scene?"

The officer nodded.

"Let's hear it!"

"I saw it happen!" shouted the lady in white. "I saw it an dey saw it!" Her finger was pointed at us.

The round-faced man turned his attention to us. He identified himself as Lieutenant Sammy something. His last name began with an "A" followed by a jumble of vowels. I remembered him simply as Lieutenant Sammy A.

"Who are you?" he demanded.

I gave our names. "Tourists!" I was quick to add.

"What did you see happen?"

"I saw her," I said pointing to the woman in white. "Out of the corner of my eye, I saw her running to the truck. She was calling out Papalou's name. I turned to look and he was slumped against the wheel, just like that." I pointed, like an idiot, at the body of Lou Addison.

"You know this man?" He hooked his thumb over his shoulder toward the corpse.

"We met him last night. We went to a luau at his place—spent the night there. Then he walked through his café while were there. That was, maybe, fifteen minutes ago."

The Lieutenant took notes furiously in a little notebook. He looked up at me. "That's it?"

"That's all I saw," I responded.

The Hole in the Bottom of the Sea

Sammy A. turned his attention to the woman in white. "Mrs. Kanahele, you said you saw it happen—talk to me."

I took the opportunity to catch Kitty's attention. She was pale—eyes bigger than ever. I extended my right index finger, rubbed it under my nose and worked my thumb like the hammer on a gun. I raised my eyebrows as if to ask a question. She got my message. Slowly she shook her head no. We had not even talked about the guns we sometimes carry. In this circumstance I was glad that Junior and the cannon Kitty carries were back in Louisville. This wasn't the time to be found with an arsenal in our possession.

"I saw dem!" Mrs. Kanahele said loudly. All eyes were fixed on us. "Dose two were kissing. I was watching Papalou getting in his truck. Den I saw dem kissing. *Oh dat's so sweet*, I thought. Den I see a motion. It's Papalou—he just slump over. I thought maybe he sick or get heart attack." She clutched her breast. "But no! Blood done come out—him dead!"

"I heard the bullet," Kitty said.

"Say what?" Sammy A. responded.

"I heard the bullet. It came right by my head. It was almost like it went right between us."

"You heard the bullet?"

"Right."

"Don't you mean to say that you heard the shot?"

"No shot—bullet. I'm a shooter, or I used to be. Before I moved to Kentucky I would go to the range once a week or so. I know what I heard."

Sammy A.'s expression took on a greater look of concern as Kitty spoke. He turned to the lady in white.

"Mrs. Kanahele, you hear a shot?"

"No shot!"

"Anybody hear a shot?" he shouted.

The gardener said, "I saw this woman running to the truck. I heard her shout—so I run too. I too heard no shot."

"Well—no shot, but a bullet. You heard a bullet—came right by your head?"

Kitty was nodding.

"You hear it?" Now he looked at me.

"I heard something," I replied. It was a zipping sound. It sounded like it went right through my ears. Actually I felt it as much as I heard it, or something like that."

"How do you know the bullet wasn't meant for one of you?" the Lieutenant asked.

I was stunned at the question. Once again, murmuring ran through the crowd.

"Lieutenant—I don't know. I just—well—I don't know. We've been on Kaua'i since Tuesday evening. We're on a second honeymoon. A shopkeeper in Hanamaulu suggested we go to Mr. Addison's luau. Well, we sort of crashed the party—we stopped to kiss, and—well that's it. I have no idea—no, no one would be shooting at us." I was gasping for air. A numbing realization was setting in. The Lieutenant might be right. *Did Papalou take bullet meant for me, or both of us? What the hell is happening?* My mind was a blur of questions. I was afraid to talk.

"Yeah, I know about the luaus up at Papalou's place —been to a couple. He attracts strays."

I didn't like the Lieutenant's comment, but, hey, I was glad to hear him change the subject.

"How can I contact you?" I told him we were staying at the Beachboy and gave the room number.

"Don't leave the island before you hear from me. Looks like you have a good alibi because you were kissing at the time. That's a new one on me!"

His comment brought a murmur of laughter from the crowd. He turned his attention from us to the ambulance that was arriving.

"May we go?" I asked.

"Yeah—I can find you. Here, call me if you remember anything else." Sammy A. handed me his card and waded into the crowd.

We walked slowly across the grass toward the building where our room was. I wanted to break into a dead run. It was all I could do to put one foot slowly in front of the other. Kitty went ahead of me as we ascended the stairs on the side of the building. She stepped onto the landing first.

"Davis, stop!" she threw her arm out as if to protect me. "Look at this!"

On the landing I saw a bag of golf clubs—no big deal.

"What about it?"

"On the landing, just behind the bag—look!"

Behind the bag I saw what I took to be a rifle cartridge—strange looking. It was large, but with a very small opening at the front.

"What is that, Kit?"

"Rifle cartridge—it's a .22-250."

"Never heard of that—22 what?"

"A guy at the range had one. He was sighting it in. He called it a varmint rifle. It had a scope and a bolt action. He said he could knock off ground hogs at two-hundred and fifty yards."

"Could that be..."

"Has to be!" she interrupted.

"What does it do?"

"You try for a head shot—small entry wound no exit wound. The man said that he could shoot a ground hog and it wouldn't even flinch." She paused. "The gun's in the golf bag."

"You think?"

"Think about it, Davis. Whoever did this has been watching Papalou—not us. Papalou makes his visit every morning, parks in the same place. He's predictable—we're not. The shooter was standing right here, waiting for his chance. When Papalou gets in the truck, he's still for a second as he puts the keys in the ignition. The shooter goes up with the rifle, takes his shot—bang, drops the gun in the bag—walks away. It was Lou Addison he was after, not us."

"My Lord!" I exclaimed. I looked off toward the truck where they were removing Papalou. The Lieutenant was shielding his eyes from the morning sun and looking our way. He stepped over parking bumpers and started toward the Beachboy.

"Lieutenant!" Kitty shouted. "You need to see this!" She took ungainly strides down the stairs. She was excited and, for a change, moving awkwardly. She ran across the grass to meet Sammy A. The two came hurriedly up the stairs.

"I think that's from a rifle," she said, pointing at the cartridge.

"You touch anything?" he demanded.

"No, nothing."

The Lieutenant crouched low, peering at the shell casing. He let out a low whistle. "Don't see that too often. Some guys here use a round like that for wild goats and pigs." He stood, abruptly. "Glenn, get up here. Wait, bring a lab kit—move it!"

Another plain-clothes officer came hustling up the steps. I watched with great wonder as they took photographs and carefully studied the area. Sammy A. pulled a plastic bag out of the kit, scribbled on a tag and picked up the .22-250 shell with the point of a pencil. "Bet you never seen that before," he said, holding up the clear bag.

"What is it?" Kitty asked—her voice filled with innocence.

"It's from a special rifle—designed for assassination. Some professional did this!"

"Surely not!" I countered.

"Watch this," announced the Lieutenant. He pulled a large plastic bag and tongs from the kit. Slowly he began to pull the covers from the heads of the golf clubs—until he uncovered the barrel of a rifle. It was a slim affair with a five-inch long bulge at the end. I took that to be a silencer.

"Look at that," he exclaimed. "Glenn, get Jimmy and the boys up here to protect the area. I'm not going to touch this! One of you guys call Honolulu!" He turned to us. "I'm going to have to ask you to leave the area. Sorry, I shoulda done that sooner." We backed away. "Glenn," He shouted. "Tape this off. I don't want people walking through here!"

We turned, walked the twenty feet to our room, unlocked the door and went inside.

The Hole in the Bottom of the Sea

Chapter Nineteen

If I could've figured out what to say, I would've said it. I guess she was right—the bullet was for Lou Addison, maybe. Questions still pounded in my mind. Ray Luzadder was a killer. I was sure of that. I had to believe that he was on the island—if all that was so, and Papalou and Ray Luzadder were two different people, then Luzadder could have taken the shot—at us. I wanted to sneak out the back door, leave the Pontiac right where it was and somehow catch a ride to the airport. Several times I started to wake up Kitty and get out of there. Hell, I didn't know what to do!

Talking was no longer on our minds after we entered our room at the Beachboy. Kitty was ready to lie down. I think she had sat up most of the night before, watching me. I grabbed a cola and headed for the lanai—and so, I sat and thought. I was at it again—so far in I couldn't back out. The weird part was that I felt like all the wheels inside me were running full speed. I was scared to death and full of anticipation all at the same time. I was alive and this was the adventure. It was hard to believe that I had found my way into this mess—and I was not about to trade places with anyone!

"Davis?" Kitty still had sleep in her husky voice.

"Out here," I called.

Mike Bradford

"Want to walk with me?"

"Yeah, I can't rest." I looked at my watch. It was after one o'clock. Too much time had passed. I guess I had been sleeping after all. My thoughts and my dreams had blended together. I found myself wondering what recollections of the last twenty-four hours were actually real.

We walked to the stairs at the opposite end of the landing. Behind us and officer still guarded the golf bag and the shell casing. Yellow crime scene tape fluttered in the breeze. There was no sign of the Lieutenant. I supposed they were waiting for experts from Honolulu. The little red Pontiac was still sitting on the street in back of the Marketplace. Across the way traffic cones lined up like soldiers defended Papalou's old Toyota truck. We made our way to the beach and walked north to the next hotel. We nosed around the lobby of the more ritzy place before heading back to the Marketplace. We talked—we muddled through all the things that had crossed our minds since the shooting. Together, we decided to check out our options, see if the police would cut us loose and head for home—and sanity. I was ready for a long snooze on my own couch, in front of my own TV, in my own little mansion.

"Are you hungry?" she asked.

"Hadn't even thought about it."

We picked up a sandwich at one of the little shops in the Marketplace. I can't remember which one or what we ate. I just remember a numb mechanical state of mind as we watched the afternoon slip away. The tourists strolled about as usual, staring in the windows. The locals were different—quiet—smiles gone. They looked at each other with wide eyes and uncertainty. Many looked at us. None stopped to speak. The children did not dance in the Coconut Marketplace that day.

"Mr. Winthorpe—Mrs. Winthorpe." I heard the voice and looked up. It was Lieutenant Sammy A.

"Lieutenant—*aloha*," I said.

"I understand you have been looking for someone." He didn't return my greeting.

"Yes, an old Navy chum."

"Is that right?"

"Yes, Lieutenant."

"Mr. Winthorpe, you were never in the Navy."

Lies have a way of catching up. I took a long look at Kitty. She was no help whatsoever. The lieutenant had checked us out. We had been weighed and found wanting.

"I'm looking for a missing person, Lieutenant—as a favor to his brother. Sometimes people tell me more if I make up a story about myself. It seemed like a bit of harmless deceit."

"You a detective?"

"No, not at all—just trying to help out a worried old man."

"Long way to come to do an old man a favor," Sammy A. said.

It was strange how my next words sprang to my lips. This strange day had rubbed the right stuff from my mind. I'd completely forgotten about our anniversary "We were taking this trip for a second honeymoon, Lieutenant. We'll be married one year on Sunday." I looked at Kitty. She was gazing back at me with the same dazed look that I knew must be on my face. She'd forgotten too.

"It seems you've mixed pleasure with trouble, Mr. Winthorpe."

"That wasn't our intention. Actually, Lieutenant, we only asked a few questions, and only talked to a couple or three people about Papalou. The rest of the time we were sightseeing. Perhaps we just managed to be in the wrong place at the wrong time."

"Perhaps—did you find who were looking for?"

"That's a question I can't answer."

"Can't or won't?" he asked.

"Can't, Lieutenant—I just don't know. I suspected that Lou Addison might be my man with a different name, but—well, I know nothing for sure."

"Who you looking for?"

"A man named Ray Luzadder—from Louisville, Kentucky. He was supposed to have drowned several years ago. His brother latched onto the notion that Ray was still alive."

"Luzadder a criminal?"

"According to the Louisville authorities, he's dead. I've heard nothing about a police record."

The Lieutenant stared off across the Marketplace for a moment. He slipped his fingertips into the pockets of his blue jeans. "What are you going to do now?"

"Give it up. With Lou Addison gone, I have no other leads, and we've both sort of developed a yen to go home. As soon as you give the OK, we'll head back to the mainland."

The Lieutenant moved his hands to his hips and arched his back as if fighting off a painful stiffness there. A troubled look was on his face as he cast a glance from place to place. I felt as if he was trying to avoid looking at us. It seemed he was struggling with what to say next.

"We have a peaceful island here. Most of the time we're out dealing with barking dog complaints or an occasional drunk. People don't even lock their doors. Some don't even have a door on their place. Shooting —violence—that's not our way!"

"I think I understand," I answered.

"Maybe, Maybe you asked a lot of questions and the one man your questions led you to is dead. People are unsure about you, Mr. Winthorpe. I am too. I know how to find you, if there's a need. I think it would be good if you left this island as soon as possible."

"Are we in danger?" Kitty asked.

"No," he answered, continuing to stare at my wife. "Maybe. Who knows?"

No one spoke.

"Oh," Kitty said finally.

"We can probably catch a flight tomorrow, I'm not sure I can work it out sooner," I said.

"That's soon enough," Sammy A. replied. "You might try a trip to see Waimea tomorrow. It's peaceful up there."

That suited me—the other side of the island would be a good place for the both of us.

"*Mahalo*, Mr. Winthorpe, Mrs. Winthorpe."

He turned abruptly, strolling away—walking the walk.

"I'm sorry, Kitty. This sort of messes up our anniversary."

"That's an understatement," she replied.

"And I'm sorry that I've got us in the middle of a mess like this when we should be having the time of our lives."

"Davis, don't apologize. Actually, I believe we are having the time of our lives. I have no idea what comes next, but this sort of thing seems to be who we are now. Call me a fool, but I like it!" Kitty dug in her purse, producing a set of keys. They were adorned with a white ribbon, tied into a bow. She slid the keys across the table. "These are for you."

"What's this?" I asked, clueless.

"Happy anniversary. I meant to give those to you on Sunday, but I'd rather do it here than back in Louisville. Those are to a new Toyota Camry—beige in color. It's a replacement for Plain Jane."

My mouth just worked for a few seconds—nothing came out. "Honey, I'm speechless. All I got you a new nightgown. I've got it hidden in our room. I had no idea. Kitty, this is too much!"

"Nonsense! What's a few thousand dollars between friends?" I think she was trying to imitate the manner of speech of Lou Addison.

"Where's the car?" I asked.
"They'll deliver it after we get home."
"Then I have the advantage, Kitty."
"How's that?"
"We can test drive your new gown tonight!"

Kitty looked at me for a long time before she responded. "OK, but I get to steer."

Saturday morning we took the advice of Sammy A. and went for an early drive to the top of the island. We drank in the fantastic sights of the Kalalau Valley and Waimea Canyon. I fed the chickens at Koke'e Lodge. We enjoyed a couple of hours of beautiful diversion before heading back to reality and whatever it was I was going to tell William Luzadder.

We discovered a Mexican restaurant by the side of the road in one of the string of small towns along highway 50, grabbed quick lunch and headed back to the Beachboy to check out and then say good-bye to Tutu.

It was after one in the afternoon when we got to her shop. With a two-forty five flight to Honolulu ahead of us, I was feeling the pinch of time. More than that, I had on regular shoes and long pants. I felt like I was giving up part of myself. There was a new person trying to emerge from the chrysalis, but our time was up we had to leave the magic island. That doesn't tell all the story—I just don't know how else to say it.

"Looks like you are prepared for travel," said Tutu in her melodic tones.

"Back to Kentucky, Tutu," chimed Kitty.

"Is it true, my lovers, that in Kentucky the grass is blue?"

"No," I responded. "The grass is green in Kentucky."

"As green as here?"

"Sometimes greener, Tutu—but different. Everything is so close here. In Kentucky the mountains are long low ridges. You will see them off in the distance and the land goes on forever.

"Like the sea?"

"Yes, like the sea."

"Then some day I will call you. You will come and take me to see this Kentucky where the land goes on forever."

"Tutu, we would be honored," Kitty replied.

Tutu stared through the sun drenched windows. "Too bad about Papalou."

My mind didn't want to seem to shift gears back to the subject of a man just dead. I stared out the same sun drenched windows. "Yes," I said. "He really seemed like a fine man."

"Many loved him on this island."

"We just dropped in to say goodbye. Our plane leaves in just a bit." I wanted to change the subject.

"I spoke to a man this morning by the name of Raymond Bautista," Tutu said. "He asked me to tell you that he hoped you enjoyed your stay on the island."

"What does that mean?" Kitty asked.

"It means that he hoped you enjoyed your stay on the island."

"Tutu, we never met this Mr. Bautista," I said.

"I know. He also asked me to tell you that his daughter, Cassie, used to take flowers to the mainland for Mr. Lou Addison."

"What!" I exclaimed.

"I told him that when I first spoke to you on the phone you were asking about bird of paradise and trying to find someone. Mr. Bautista told me Cassie had taken bird of paradise for Papalou. A coincidence—that is all."

Wide-eyed, Kitty stared in disbelief. The moment seemed unreal. Now we had an actual connection with Casandra Bautista, Lou Addison and the flowers on Mable Luzadder's grave. At the moment it seemed that the circle was complete.

"Mr. Bautista also asked me to tell you that he said thank you."

"Why, Tutu, why does he say thank you?"

"Who can say? Mr. Bautista knows his reason."

"Maybe I need to talk to him."

"No, I think not. Davis, I think enough has been said. As you told me, you have a plane to catch. *Aloha*, my lovers."

"*Aloha* and *mahalo*, Tutu," Kitty said.

"*Aloha*," I said, turning for the door.

The Hole in the Bottom of the Sea

Chapter Twenty

The islands fell away behind us as cloud covered smudges of green against the unending sea of blue. *"The sea goes on forever,"* Tutu had said. I stared out the window of the plane at the featureless expanse. The song kept repeating in my head. What kind of fool writes a song about a hole in the bottom of the sea? "We'll come back and finish this trip," I said to Kitty. I turned to look at her. She was slipping away—probably to dream of a new adventure.

"Yes," she murmured. "And bring Tutu back to visit Kentucky.

After calling William Luzadder, I'd requested a return route that would take us through Kansas City and provide us with a lengthy layover there. I had a report to make to the man. I didn't have the words yet, but I knew I had to see him. I guess my plan was a mistake —at least it wasn't smart. We flew all night, with an untimely change of planes in Los Angeles. We were then off to Salt Lake City and, finally, Kansas City. A dull numbness crept into my bones as we stepped into the rent-a-car bus. We still had to catch a flight to Cincinnati before our final leg to Louisville. Kitty's charming ways had totally disappeared. It was pretty obvious that our trip to paradise was over.

"Mr. Luzadder, we found a man," were my first words to him.

"What does that mean?" he responded.

"I wish I knew. Our search led us to a person named Lou Addison and we have reason to believe he was the one sending flowers to Louisville."

"Who the hell is he?" William's question was abrupt and terse.

With the length of notice I'd given, Alice had taken the opportunity to prepare a meal for us. Somehow the thought of pot roast cooked with potatoes and carrots had a great appeal to me. I had enjoyed Hawaii, but I was tired of fish and fruit. On the table I also spied, green beans, mashed potatoes and gravy. A glance through the kitchen door revealed a coconut cake and coffee brewing. I hoped William would keep his pertinent question on hold for a bit. What I really wanted was a great meal followed by a nap. I had four hours and a half to talk to William and get back to the airport.

The diversion provided by the meal lasted about six minutes. We had time to offer a hasty prayer, fill our plates and settle to the feast.

"Let's have it Winthorpe. Who's this Lou guy?"

"He used to live in Memphis—went to Hawaii a few years ago where he runs a flower shop, a small café and a few more business interests on the island of Kaua'i."

"Got pictures?"

"One short video. We can look at it as soon as we finish the meal."

"I'm not that hungry," Kitty announced. She left the table and proceeded to pull cables out of the video camera carrying case. By the time Alice brought dessert and coffee to the living room, Kitty had the tape queued up and ready to show.

"Mr. Luzadder, this is in an area called the Coconut Market place," Kitty said. "In just a few seconds the picture will show a man and a woman standing in front of a café—wait—there!"

The shot of Papalou and Mary Mott lasted for eight or nine seconds before they walked toward us and moved out of the picture. Lou had dropped his head to look at his mail. The ball cap obscured his face for the last little bit.

"What in the world was that?" William bellowed.

"The camera was on its side," Kitty replied.

"Well, back it up!"

Kitty did as she was told. As the shot came up, we all leaned to one side to get the picture in perspective. Kitty pressed the pause button. The image was a little shaky but we had a full-face picture of the man in question.

"Alice, go over there and turn that TV set on its side. Maybe we can see this damn thing!"

Alice laughed at his tease—twittered might be the better word to use.

"Winthorpe, you go all the way to Hawaii and this is what you come back with?"

"Well—uh," I muttered. "This was the only opportunity that presented itself…"

"Look at it!" He interrupted. "You've seen the picture of my brother. That's not Ray—face isn't right. He looks short."

"The woman is rather tall," Kitty said.

"Ray hated hats—he wanted his hair to fly in the breeze for the ladies. This man's gray and almost paunchy."

"A lot of time has passed," I ventured.

"This is true, Winthorpe, but the face isn't right."

"He could've had surgery."

"What, plastic surgery? Why would Ray do that?"

"No idea," I responded. "Just trying to put pieces together."

"That's not my brother!"

"Then that's all I have for you, Mr. Luzadder."

"The hell you say—you know his name. You got his number? Let's call him. You may be too shy, but I'm not afraid to ask. Alice, get the phone."

We didn't answer. William caught the glances that Kitty and I exchanged.

"What—there is more, isn't there?" William asked.

"There was a shooting," I said. "The man in the picture is dead."

William was silent.

"Turn it off please," Alice said.

The silence continued for several long seconds.

"That man—is not my brother," William said again. He presented each word with measured tone.

"He's our last connection," I said.

"Who shot the man?" William asked.

"Not sure," I replied. "The police are still looking into it."

"Was he shot in a robbery—what?"

"As I heard it, he was shot with a hunting rifle." I glanced at Kitty. She had a slight look of surprise on her face. I had no choice, as I saw it. Sometimes there is very little difference between a lie and the truth. In a sense of the word, what I had just said was the absolute truth.

"Hunting accident?" he asked.

"That seems to be the logical assumption."

"Poor devil—you said he ran a flower shop. Could this man have been sending flowers for Ray? Maybe he was an old friend that just recently heard of Ray's drowning and maybe sent flowers to Mom's grave. You know, since Ray was never found."

"Maybe—the few clues I had led me to the conclusion that the flowers came from him. As to why this Addison guy started sending flowers to Louisville, I don't know, but I do have reason to believe he's the one. The rest is a mystery. Either this man is—was Ray Luzadder, in hiding, or Ray's still out there somewhere, or..."

"Ray is at the bottom of the Ohio—still," Alice interrupted, with soft measured tones.

William Luzadder stared at the floor for a long time. I was content to wait—let him make the next move.

Finally he spoke, "This guy in the picture—that's not Ray. Wonder who the hell he is."

"I'm not sure I know the answer to that. What I've told you is all I know, William, and we really do need to head for the airport."

"Can I have the tape?"

"Our pictures of the island are on there. I'll send you a copy."

"I guess you expect to be paid for this sidegadlin picture!" He said. There was tension in his voice.

"You did ask me to work for you, didn't you?"

"I did, but I didn't expect no trip to Hawaii!"

Kitty responded, "We've put a lot of time in on this over several months, Mr. Luzadder. If we billed you for time and expenses the amount would probably blow your mind. Make it fifteen-hundred and we call it quits."

Luzadder stared at her for what seemed like forever, "Make it a thousand."

"Done," Kitty said flatly.

"Alice, get the checkbook!"

The Hole in the Bottom of the Sea

Chapter Twenty One

So ended the strange Luzadder adventure—for a while. I laid the matter behind me and moved on to other things. I had a new car to check out—and one other important matter. A few weeks after our return to Louisville Kitty planned a party to celebrate our new home. We were finally completely out of the little house on Peachtree and enjoying life on a different scale. Winston and Shannie were there and the ever present Garrett, of course. Dr. Kepple and Indigo Matthew were on hand along with new friends from Old Louisville, plus friends of mine from way back when. I had hoped to include Maddie Wolfe, but she was still out in Colorado camping alone in the Rocky Mountains, or something.

As soon as the crowd had gathered and seemed to be on their way to being well fed, Kitty took the floor. "I am most happy to announce to all of you and especially happy to announce to Davis that our first child is due in June."

"Damn!" Winston Pence's rich exclamation filled the room.

Indigo Matthew knew that it was time to pray. Dressed in a magnificent multicolored caftan, she swept to the end of the room. "Now all you children hush. The Lord is going to bless this happy occasion! Dear

The Hole in the Bottom of the Sea

Lord above," she began. I hadn't taken a breath since I heard Kitty's words. My senses swam away from me. I didn't hear another word Indigo had to say.

"Actually, Davis, I think it happened that Wednesday night on Kaua'i. Isn't that delightful? We got pregnant in Hawaii! We have to fix up that second room—the one next to ours. We need clothes, and names. We need names!"

"Kitty!" I raised my voice. "You're chattering, honey." She came to my arms.

"Are you as happy as I am?" she asked.

"If I could feel how happy you are—then I would double it," I responded. "You did sort of catch me by surprise. You could have told me before you let the others know."

"Oh, Davis, I couldn't. I was so afraid you wouldn't be happy about it. I just had to have our friends here when I told you. You should have seen the look on your face! It was so precious…"

I watched my delightful sweetheart as she chattered on. Everything in me mellowed out. I fought back tears. We were going to have a child, my Kitty and I.

The weeks rolled by quickly after that. A little before Christmas a card came from William Luzadder. The usual two-hundred bucks were inside. I took me a ride down to Towboat Annie's and did the Ohio River thing. Ducks came paddling over, hoping for a free meal. I watched the wreath sink into the swirling dark water. It was December and it was cold. I wondered how long William Luzadder would keep up this remembrance of his brother—now twice dead. My deed was done. Life went on.

Kitty bought the house on Maramassee Island. We brought all our crew and lured brother Sal and his family to the shore for the week between Christmas and the New Year. It was a grand christening for the beach house—*God, I owned a beach house!* More than that, I owned a company, Dakpro, Incorporated. Kitty said we should shelter our holdings and form a life trust for the family. We created Dakpro as part of that strategy. Dakpro? That stands for Davis and Kitty properties, what else. I was President and Kitty was Secretary/Treasurer. Yup, you guessed it. We used that company well! Kitty had to shelter a whole wad of bucks to avoid capital gains. I don't need to include details here, but, hiding behind Dakpro, Kitty and I bought as much of the world as one could with a mere six million.

I guess it was a matter of guilt on my part, but I made arrangements to have the body of Danny Cutshaw moved from the Potter's Field to a space we purchased in the old St. Louis Cemetery. We bought a nice stone to be placed at his new resting place. Kitty and I went over with Garrett and Winston. We stood by with the rest of the grounds crew while my preacher friend, Charley, said a few words. It gave me some closure over the death of the nice little man. I had no idea how he found out about the ceremony, but Curtis Cooper also showed up. I'd gone to see the Sergeant after our return from Kaua'i. I told him the whole fascinating story. It was the first time Cooper had ever shown much interest in a story I brought his way. He told me that he'd gotten no sympathy when he suggested that the LPD take a closer look at Danny's death. His passing remained on the books as accidental. We all chatted for a few moments after Charley pronounced the final benediction. Kitty leaned sadly on my arm as we made our way back to the Town Car.

Our baby came in June. I felt as if I was the first man to ever become a father. When I was a boy there was a Doctor in Louisville who was especially kind to our family. He was a community leader and very helpful to us in some hard times. He was with us when dad died. I told Kitty about my Doctor friend, now deceased. I told her I wanted to name a son after him. The idea seemed to click in her mind, and on the big day, I pronounced the words, "Charles Allen Winthorpe." This began my years with a kid named Charley. Another child was to come, but I'll add that to the tale when the time is right. We had a big to do on Park Avenue the day Charley came home.

"I can't figure it!" Winston Pence announced. "I got this blond-headed buddy who marries a black-haired woman, and then out pops a red-headed child. I don't think I'll ever understand white folks!"

I stared at Win with a stunned expression. He was always so proud of his ancestry and he knew the stories of where his people came from. He had a proud African heritage and was quick to tell about it. I enjoyed no such accomplishment—just bits and pieces. My name came from English decent, but there were some Scots and Irish in there. My great-grandmother on my father's side was Italian. I'd never told Kitty that. On my mother's side, my great-grand mother was a Cherokee Indian—Native American. I had no idea where the red hair came from. I spread my arms wide and blurted out the words, "I am a child of the universe and this is my son."

Winston laughed at me—and you guessed it— Indigo Matthew prayed. It was a long beautiful poetic bit about how all of us are God's little children. Winston held my son as we stood in a tight little circle. For me, life—the essence of it, was complete. As a man, I felt fulfilled. Kitty was in my arms.

A couple of years passed after the shooting of Lou Addison. It took a while for the facts of the matter to come to me, and I had nothing to do with the solving of things. I just stumbled onto the truth about what had really happened.

I was home alone one Friday night, watching the baby. Kitty was at a concert down at the Center for the Arts with Indigo, Dr. Kepple and Maddie Wolfe. Charley had fallen asleep for the night. I was bored. I sank into my big leather couch in the office. I was going to have one of those private guy times, channel surfing and snoozing. A bowl of chips and a warm bottle of beer rested on the table beside me. I came upon a show on one of those documentary channels that caught my eye. The program told about some super-secret, upper-level, renegade operation in the Federal Government. An assortment of discontent agents from various agencies had formed an outfit that they called the *Moab Group*. The name had something to do with the Bible. These agents were unhappy with certain criminals who got off, but were known to be guilty. In addition, the members of the group didn't like the protection programs that gave new identities to criminals who would testify in exchange for freedom. They also got all worked up with some of the bosses in high crime that were untouchable. So the agents formed this group of assassins to off these guys—this group of assassins made themselves into judge and jury. It was interesting stuff and I watched intently.

As the program ended, I was ready to hit the channel button. I held up when they started putting up the names of these guys in the Moab Group. It was one of those black-screen with white copy things. They displayed their code names and what had happened to each conspirator. The stuff would come up one screen at a time, slowly fading out while the next item appeared:

> *Clarence Langston, FBI,*
> *Code Name, Ehud*
> *Three life sentences*
> *Leavenworth U.S. Penitentiary*
> *Leavenworth, Kansas*

Fade—next screen...

> *Solomon J. Greene, CIA*
> *Code name, Israel*
> *Life in prison*
> *Terre Haute U.S. Penitentiary*
> *Terre Haute, Indiana*

On it went...

> *Carter "Happy" Foxx, CIA*
> *Code name, Gilgal*
> *Life in prison*
> *Allenwood Federal Prison Camp*
> *Montgomery, Pennsylvania*

Next...

> *Rachel Cooper, DEA*
> *Code name, Jordon*
> *Life in prison, two consecutive terms*
> *Federal Correctional Institution Marianna*
> *Marianna, Florida*

And another...

> *Raymond Luzadder, CIA*
> *Code name, Ephraim*
> *Missing, presumed dead*

Fade to black—music starts, one more screen...

> *"And they struck down at that time about ten thousand Moabites, all robust and valiant men; and no one escaped...*
>
> Holy Bible, Book of Judges 3:29

Fade to black, roll credits...

If I had been hit with a bag of cement, I would not have felt more strangely. I think my mouth hung open for about three minutes.

When Kitty came home, she asked, "How's the baby?"

I wasn't ready to tell her about the rebirth of the Luzadder affair. "The baby's fine," I said.

She smiled at me with those cupid lips. "How are you?"

"I'm fine," I lied.

"I'm going upstairs, "She said. Again, that smile—a funny little smile.

I listened to the stairs creak as she took them one at a time, and to the creak of the flooring in our bedroom.

It's strange what little things send up red flags in the mind. Her smile wasn't right. The speed with which she ascended the stairs wasn't right. Something was on her mind—my Kitty, my mystery. It was September again, and I had known this woman for just over three years. (To be exact, it was three years and fourteen days.) There was something behind those dark eyes.

There was something behind that wonderful smile that could come and go so quickly. That was it! That's why her smile was not right. The smile was happy. The eyes were sad. I believe that there's a crossed connection between the eyes and the lips. The lips are wired to the brain. One can fake a smile. The eyes are wired to the heart. The eyes are less likely to lie. Was Kitty lying to me? Not really, but her eyes gave her away. Something was wrong and she wasn't telling. Three years had given me time to understand this much about my lady. She was still hiding something. She was hiding something and I didn't have a clue. I heard her singing softly. I knew she had Charley in her arms. I loved her and I loved that boy. We were together, the three of us and I could wait. I knew that someday, when it was the right day, my Kitty would let me in on the rest of her secrets. Yes, there we were, Davis and Kitty Winthorpe, liars and lovers.

The following Monday I made a call to some people I knew and got permission to visit Solomon Greene at the penitentiary in Terre Haute. Greene and Luzadder had both been in the CIA. I figured there might be some history between them. I hoped against hope that Greene would be willing to give up information. As it turned out, he was more than willing to talk.

He was a tallish, odd-looking man—bald, blonde and awkward. Wide, squared shoulders made his head look too small for his frame. His hips didn't seem to fit his body right, creating an awkward gait. He constantly shifted his gaze from place to place. It seemed as if he

The Hole in the Bottom of the Sea

needed to use his beak-like nose to steer his eyes. Once he had pointed his nose in a new direction, he would lean slightly as if trying to focus. Those blue eyes were not friendly. A neatly trimmed mustache and set of well organized chin whiskers presented a certain aspect of evil.

I told him about the program on TV and that I had gotten his name from the list at the close of the documentary.

"So?"

"Curiosity—I was wondering if you knew Ray Luzadder."

"Ray was a schmuck and a turncoat! He deserved what he got!" Greene wasted no time expressing his opinion of Luzadder.

I admit that I've cleaned his language up a bit.

Greene went on to tell me that he had seen the program. Actually, he had been interviewed by the production team and helped write part of the script.

I said, "The program used the words, *missing, presumed dead*. What does that mean?"

Greene leaned back in the swivel chair in which he sat. There was a plate glass window between us, with a speaking port. He leaned back as far as he could, putting his feet up on the shelf in front of him. He looked at me with what seemed to be a violent confidence. He repositioned himself several times.

"Well now, I guess *we* know that there is always more to a story." He spoke in a contemptuous manner. Leaning back, as he was, he almost shouted the words.

"Maybe you could fill me in?" I tried to counter balance his hostile manner with soft and even tones.

Greene moved like a cat, uncoiling so fast that I had no time to react. He slammed both hands on the shelf as he stood. His mouth was right at the speaking port when he shouted, "Who the hell are you and why you asking about Ray Luzadder?"

My nose was up close to the port. It was almost like an explosion in my face. I remained calm. "His brother, William, is a client of mine. He's got some age on him and he's ill. He just wants to know what happened to Raymond." It was almost true—what I said.

"You a lawyer—detective, what?" Greene was still shouting.

"No, I use the term *client* loosely. I'm really more of a friend."

Greene took several steps backward to retrieve his chair. He shoved it toward me with his foot. As the chair bounced back, he caught it and sat down. An armed guard took a few steps in our direction. Greene waved the guard off, put his elbows on the shelf and leaned up to the port.

"Well, *friend*. Let's see what brother thinks about this!"

From the story Solomon Greene told me I have formulated this scene:

The large room would always be very dark, so dark one could not tell its shape nor discern the corners. In the room was one dim light, suspended above a round table. The light was in a canister fixture just above the table. It was close enough to the surface that it only cast a circle of light. The persons seated around the table could not be seen.

A ritual of silence would be performed. Five people would enter—each by a different door. Their footsteps would echo in the darkness as they approached their seats. Once seated, each would softly pronounce their code name. The first person in would carry a short sword. The sword was double edged—about eighteen inches in length. After the final person arrived, the first would place the sword in the lighted area in the middle of the table. A full minute would pass, and Number One would place a long piece of paper across the sword. There would be a name written on the paper. Following this he would distribute five manila folders. The people at the table would pass the folders around until each had one. As if on command, each would open their folder and read the information inside. The folder would contain a vivid description of the life of crime led by the person whose name was written on the paper across the sword. There would be photographs, Grisly pictures of victims. Pictures of the intended—addresses—information.

When each individual was done with the reading of the material he (or she) would close

Mike Bradford

> *the folder and place their left hand on top of the folder as a signal.*
>
> *When the last hand was placed, Number One would say, "Who has a message from God?" The light would go out. There would be total darkness in the room for one minute.*
>
> *When the light came back on, the strip of paper would be gone. Number One would say, "To restore the land."*
>
> *All would respond, "To restore the land."*
>
> *They would exit in silence.*

"Who was Number One?" I asked.

"Ehud."

"And Five?"

"Ephraim. Your sweetheart, Raymond."

"Does anyone else know about the Moabite Ritual? They didn't tell about this on TV."

"Should have," Greene said. "Would've been a great scene—dark room—spooky sounds!"

"Yeah, right. Was this a secret, or what?"

"Yeah, it was a secret ritual. Maybe others knew— I don't know. Ehud worked with us as individuals. If there are more to the group, who knows? There are four people in the world I know for sure who know this story, plus you. There's also one in Hell."

"Ray Luzadder?"

"Yeah, Old Ray Boy, and I hope you're soon to join him."

I took this as a threat. I was sure Greene knew Raymond was dead, and this man still had connections.

The Hole in the Bottom of the Sea

I began to think about Kitty—and Charley. It was my turn. I had to speak. "I mentioned that the program said Luzadder was missing and presumed dead."

"Yeah, right—you believe that?"

"What should I believe? You implied there's more to the story."

"You should believe two things. One, Ray Luzadder, a.k.a. Lou Addison, has his feet pointed up, rotting in paradise! Two, I am way past being tired of this conversation."

"Paradise?" I said. I wasn't going to back off now.

"Yeah, Hawaii." He said the words with an odd, mocking inflection. He reminded me of one child taunting another on a playground. No, that's wrong. His tone was not at all childlike. It was evil.

I knew enough now. At least I thought I did. Greene had used the name Lou Addison. He had to know more about what happened. So I asked the question, "You brought it up. So, what's the deal—is there more to the story?"

"There's always more to the story. This is the best part."

"I'm listening," I responded. It was a nudge. For a man tired of a conversation he seemed to be full of something that needed saying.

"Ehud would set all this stuff up. He would select the next Fat Man, and put everything together. It was up to the taker to figure out how to do the intended."

"Fat Man?"

"Oh, it's in the Bible somewhere—Judges. Look it up."

"Taker?"

"Oh, hell, yes—the taker—the person who picked up the paper with the name on it. Try to keep up!"

I waited several seconds. "Did you know who Ehud was?"

"Sure I did. We all did. Ehud was Number One, Clarence Langston. None of the rest of us knew each other—supposedly. Ehud would identify potential members. *Discontents* the media called us. He would feel us out, then recruit us."

"You knew Luzadder, didn't you?"

"Oh yeah, Old Ray Boy and I had worked together. Ehud didn't know that. Made no difference. Ray and I had an edge. We could do the intended together. That was against the rules. We were supposed to work alone—actually, we weren't supposed to even talk to each other. So, yeah I knew Ray Luzadder. Ray was a specialist in the CIA—deep cover, special ops. He took care of dirty little tasks, if you know what I mean."

"And you—what did you do, uh, for the CIA?"

"Oh, call it what you will—I was a mechanic. I cleaned up messes. If things got nasty I could run the cover up. You might call it public relations."

"You an assassin?" I asked, pushing Greene a bit too much.

"I am whatever I need to be!" he snarled. "And I'm done here. Tell brother William that Ray deserved what he got." Greene got up to walk away.

"What happened to Raymond?" I shouted through the port.

The guard announced, "Sorry, time's up."

"Up yours!" Greene retorted. He sat back down.

The guard came toward him.

"You don't need this!" He pointed at the guard, raising his voice. "Two minutes," Greene commanded, holding up two fingers.

The guard retreated.

"Raymond picked up the paper on this one Fat Man. We had this method Langston had taught us. *Befriend and destroy* is what he called it. It came from the story in the Bible. We would befriend the Fat Man, then we would kill him."

"Any women?" I asked.

"A few." He thought for a moment. "A few," he repeated. "This one Fat Man was an untouchable. That is to say we knew he was dirty, but couldn't put him away. He had some crooked cops and lawyers looking after him. He even bought a Judge or two. Ray knew the Fat Man was a nut about these little airplanes, ultralights. Ray Boy was into these things too. He saw the connection and picked up the paper. So, Ray moved his rig to the little airport where the Fat Man stored his ultralight. Next thing you know, they're flying together. Ray started telling the Fat Man about how he would do touch-and-go landings on the surface of the Ohio at Louisville—like that, Fat Man bought it. They packed their rigs in a truck and drove to Louisville. Ray cut a wire on the Fat Man's rig so it wouldn't start. Ray acted all disappointed and told the Fat Man to take his rig up. That's it. Ray rigged a little explosive device that would pop and blow the ignition wire loose. Engine quits—bloop! Fat man's in the drink. Ray knew the wreckage would fold up and trap the guy. We did it in December so the water would be cold enough to weaken him quick. Ray Boy was supposed to make sure the Fat Man was strapped in real good and send him my way."

"Your way?"

"Yeah, we were together on this one. The device was set up with remote control. I was leaning on the rail at some down-by-the-water bar, putting down a highball. I watched the bastard fly under the bridge, touch the water, one, two, three times. When he touched on number four, I pushed the button—bloop! I threw back the rest of my drink and said, 'Here's a message from God.' A cute redheaded waitress was leaning on the rail with me—watched him go in.'Oh my God!' she shouted. She turns to me and said, 'Did you see that?'"

"I said '*What happened?*' That's what I said to her, acting innocent, and all."

"What's this *message from God* business?" I asked.

"Here's a message from God? Ray said the same thing as the Fat Man took off, *Here's a message from God.*"

"How do you know that?" I asked.

"We always said that. Ehud told us to. It's more of that Bible stuff."

"You still haven't told me what happened to Raymond. The papers in Louisville said Raymond died in the crash."

"Raymond got holy on us. He was questioning the appropriateness of what we were doing. He told me that it was immoral and illegal, and we had to quit. I told him that doing what's legal and doing what's right were two different things. We were righteous in what we did. Ray Boy turned pansy on us and was wanting out."

"Why didn't he just quit?"

Nobody quits the Moab Group. Ray knew that. So, he was looking for an out. I don't think he planned the Ohio River thing. He had some preparations in place and that situation just gave him opportunity. We used Ray's ultralight that day so it would be easier to rig the engine. When they couldn't find the Fat Man and thought it was Ray in the drink, Ray skipped—disappeared."

"What then?"

"We put his name on the table."

"Who took the paper on Raymond?"

"Didn't know—not at the time. I wanted it, but when I reached into the dark the paper was already gone. I figured Ehud, Langston, had it, so I went to him. I told him what I thought and confessed to him that we had done this one Fat Man together. Langston didn't know who took the paper either, but we agreed to work together on it—you know, go after Ray."

"You said earlier that Ray was dead in Hawaii. How do you know that?"

"Ray was a mamma's boy. He started sending flowers to his mother's grave. Some snooper in Louisville wised up to it and started asking questions."

"What's a snooper?"

"You know, newspaper reporter, private detective, ex-cop. Who knows what he was? Who cares? I don't even care why he got into it."

I felt the weight come off. Greene had no idea who I was.

"What next?" I asked.

"Ray Boy hired a mechanic to scare the guy off. The mechanic messed up and got in jail. He was one of our pocket guys. He did dirty work we didn't want to get too close to. After the cops nabbed him, he called Ehud. He knew Ehud had the connections to get him out and offered to give up information in exchange. He let it out that Ray Boy called him to set up the job— even gave up the snooper's address."

"What happened next?" This story was getting too close to home!

"Langston got enough from the mechanic to find the snooper. So, he had people watching the guy. You know, he put a tail on him. When the dumb ass snooper found Ray, the tail called Ehud. Ehud flew to Hawaii and did Raymond himself." Greene put his finger to his head like a gun, dropped his thumb and said, "Pop!"

"What happened to the snooper?"

"Who knows? He was some dumb cluck in over his head. He had no idea what went down. Ehud popped Ray, and we forgot about the snooper. He's probably back in Louisville boinkin' some waitress."

Time crawled by slowly as I drove back from Terre Haute. I had led the executioner to Raymond Luzadder. I remembered that day in front of the house on Park

The Hole in the Bottom of the Sea

Avenue—the day we left for Hawaii. I remembered the guys tossing a football in Central Park. I remembered a man on a park bench, reading a book. Was one of them following us? Someone was on the plane with us, maybe—in the restaurant—on the beach. God! Where! What! For all he was—for all he had done, Ray Luzadder was dead, and, right or wrong, his blood was on my hands. I had asked the questions that put Sally Patton, Casandra Bautista and Danny Cutshaw in their graves. I realized that to be true. Every story has to have a villain—I suppose. In this story the villain was a snooper named Davis Winthorpe. While I drove back to Louisville that day, something broke inside me. I will never be the same. The light of day will never look the same. My beautiful boy with hair so red will always remind me of days so strangely spent when he was conceived in paradise.

I never told William Luzadder about my trip to see Solomon Greene. And I confess—I am too weak. I've never told Kitty. William still sends me a card every Christmas. I put the two-hundred in the offering plate at church. I buy a wreath with bucks out of my own pocket. I weight the wreath with a brick and go alone to Towboat Annie's. Leaning on the same rail, I drop the package into the Ohio, and watch it go down—It goes way down. Every time part of me goes down with it—down, deep down, to the hole in the bottom of the sea.